More Praise for *And Then I Found You*

"A touching story."   —*Kirkus Reviews*

"A Patti Callahan Henry story can be counted on to contain one or more of the following: secrets from the past, lost love, and a damaged heroine who keeps others at arm's length. Her latest novel sticks true to form, with a twist—Henry drew inspiration from her own sister's true-life story."   —*Booklist*

"A quick read with high marks for heartstrings tugging . . . The whole reading experience was like watching a Lifetime movie in my jammers on a Sunday afternoon . . . and I loved it."   —*Book Riot*

"A frothy story somewhat akin to the restorative bubble bath. Enjoyable reading."   —*Sacramento Book Review*

"*And Then I Found You* is as authentic as it is riveting and ultimately unforgettable. Your past will find you—and it can change your life. I think it's the most soulful book Patti Henry has ever written."
                    —Dorothea Benton Frank, *New York Times* bestselling
                    author of *Porch Lights*

"In *And Then I Found You* Patti Callahan Henry explores the labyrinth of a woman's heart—mother, daughter, sister, friend, lover. Moving and beautifully written."   —Mary Alice Monroe, *New York Times*
                    bestselling author of *Beach House Memories*

"Patti Callahan Henry has a singular gift—she can connect her characters so deeply to the natural world. She leads Katie Vaughn by moonlight, with a touch as light and deft as a white feather, unafraid to plunge her into the deepest sorrows so that she can emerge changed and beautiful. You can't help but root for Katie. *And Then I Found You* is Henry at her best, brimming with heart and compassionate wisdom." —Joshilyn Jackson, *New York Times* bestselling author of *A Grown-Up Kind of Pretty*

"Patti Callahan Henry asks the big, equivocal questions about what it means to be a mother, a child, a family, and the answers she finds in *And Then I Found You* will surprise you, provoke you, and rearrange your heart." —Jacquelyn Mitchard, *New York Times* bestselling author of *The Deep End of the Ocean* and *What We Saw at Night*

Praise for *Coming Up for Air*

"An affecting Southern tale about second chances and banishing the ghosts of regret . . . Romantic storytelling at its simple best." —*Kirkus Reviews* (starred review)

"Elevated by Henry's subtle, sometimes excellent characterization . . . Ellie's earnest quest for true happiness will resonate with many readers, especially fans of Kristin Hannah and Susan Wiggs." —*Booklist*

"*Coming Up for Air* is heartwarming with a touch of magic. Patti Callahan Henry's elegant writing takes you on an emotional journey you won't soon forget . . . nor will you want to." —Diane Chamberlain, *New York Times* bestselling author of *The Lies We Told*

"A beautiful, emotionally engrossing story about marriage and motherhood, loss and longing." —Emily Giffin, *New York Times* bestselling author of *Something Borrowed*

"Set in a world of books, book clubs, bookstores, and beaches, *Driftwood Summer* is a wonderful novel for those who appreciate the importance of both literature and family." —*Booklist*

"Callahan's characters are interesting. . . . [a] well-written novel" —*Romantic Times*

Praise for *The Art of Keeping Secrets*

"Patti Callahan Henry's characters are complex and well drawn, and the sea sings in every syllable." —Anne Rivers Siddons, *New York Times* bestselling author of *Burnt Mountain*

"Henry gently draws readers into her story and then keeps them fully engaged until her tale is completely told. Readers who crave books that sparkle with the sheer beauty of language can rely on her." —*Booklist*

"This beautifully written story starts with an intriguing premise that immediately grabs the reader's interest. Henry uses universal concepts such as belief and faith to delve into the difficult question of how well we really know anyone, even those closest to us. Once again, the setting is the visually vivid South, with characters you quickly come to care about. This is an emotionally wrenching but ultimately healing tale." —*RT Book Reviews* (4½ stars, Top Pick)

and then
i found you

ALSO BY PATTI CALLAHAN HENRY

Coming Up for Air

The Perfect Love Song: A Holiday Story

Driftwood Summer

The Art of Keeping Secrets

Between the Tides

When Light Breaks

Where the River Runs

Losing the Moon

and then
i found you

. . . .

PATTI CALLAHAN HENRY

St. Martin's Griffin

New York

For Barbi Callahan Burris

and

Catherine Janelle Barbee

for brave love and courageous hearts

AND THEN I FOUND YOU. Copyright © 2013 by Patti Callahan Henry. All rights reserved. Printed in the United States of America. For information, address St. Martin's Press, 175 Fifth Avenue, New York, N.Y. 10010.

www.stmartins.com

The Library of Congress has cataloged the hardcover edition as follows:

Henry, Patti Callahan.
    And then I found you / Patti Callahan Henry. — First edition.
      p. cm.
    ISBN 978-0-312-61076-0 (hardcover)
    ISBN 978-1-250-03678-0 (e-book)
  I. Title.
    PS3608.E578A85 2013b
    813'.6—dc23

                             2013004029

ISBN 978-1-250-04977-3 (trade paperback)

St. Martin's Griffin books may be purchased for educational, business, or promotional use. For information on bulk purchases, please contact Macmillan Corporate and Premium Sales Department at 1-800-221-7945, extension 5442, or write specialmarkets@macmillan.com.

First St. Martin's Griffin Edition: May 2014

10 9 8 7 6 5 4 3 2 1

Acknowledgments

. . . .

This novel was inspired by a true story that happened in my family, and most directly to my middle sister, Barbi Callahan Burris. I am forever grateful for her courageous decision and eventually for her brave willingness to share her story not only with me, but also with the rest of the world. Although this is not her True-Life story (that is hers to tell), I could not have written this fictionalized version without her open honesty.

And to Catherine Janelle Barbee and her mother, Colleen, her father, Chris, and her brothers Christopher and Connor, who have opened their lives and hearts and home to me, I am grateful beyond measure.

Any essence of courage, heartbreak, healing, and redemption in this novel would be absent without Barbi and Catherine's willingness to share their memories, fears, and stories.

I want to thank so many others who have contributed to this novel's ultimate storyline:

—To John Cohen and Brenda Loringer of Wingate Wilderness: You changed our lives and I hope I've offered some lasting tribute to your incredible work.

—To Jeannie Callahan Cunnion (and her beautiful family—Mike, Cal, Brennan, and Owen) for her adoption advocacy and eye for detail. I could not have written sections of this book without your expertise.

—To my editor, Brenda Copeland, who came into my life at the right moment for the right story. I am deeply thankful for your patience and finesse with words and editing.

—Always to my agent, Kimberly Whalen, for still, all these years later, collaborating with me and with my stories.

—To those who read the novel early and offered insight, input, and kind words: Jaquelyn Mitchard, Mary Alice Monroe, Dorothea Benton Frank, and Joshilyn Jackson.

—To my newfound dear friends in Birmingham, Alabama, who sustained me during this move to a foreign city while I was in the middle of writing another novel: Cleo O'Neal, Kate Philips, Lanier Isom, Kerry Madden, Michael Morris, Cate Sommer, and all those in Mountain Brook who brought me cookies, cakes, and flowers to welcome me here. This city has also welcomed me, and I hope I've done it some justice by showing off its prettiest parts in this story.

—To my warm and wonderful readers, who have followed me since the beginning and push me to continue (special shout-out to Ashley Gross): Your words of encouragement allow me to write mine.

—To my long-lasting and true friends from Auburn to Atlanta to Birmingham, who encourage and listen and mostly make me laugh, you know who you are and how deeply I love you.

—To the librarians, booksellers, St. Martin's sales reps, book-lovers, and bookstore owners who put my books on the shelves and nominate them for awards and talk about them to readers, I am pro-foundly humbled and grateful.

—To the most innovative, kind, and creative publishing group at St. Martin's Press: Sally Richardson, Matthew Shear, Matthew Bal-dacci, Jeff Dodes, Brenda Copeland, Stephen Lee, Lisa Senz, Sarah Goldstein, Lauren Hesse, Laura Chasen, Paul Hochman, and the women at Wunderkind PR, Tanya Farrell and Elena Stokes, I am blessed to have all of you on my team.

—To Cammy Hebert and the fairytale design group at Show Me Your MuMu—an inspiration.

—And where would I be without Brooke Wahl? Without her, I'd be buried under a pile of paper, notes, and lists. Brooke, I am so glad you came into both Meagan's and my life.

—To a young woman who has encouraged me from the very be-ginning and is my daughter-from-another-mother, Tara Mahoney, I love you.

—To my sisters-in-law, Anna Henry and Serena Henry: If I could have chosen you, I would have chosen you. I love you so very much for not only listening and brainstorming and caring about my work, but also for being the lovely souls that you are to me.

—To all the nieces and nephews—Kirk, Sofia, Colin, Gavin, Cal, Brennan, Owen, Sadie, and Stella—my life is full of laughter because of you.

—To my parents, Bonnie and George Callahan, whose love is un-ending.

—To my family, of course, because without them there would be nothing else—Pat, Meagan, Thomas, and Rusk Henry.

and then
i found you

The way to love anything is to realize that it might be lost.

— G. K. CHESTERTON

prologue

. . . .

BLUFFTON, SOUTH CAROLINA

1988

March twentieth was full of First Things, and to thirteen-year-old Katie Vaughn it was the day that started all the other days in her life, the beginning of everything that might come after.

It was midday, recess, when Katie hung upside down on the monkey bars. A net of freckles covered her pale face and her copper hair dipped into a puddle—a disgusting soup made of mud and the lime-green slime of newly mowed grass. But it didn't bother Katie. She knew how to hang upside down, swing up to grab the bar, and do a full loop before landing five feet out from the bars on the solid earth below her feet. Katie was showing off and she knew she was, but if you know how to do something better than anyone else, Mom had told her, you should be doing it.

That day—that first day of spring—no one else would go near the monkey bars what with the slimy puddles, but Katie's skill had no match at Wesley Prep. She did her loop and then landed on the grass, smiling in that way of the humble when Jack Adams turned to smile at her, and damn if that wasn't when she felt her feet slip across the unstable ground. Losing balance, she landed with splayed legs, her hair spread like seaweed in the mud.

"Shit."

Sometimes kids say what they feel instead of what they're told is proper, and this was one of those unfortunate times for Katie Vaughn. The word was out of her mouth before she even knew it. This was the first time she'd ever cursed, and the word felt like biting into a lemon with the quick stab of bitter juice. It tasted good until she looked up and saw the principal looking down at her and frowning.

"Young lady, did you curse on my school grounds?" Mr. Proctor asked.

Katie looked him directly in the eyes. She'd already done one bad thing, and wasn't set to lie about it. "Yes, Sir," she said.

"Follow me. We'll call your mother," he said, pronouncing the words as if a period existed behind each one. He walked away, obviously expecting her to follow.

Katie glanced at Jack and shrugged her muddy shoulders; she could have sworn he was laughing.

After she'd been sent home to "clean her clothes and her mouth," Katie sat in the alcove of her bedroom window until evening. A small room with a single white-painted iron bed, this was Katie's hideaway. Wallpaper made of climbing pink roses filled the room like a false and always blooming garden. The dark wood hand-me-down furniture had all been painted a shade of pale pink, meant to match the rose wallpaper but missing its mark completely. Which was maybe what had happened when she'd tried to impress Jack and instead fallen into the mud: an absolute miss.

She still sat at the window waiting, although she didn't know what she was waiting for, until Jack threw acorns skyward to ping against the glass pane.

Katie opened the window. "Hey," she called out, swinging the pane out on its rusty hinges.

"Come out," he said, glancing around like a boy who is afraid he'll get caught. "Or are you grounded?"

"I'm not grounded," she said. "My mom knows that sometimes the right word is just the right word."

He laughed and threw a pinecone toward the back yard. He was a boy accustomed to having something to throw at all times. "Well, come on out."

Yes, this was what she'd been waiting for—to walk under the moon with Jack Adams.

Every night Katie checked on the moon to make sure it still hung by the invisible forces above, as if the moon could be anywhere else but the sky. She always wanted to know that Luna followed her as her grandfather had told her it did. It hadn't disappointed her yet.

Spring in Bluffton, South Carolina, was thick and swollen with possibility and, running outside, Katie felt the earth in her body. She and Jack walked down the stone pathway that led to the May River— her river—a flowing body of water so wide and rich that Katie believed the world must have been born in its basin. Scientists were wrong about where the world started because her river was the original Garden of Eden. Jack took her hand, winding his fingers through hers like the kudzu that twined over her front porch lattice.

They sat on a shattered oak log, quiet until Jack spoke. "I can't believe you aren't grounded. I mean, my dad would have made me pick out my belt if I'd been caught by mean Mr. Proctor like that."

"Well, you're a boy and you can't say that around girls, but the best I can figure is that it matters more *why* you say something than *if* you say it. If I'd have said that to my stupid little sisters or the teacher, I'd have been locked in my room for a week, but I said it because I fell and landed almost inside the earth."

Jack laughed. "I love the way you say things. You're funny, Katie."

And then he did the one thing, the only thing, she'd ever wanted him to do—he kissed her right there under a half moon next to her favorite river. It was a quick kiss, his lips brushing hers and releasing before she could fully kiss him in return. He turned away. "Guess I should've asked first," he said.

"Ask me now."

He looked at her and smiled. That kiss—the second one—was even better than the first. Katie considered it the *real* first kiss because it lasted long enough for her to taste the lemonade on his lips.

They sat in silence, crickets singing their praises, or so Katie believed.

Jack dug his forefinger into a hole of the log, plucking out dirt and flicking it onto the ground. "So, you're my girlfriend now, right?"

Katie stared at Jack with what she hoped was an adorable wide-eyed look. "Of course."

"You know, today is the first day of spring," Jack said. "And my crazy mother believes that anything you promise on the first day of spring is a promise you can never, ever break."

"I didn't promise anything today," Katie said. "So nothing to break . . . yet."

"Me neither."

"Well, I better get home for dinner or I *will* be grounded," Katie said.

They walked hand in hand to the fork in the path. One way led to his house, the other to hers. Jack glanced toward Katie's unseen house as if Katie's mom and dad had seen what happened on the riverbank.

"I can make it home from here," Katie said, knowing she didn't yet want to go home.

"You sure?" he asked.

"Yep," she answered, and then kissed him quickly, and crooked so their front teeth clacked together. She ran up the path and when she knew he could no longer see her, Katie stopped and took a hard right to her favorite willow tree—the one with a trunk as thick as three men, the tree she hid under and in. Her fortress. Flopping down on the ground under the willow's guardian limbs, Katie spoke out loud. "Today I said my *first* curse word. Today was my *first* kiss. Today is the *first* day of spring, and now my *first* promise: I will never, ever love anyone but Jonathon Gray Adams—my Jack."

Some people wish upon stars, others on birthday candles, but Katie Vaughn made a promise under a half moon and in that moment, nothing felt more important than this vow made on the first day of spring— one that couldn't and wouldn't be broken.

And when the night is new
I'll be looking at the moon
But I'll be seeing you.

SAMMY FAIN AND IRVING KAHAL, 1938

one

. . . .

BLUFFTON, SOUTH CAROLINA

2010

The unopened letter perched on the side table like a single wing about to take flight. Katie Vaughn—who at thirty-five went by Kate—wanted to open the letter, but waited.

For Kate, the first day of spring held more than blooming daffodils. It was still a day of firsts. Kate had a ritual, a sacred ritual. She made sure that she did something she'd never done before, something that would count as new on the first day of spring. Six years ago she'd opened her boutique. The year before that she ran a marathon with her sister. Of course there was that trip to Charleston with Norah. Then four years ago the midnight swim in the darkest water with Rowan, the first time he'd visited her in South Carolina. It didn't matter what she did or said or saw as long as it hadn't been done, or said, or seen before.

This year, Kate's parents, Nicole and Stuart, would meet Rowan's parents for the first time. After four years of dating, Kate and Rowan had finally found a day and time when both sets of parents were not only willing, but also able, to meet. They'd tried this before, but someone always had a reason for backing out: a cancelled flight, a threatening hurricane, a bout of the flu or, mostly, overwhelming job responsibilities. Holidays had become a source of agony—who would get Kate and Rowan?

Kate wasn't sure she was ready for this meeting, but as she knew: Life moved ahead without her permission.

And yes, it was time. Four years of dating and the parents should meet. Or so she was told.

The door buzzer forced its cracked sound into her loft, and her mom's voice came through the intercom. "Buzz me up, darling."

Kate's loft was on the second floor of a historic brick building above the boutique she owned. Her living space ran the length and breadth of the building and overlooked an oak-lined street front bordering the lush Broad River.

When the elevator doors opened, Kate's mom, Nicole, appeared with a cigarette balanced delicately between her fingers, like a gymnast on a balance beam.

"Mom," Kate held her nose in disgust. "Not in here. Seriously."

"Oh, darling," Mom came close and kissed Kate's cheek with the cigarette held up and out. Nicole ambled to the kitchen sink, taking one long draw before turning on the faucet to douse the embers, then tossing the offending cigarette into the trash.

She wore a pair of white linen pants and a pastel button-down—an outfit she wore almost every day with the shirt changing shades until Labor Day, when she donned khakis or pressed denim. (Never jeans, she'd said. Only boys wear jeans; girls wear denim.) Her copper hair was cut short and tossed with gel in a style Kate knew was supposed to look casual, but looked messy. "I was downstairs shopping in your store for something to wear tonight, and thought I'd come up and say hello."

"Did you find anything?" Kate asked, already knowing the answer.

"Oh, I tried. But you have such trendy things and it's all so expensive. I couldn't afford it even if I liked it."

"Well, then it's a good thing you don't like any of it. I know you have something in that closet of yours. It's not like this is some fancy dinner."

"But I want to make a good impression." Nicole glanced at the unopened letter, tapping her finger on its edge. "Also, I wanted to check on you because I know what today is and I know it's . . . hard."

Yes, everyone fumbled to find the just-right word for what the day was and what the day meant, and *hard* was as good a description as any other. Kate smiled. "Thanks, Mom. Really, it's okay this year."

"Ah," she said. "Love will do that."

"Do what?"

"Make everything better."

Kate laughed. "You're funny. I've never said I'm in love."

"Well, dear Lord, you've been dating him for four years and I can see it. *And* you've never asked us to meet anyone's parents. It's time, sweet pea. It is time to fall madly and terribly in love."

Kate stood. "Tara and Molly are going to be downstairs any minute and I've got ten million things to do before tonight, so hug me, then go home and pick out an outfit, okay?"

They talked for a few minutes about times and logistics for the evening. Even as Kate promised that her parents didn't need to do anything but show up, Nicole won out with her insistence that she would bring an appetizer and her husband's favorite whiskey in case Rowan was out.

"Dad can live without his whiskey for one night."

"Maybe one night," Nicole said, "but not tonight." She hugged her daughter. A dark smudge of lipstick was smeared across Nicole's front tooth, and Kate made a brushing motion with her finger across her own teeth.

Nicole reached up and wiped the lipstick off her teeth without a word: mother-daughter silent language.

They hugged good-bye and Kate stood in front of the closed elevator for a moment, thankful that her mother—no matter what excuse she'd used—had come by. No one in Kate's tight-knit family ever really knew what to do or say on this day. Each family member—Mom, Dad, and Kate's sisters, Tara and Molly—had all tried different ways to deal with it. They ignored the day. They sent cards. They made phone calls. They made visits. A lot of visits. Kate's little sister, Molly, had once brought over a tiara and set it on the kitchen counter like a monument where it had stayed for almost a year until Rowan had asked what the sparkling crown was for, and Kate had hidden it in the box with all her other memories.

Kate was the oldest of three sisters and the one who baffled her parents the most. She didn't conform to the Vaughn Family prototype: studious and bent on traditionalism. Fifteen years ago, when she still went by the name Katie, her family had begged her not to leave for south-of-nowhere Arizona, which was—in their humble opinion—far too close to the Mexican border. They told her not to leave South Carolina and all she knew. Jack had warned her that if she went, their relationship might not make it through the absence. But Katie left. At twenty years old, she hadn't imagined ever losing anything of value: love, confidence, or, least of all, Jack Adams. Doing something so terrifying and wonderful as living in the wilderness and helping young girls could only hold the best of things. Young Katie hadn't—*couldn't*—conceive of all she would lose inside a single choice that had felt so right.

Maybe there was something to the supposed magic of March twentieth, because Kate hadn't fully loved another man since her promise under the willow tree. Kate often joked to her best friend, Norah, that on that first day of spring, after that first kiss, she should have made Jack also promise to always love her. A one-sided promise hadn't done Kate any good at all.

"It could be that a girl only loves like that once," Kate had told Norah. "Only once and then after that, love is more sensible."

Norah had completely disagreed. But Norah was a romantic; Kate was a realist. Or so she said.

And now there was Rowan.

Kate knew that Tara and Molly would be waiting downstairs, wandering the racks and asking to open the new boxes in the back room. The biggest perk when your sister owned a clothing store? First pick of the new shipments.

But Kate was wrong. Tara and Molly were sitting on stools behind the checkout counter, talking to Norah and holding their ever-present Starbucks cups.

"Kitty-Kat," Molly said.

"Katie-Latey," Tara said.

Kate laughed and pointed at the imitation Paris Train Station clock hanging on the back wall. "Two minutes. I've got two minutes until late is late."

"Your definition of late and our definition aren't quite the same," Molly said.

"Just today, can we take a break from pointing out my faults?" Kate asked, trying to smile at her sister. That was the thing with Molly— she knew what dug the deepest and hurt the most, and sometimes she couldn't help but use that superpower.

Norah, always the peacemaker, always knowing when the sisterly jabs were building, quickly interrupted and changed the subject. "We were talking about tonight, and wondering why we, the most important people in your life, weren't invited."

Norah stood between Molly and Tara. She was a light, a candle, a beacon really. Kate and Norah had been best friends since third grade and whenever Kate felt lost, she looked to Norah exactly as she did when she asked, "Do you really want to sit through a dinner with the Vaughn and Irving parents?"

The three of them looked at each other in alternate glances and laughed. "Um, no," Tara said, standing.

Norah smiled at Kate and winked. Norah drew stares wherever she went, and yet she pretended she didn't notice. It was her beauty, yes—with her long, dark hair and almost six-foot height, with her eyes so dark they appeared mystical—but the stares were mostly a result of gazes being drawn to Norah's face where, at birth, a pair of forceps had gashed her left eye, leaving a dip and scar that made it appear as if Norah had wept enough to form a half-inch-long furrow into her cheek. Norah was told many times that there were methods and lasers and surgeries that could fix this, but she shrugged and nodded. "Yep, that might be a good idea one day." Yet one day never seemed to matter to Norah. Only that day, the day she was living, was important to her.

"So, we're here to pick out your outfit for the evening," Tara said, her cheeks puckering inward as she took a long draw of her coffee, which she always desperately needed what with a ten-, a four-, and a two-year-old under her feet and in her hair and in her bed (her words exactly).

Kate laughed. "No way. I've got that under control. We're going out to lunch and that's it."

Molly moaned. "Come on, Kitty-Kat. Let's do something funner than that today."

"Funner is not a word, Molly." Kate kissed her baby sister, who wasn't a baby at all but twenty-seven years old, on the forehead.

"Then let's go do something that is memorable and silly instead." Molly held out her hands. "I say kayaking out to Goat Island and drinking moonshine until dusk."

Their joined laughter was a sacred sound. Kate shook her head. "I'm all in on the kayak, but since I want to appear vaguely human to the Irving family, I'll skip the moonshine."

The front door to the boutique was open, propped by a concrete garden statue of a little girl holding out her skirts. Birds called and the breeze rattled in the palmetto fronds, sounding like blessed rain. "God, I love spring," Tara said as she stood. "It's like anything, almost anything at all could happen." She held her arms out wide, coffee cup still in hand as a permanent appendage.

Norah glanced at Kate, who attempted to smile back. Yes, anything could happen and mostly had.

"Where are the kids today?" Kate asked.

"Dearest hubby took the day off. He knew I wanted to spend it with you," Tara said.

"It wasn't necessary, but thanks," Kate said and hugged her sister with one arm, keeping the full force of the day's meaning close and distant in a dance of opposites.

"Let's go then." Molly jumped off her stool.

"I wish you could come," Kate said to Norah.

"I almost asked Charlie to cover for me." Norah smiled.

"Your husband's too cute; I wouldn't trust Kitty-Kat's clients," Molly said.

Norah laughed. "Good point. Anyway, I tried to get Lida to cover, but she has that mysterious stomach bug that grabs her every few weeks."

"Sure thing," Tara said and rolled her eyes. "The bug that sits on the bottom of the freaking tequila bottle."

"Stop," Kate said.

"I swear, Kitty-Kat, you take in humans like some people take in animals. I think you should move on to stray cats." Molly poked Kate's arm with one slender finger.

This never-ending subject irritated Kate, but she smiled. "I know."

And she did know. Lida had once been one of the girls she'd counseled in the wilderness of Arizona. Now twenty-six years old, Lida could hold it together for weeks and sometimes months, but then she'd slide back into that dark place, a place where someone who hadn't visited that same hell could never imagine or understand. The last thing Kate had energy for that morning was rehashing the pain that led Lida to do things Molly and Tara couldn't fathom doing. Kate knew all about doing things she'd never once imagined doing. Explaining rarely helped.

Kate met Rowan Irving when she was on a buying trip for Mimsy Clothing. It was Rowan's smile that caused Kate to grin in return. This was what she'd been waiting for: an open door that would shut all others. It had been nine years since she'd last cracked open her heart, and it was time to try again.

When she met Rowan, she'd resolved to forget the pain of the past. Time to move on, she'd told herself. Somewhere deep inside she'd remember what happened, but the world would never know or see. She would make a new life starting right there, right then. Nothing of the past would build the future.

Rowan's eyes were brown, his eyelashes long and dark. His face was square and solid. He seemed able to hold the weight of her world without wavering. They sat across from each other at a bar table and laughed about the karaoke singers onstage. "Do you sing?" he asked.

She started to answer in her usual way, which would be "Oh, no, I could never get on that stage." And then she remembered: Begin Again. Begin Anew.

His eyes were smiling. She'd never really seen anyone's eyes smile like that, so fully. "Yes," she said. "I try."

"Okay, go for it." He pointed at the stage.

"You'll go with me?"

"I don't karaoke."

"Tonight you do," she said, enjoying this new self who flirted and took chances and tried to talk a man into singing with her as if she were tasting a new flavor of ice cream.

"No way," he said.

She leaned toward him, making chicken clucking noises.

The chair rocked as he leaned back to laugh. He slammed his hands on the table. "Is this a dare?"

"Just seeing if you're worthy of my attention."

"Throwing down the gauntlet."

She stood. "Guess so."

"You have no idea how awful this will sound." He stood and took her hand as they walked to the karaoke stage.

"See, that's the thing with bar karaoke, the worse it sounds the better it is."

"Then this will be the best of the night."

Kate flipped through the songbook. When they started with Meatloaf's "Paradise by the Dashboard Light," the bar was packed. By the time they got around to "Brown Eyed Girl" by Van Morrison, the place had almost cleared out.

It was closer to morning than night when they left the bar. "Can I call you or something?" Rowan asked.

"I live in South Carolina. That's really . . . far away."

He grinned. "Not for a phone call."

"No, not for that." Kate wrote down her number, then left without touching Rowan Irving.

They'd been dating four years now; their mutual love of the outdoors, rivers, and an ever-changing landscape were the solid base for all that came after. If Kate had ever made a list—which she hadn't—Rowan would fill the imagined boxes of a perfect mate. She wanted those facts to move from her head the mere twelve inches toward her heart and settle in with deep love, something past admiration and comfort.

He was from Philadelphia, and when their long distance dating became more annoying than romantic, he'd moved to Bluffton. He'd said it was for the job offer—landscape architect for one of the most prestigious firms in the Low Country—but they both knew that it was love that brought him to South Carolina and love that kept him there. They hadn't moved in together or even talked of engagement, but Kate understood a commitment was close, and fear was tucked inside the beautiful possibilities.

The evening with the Irving and Vaughn parents went better than she'd hoped, except for the moment when Mr. Irving, in his ascot and pressed pinstripe suit, asked why Kate was Katie to her parents, but Kate to everyone else.

"Oh, she decided to shed her old self," Stuart, Kate's dad, said with a dismissive wave.

"Why would she shed her old self?" Mrs. Irving asked, twisting a napkin in her hand.

Kate laughed, a false sound. "Oh, there was no shedding involved. One day I thought Katie was too cutesy. That's it."

"Oh." Mrs. Irving lifted her hand to twirl her pearls, and attempted to smile, but Kate saw the underwriting: *liar.*

Other than that four-sentence conversation, the night had gone well. Kate's dad hadn't drunk too much whiskey. Her mother hadn't lit a single cigarette. The steak dinner, which Rowan had cooked to impress her family, wasn't burnt. No one brought up The Future or, for that matter, The Past. So, all in all, a success.

The evening was ending, coffee brewing in the kitchen. Rowan lived in a two-bedroom guesthouse behind a much larger house in the Bluffton historic district. A landscape designer, he lived there gratis in exchange for taking care of the yard and gardens surrounding the house. His den was crowded with leather furniture—the complete opposite of Kate's cream and linen slipcovered aesthetic. She wondered how the two of them would ever combine not only their lives but their tastes. His windows overlooked a boxwood labyrinth with a large fountain in the center. The family gathered there as Kate slipped into Rowan's bedroom to catch her breath.

She sat on the edge of his bed and placed her wineglass on the bedside table. Kate hadn't yet told Rowan everything she needed to tell him about her history, and she knew it was time. After the parents left, she would tell him everything, all that was getting in the way of their future together.

What future? Kate sank sideways into Jack's pillow. What would their future look like together? She couldn't imagine it. She saw their separate lives as scattered remnants, and she wasn't sure the pieces could ever come together to form any kind of whole. Was wanting to want it good enough?

Dixie, Rowan's goofy and hyper golden retriever, came bounding into the room. Seeing Kate on the edge of the bed, the dog assumed it was playtime and jumped toward her, knocking the red wine onto the khaki bedspread and across Kate's pale green sundress.

"Dixie," Kate hollered, and ran into the bathroom for some towels. Mopping up the spill, Kate shooed Dixie off the bed and watched the wine drip into the top drawer of the bedside table. She yanked the drawer open to shove the towel under the rim of the table when she saw the box: a small white box with two bloodred drops of spilled wine on its top. She opened the box a fraction of an inch to see the ring—a round and brilliant engagement ring.

She jerked back.

"Kate," Rowan's voice called from the hallway.

She shoved the drawer shut. "In here," she called. "Dixie spilled my wine."

Her parents appeared at the doorway along with Rowan and his parents. Kate cringed. "Sorry. I was coming in here to use the bathroom and Dixie jumped up on me and . . ."

All gazes moved to the bed, which was of course not a bathroom. "Let's go have some coffee," Kate said, guiding the crowd back to Rowan's den.

"Who wants dessert?" Rowan asked as they stood facing one another.

Kate felt the panic rising—a grip on her throat, a beehive in her gut. It always happened this way. Just when she thought she could love, just when she thought a man would be able to enter her life, she panicked. She wanted, more than she wanted anything, to make this dread end.

She smiled past the anxiety and then lied. "I'm exhausted. I think I just need to go home and hit the sack."

Rowan looked at her and squinted, knowing her voice was off-kilter. "Okay," he said, drawing out the end part of the word into a long "eh" noise.

Good-byes were said and hugs were given and when only Kate and Rowan remained in his den, he asked the questions she couldn't answer. "What's up with you? What's wrong?"

Home in her loft, leaning against her bed's padded headboard, Kate closed her eyes and took in a long, deep breath. *What is wrong with you?* Those weren't Rowan's exact words, but close enough to taunt her.

The sight of that ring should have sent any girl into spasms of happiness.

What is wrong with you?

The answer to that damn question seemed as far away as the moon: inaccessible, remote, and frozen.

She slumped down under her covers, bringing the white duvet to her chin. Maybe the unassailable answer to what was wrong was to really and finally once and for all *talk to Jack.*

No.

See Jack.

No.

When all the mistakes had been made and all the running had been finished, a girl does not go back to the boy to undo what can never, ever be undone.

two

. . . .

ARIZONA

1995

It's easy to find where some things begin: a fire started, a secret told, a book opened to the first page. But Kate couldn't understand exactly where she and Jack had gone wrong. God, how she wanted to find that starting point and place a pin on it, a red-flagged pin of blame and reason.

During their junior year of high school, Jack's family had left for Birmingham, Alabama. Maybe that's where it started, with his parents' decision to move. Or perhaps it all began the month Jack graduated early from Clemson and decided to go to law school in Birmingham, leaving Katie to finish at Wake Forest, bored, alone, and restless. Yes, maybe she could thrust that pin into both those past events, but again and again she believed that the beginning of the end was the day she decided to take the job after her college graduation. No malice or meanness existed in this decision; if anything she'd thought she was doing the right thing for both her life and their relationship.

That last semester of college, Katie missed Jack fiercely, knowing their time apart during college would soon be over. Distracted and detached, she wandered the University gymnasium during a job fair and weighed her options: move to Birmingham and get a job while Jack was consumed with law school or find a summer job that wasn't permanent and wait for Jack's schedule to slow down. She imagined her loneliness in a city she didn't know, and in which she had no friends.

In the muggy gymnasium, a job fair had been set up. Tables were lined up like multicolored dominoes, one after the other with tall signs stating what company or employer was represented. Balloons meant to attract were wilting in the heat, drooping pitifully. Students milled around after scribbling their names on the sign-in sheet to prove to the academic advisor that they'd showed up as promised. Katie wandered past the secretarial jobs, the nursing home employer, and the trucking company where the man behind the table spit dark liquid into a plastic cup while grinning at her. "Missy, you want a job that'll take you on the open road for the summer?" Katie laughed, shook her head.

Katie turned her back on the trucker to see the Winsome Wilderness sign. Two girls Katie knew from her Adolescent Psychology class—Jeannie and Meg, both pegged "granola-girls"—were standing behind the table. These girls were not quite hippies and not quite ragged stoners either. They wore cutoffs and cute embroidered tops, and considered ChapStick to be makeup. They were beautiful though, with their long hair, and they were always smiling. That was the main thing Katie had noticed about them.

Photos, feathers, and bundles of sage were scattered across the red-clothed card table. Twig frames showcased pictures of smiling young girls looking over their shoulders as they wound their way through red rocks. Other photos showed girls gathered around a campfire, the glow of the fire reflected in their young faces. Katie picked up a speckled brown feather lying on the edge of the table.

"Hawk," one of the girls said.

"Huh?" Katie looked up at Meg and Jeannie.

"That's a red-tailed hawk feather. Means wisdom." Meg, or the girl Katie thought was Meg, said.

"Okay." Katie smiled at both girls.

"I'm Meg," she said. Yes, Katie was right. "We're in Psych together, right?"

"Yes," Katie said and glanced at the other girl. "And you're Jeannie, right?"

They both nodded.

"Are you looking for a summer job?" Jeannie asked.

"I am," Katie said and lifted a sheet of paper with typed facts and an attached application. "What is this?"

"A wilderness program. Aren't you a social work major like us?"

Katie nodded.

"This is sort of like Outward Bound, but for kids who need more help and therapy and like that."

"And like that?" Katie asked. "Like what?"

"You don't have to do the counseling or anything crazy. You get to camp with them for weeks. You're called a field guide." Meg smiled and gazed past Katie as if she was imagining heaven during a frenzied religious tent revival.

"Well, then what do you *do*?" Katie placed the application back on the table. She was being polite. She'd already decided that this hippie-fest was not for her. Sure, she'd studied social work and, sure, she loved the outdoors, but talking to troubled kids over bonfires was not for her. Singing koombaya and sleeping on the dirt was for someone else entirely.

Katie's mind was set until Jeannie spoke. "It's a miracle what happens out there," she said. "You'll never be the same."

Katie wanted to be something and someone different than she was—someone who didn't sit around and wait for Jack to finish law school and pay attention to her. She wanted to be a girl with purpose and a meaning. And the words—*you'll never be the same*—were a siren call.

"How so?" Katie asked.

"We're shutting down for the day. You want to go get a beer with us?" Jeannie asked.

"Sure," Katie said, without any nudge, whisper, or thought that this might be the very moment she thrust the pin of change into her own life.

It wasn't until after she took the job at Winsome that Katie remembered an afternoon with her mother, a hazy afternoon that began her essential desire to be in the wild, to refuse to give in to the demands of others, or even the demands of love.

It had been an afternoon of unruffled peace, just fourteen-year-old Katie and her mom on the pier, eating their melting ice cream cones and watching the Hilton Head boats coming in and out of the marina. They'd shopped the small trinket stores, and Katie's mom bought her a brand-new shark tooth necklace, which dangled off Katie's slim neck. She fiddled with the point of the tooth, pressing it into the skin of her thumb as she watched the boats move in and out of the slips as easily as fish.

"I want to be like one of those," Katie said to her mom.

"One of what?"

"Those boats. I mean, not really a boat, but something like a boat."

Her mom had laughed, fully, sticky with ice cream. "Something like a boat?"

"You know, like all free and wild and not stuck anywhere at all."

"Katie, dear, don't say *like;* that's a bad habit. And yes, we all want that when we're fourteen," her mom said, quietly. A sad tone arrived; Katie knew all her mom's tones the way a pianist knew all the keys.

"I'll want it forever," Katie said.

Her mom's ice cream cone melted down her forearm unnoticed or touched. "I hope you do. I hope that whatever it is you want that you don't give it up just because someone else asks you to do so. Anything you want, Katie, anything, don't let someone else talk you out of it."

"I want another shark tooth necklace," Katie said, grinning.

Her Mom had smiled, but with only the bottom part of her face. "Nice try." She put her hand on Katie's leg. "You think you love that boy, don't you?"

"He's not a boy. He's Jack. And I don't think I do, I know I do."

"You're fourteen."

"You didn't love anyone when you were fourteen?" Katie licked the edge of the cone, scooping the last of the ice cream into her mouth..

"No, I loved my Raggedy Ann doll. That's about it at fourteen." She handed the remainder of her cone to Katie.

"Really?"

"Really."

"Well, Jack is the most amazing boy in the world."

"You'll let him talk you out of your dreams. That's what love does sometimes—talks you out of your dreams."

"Not me," Katie said. "Jack would talk me *into* my dreams."

It should have been simple. Katie wanted to take the Winsome Wilderness job to make a difference in the world, to help those who were helpless, to reach out to a child who didn't have what she'd been given. But somehow it turned complicated, like a mathematical equation Katie could never solve.

Jack begged her not to go, saying "Why do you want to be so far away from me? There are social work jobs all over Birmingham; you don't have to be across the country to help kids." Her dad told her she was crazy, saying "You're too far away. The money isn't even good." And then there was the panicked plea from her mom, "If anything happened to you, I'd never know and you'd be stuck in the middle of nowhere." Katie did her best to soothe their worries and promised to be home soon.

The job entailed camping out with thirteen- and fourteen-year-old girls, helping them learn the ways of the wilderness while keeping them in line until their therapists showed up to counsel them two days a week. Katie and the other guides were to impart stories and lessons to the girls, but the main goal was to allow nature to do the work.

On the nights she wasn't camping, Katie shared a two-bedroom apartment in Timber, Arizona, with five other girls and a mass of bunk beds, knowing that rarely would any of them be there at the same time. It was the perfect way to have a home base and also save money. Perfect, that is, except for the rare times when all of them had off the same week. Field guides, they were called. After one week of intense training and an assurance of her love for nature's unreliable behavior, Katie went off into the wilderness. No cell phones. No TV. No cars. No cable. Only nature. And Katie fell in love—with the wilderness, with the girls, with the work.

The pain humans inflicted one on another, even in love, had done damage to these girls in ways Katie had never known. She watched as they arrived angry and hurt, slowly opening to nature's erratic and tender wildness. They learned self-reliance by crafting necessary items. They took what they'd been given in the wilderness and created something out of it: a spoon, an arrow, a pouch of leather, and, most importantly, a fire. Then they took what they'd been given inside— all the wonderfulness inside—and created a new life. The creative spirit reigned in the wilderness, and each girl who graduated took a piece of Katie's heart with her.

After three months of summer work, Katie decided to stay on with her job. She'd always thought of work as something to fill time and make money, a nuisance that preoccupied her from greater things. She soon discovered that this work filled her up, changed her as she grew into either new Katie or the real Katie; she wasn't sure which and frankly didn't care either. Katie had always needed a goal, an end point, something to work toward with greedy need. But this job—and it was so much more than a job—took her to a place both inside and outside herself she never knew existed. Helping wounded young girls to heal instilled in her a generous feeling, one that extended past her own demands and desires. Meg had been right—working with these girls was a miracle. Although she missed Jack, most thoughts of self were buried under the work she was doing.

Needing to see Jack and also explain why she was staying longer at her job, Katie gathered her savings and bought a plane ticket to Birmingham. When she arrived at the off-campus apartment that Jack shared with two other law school students, a party was in full swing. A real college party with a sweaty keg floating in a trash can and girls sitting on countertops and floors.

The room smelled like sweat and old beer. Katie wound her way through the apartment until she found Jack in his bedroom, standing in front of his closet, talking to his roommate about who would pay for the keg this time around.

"Baby, you're here!" he said, when he saw her standing in his doorway. He moved towards her and in two steps lifted her off the floor.

"I'm interrupting a party, I think."

"You don't interrupt anything of mine," Jack kissed her, an unassailable kiss that made her weak and indecisive about anything and everything.

"You two are ridiculous," the roommate said and laughed, slamming the door behind him as he left them alone.

"So," Jack said, "Tell me that you're here to say you are never returning to that faraway place where I can't even get you on the phone. Please say that."

She couldn't.

"I committed to this year." Katie cringed as she said the words. "You're so busy with school, and I love what I'm doing. I thought one more year and then you'd be almost done and we would . . . settle in a little bit."

He sat on the edge of his single bed, unmade and rumpled. "A year is a long time. A really long time. You'll miss so much."

"But then I'll have everything else forever." She had practiced this steady proclamation on the plane.

Jack didn't answer.

"I have to do this. For the first time in my life, I'm making a difference in someone beside myself. There's this girl, Sara—her dad died last year. She was the angriest person you'd ever met, and she graduated last week with a new heart. You can't imagine the beauty out there. The mountains turning to desert to mountain again. The—"

Jack held up his hand. "I know. I know. I read it all in your letters. The feathers you collect. The things you've learned to make. You sound happier than you've ever been."

"Not ever been, but happy, yes. Making a difference, yes. If I stayed here, I'd be passing the time waiting for you to graduate. So this seems a much better way to wait. Right?"

"You see this as a way to wait? Wait for what?"

"You, of course."

"I would never leave you for a year," he said.

"I'm not leaving you. I'm taking a job. There's a huge difference."

"It doesn't feel like there's any difference. What about us?"

"Us?" She kissed him. "There is always us. You're going to be buried underneath a stack of books taller than me. If I don't do this, if I don't try this now, I know I will regret it for the rest of my life."

"We made it through four years at separate colleges, now it's time to be together."

"I'm begging you to understand." She took both his hands and squeezed them. She tried to explain that if she didn't do this one thing she would never again do what she wanted, that if she could let someone—even Jack—talk her out of doing this, that she would never again follow through on anything important in her life. Never. "It's one year. That's all." She wiggled onto his lap and kissed his neck. "Love is enough. It always is."

"Sadly, sometimes it's not enough."

"You are so pragmatic. My lawyer, Jack Adams."

"Please don't go."

"I have to. That's the thing, Jack. I absolutely have to. But I believe in us. I do."

At that four girls burst into the bedroom, calling Jack's name. They stopped short when they saw Katie. "Sorry," one tall brunette said as she shut the door.

"Well," Katie stood and looked down at him. "I guess you aren't going to be too lonely while I'm gone."

"Don't turn this around," he said. "I'm not doing anything wrong. At all."

"I'm not either," Katie said.

"If I'm not doing anything wrong and you're not doing anything wrong, why the hell does everything feel so wrong?" Jack asked, squinting at Katie as if a bright light shone into his eyes.

"I don't know," she said in a whisper. "I really don't know. But I can't fight about it, and I can't leave with us angry."

"Let's get out of here," he said.

The camping and wilderness routine returned to Katie as if her visit to Jack had been a quick dream. She opened her eyes in the dead of night, her head lying on a bunched-up sweatshirt. As usual, the first thing she looked for in the night sky was the moon, but it was a new moon, not invisible exactly, but translucent. The arching bell of dark sky reached to touch the edges of the earth, holding its innumerable stars. A young girl next to Katie whispered. "There are a million more stars here than where I live in New York."

Katie smiled into the dark, once again explaining. "There are always the same amount of stars, but here you can see them. Just like you'll soon be able to see all the beautiful things in you that were there all along. It takes the wilderness to open your eyes."

"Whatever," the girl said in the hoarse and angry whisper they all seemed to arrive with.

That night Katie missed Jack with a deep ache. It was a feeling that snuck up on her in the quietest moments. How was it possible to both love where she was and yet miss where she wasn't?

She'd seen the sun set and rise on the same seemingly endless terrain. She'd eaten food she'd never heard of and slept less than she knew a human body could sleep and still function. She collected feathers, which she often found exactly when she was thinking about something that needed an answer. She knew her days by the phases of the moon. The shooting stars—twenty or thirty a night—were her lullaby and passageway to sleep. What was once foreign was now familiar.

Many times Katie felt that her family was frozen in time, but much happened that year. After an early graduation from University of South Carolina, Tara had eloped with her boyfriend, Kyle; now she wrote witty columns about marriage for the local paper. Molly was in her sophomore year in high school and her letters were full of exclamation points and drama. Her parents were living a second dating life, their first cut short by marriage.

No one in the family—not one—agreed with Katie's job choice. They believed she was running away from life when she told them over and over that she was actually not running anywhere, but maybe, just maybe, was learning a new life while touching the lives of others.

Jack wrote letters and she wrote back, long letters about everything she saw and felt in this strange terrain. In every correspondence, she told him, *I wish you could see what I see.* She missed him, his voice, his touch, and yet the longing for him couldn't stand against the need to stay at her job. With every girl's life that changed, a new young girl was beginning to see her way through a cloud of chaos, and Katie couldn't leave her alone in that misery.

What Katie wasn't able to explain, the phenomenon that lacked words, was how passing time in the desert was different than actual-time at home. Scientifically, of course this time alteration wasn't true, but in the paradox that was nature's way, it was vivid and unerring. Ten days strung together were only two days. While at home a month passed, in the desert it was a week or less. She didn't feel she'd been gone too long and they—her family and Jack—felt she'd been gone forever. A lifetime perhaps.

Jack's written words filled those empty missing-him spaces until they'd be together. The delay, Katie thought, was where the love grew larger in longing.

The first year had passed and each time she was pressed to come home to Jack, she gave it a time limit, *Just one more month,* Katie would write. *There is this new girl, Steph, and she is making so much progress. Her dad almost destroyed her, but she's coming out of her shell. She has a month left . . . then . . . then I'll come home.*

And then, *They need me two more months because they lost their best field guide. I promise, just two more*—Even inside these explanations and excuses, Katie only felt as if their love was waiting, never as if it were leaving. Until the week Jack's letter ended with, *We should both be free to date others by now.* But Katie didn't take it literally, only as a hint that they could, but of course wouldn't.

It was Katie's mom who sent the most pleading letter, asking why Katie didn't love them anymore. Katie tried to assure her parents and sisters that it wasn't love's absence, but her own love of the girls, that kept her in the wild.

Her teenage sister, Molly, responded with, *You sound like those stupid boys who say, "it's not you, it's me."* Katie told her sister that although the adage might be stupid, it was true. It wasn't that she didn't want to come home to the family; she just wanted to be exactly where she was. And she meant it, too, until Tara wrote a quick and cryptic P.S. on the bottom of a letter: *Saw Jack in Atlanta at a concert. His date seemed nice.*

three

. . . .

BLUFFTON, SOUTH CAROLINA

2010

Mimsy Clothing had opened for the day, and Kate stood at the front counter rearranging the bracelets hanging on a dress-shaped wire. Exposed brick walls were adorned with black and white photographs of South Carolina, while free-floating iron racks were loaded with women's clothes. Unadorned iron-framed windows allowed light to pour like lemonade into the store. Carla Bruni sang in French through the overhead speakers, and Kate sang along in words she didn't understand but had heard a hundred times.

The front door opened and a gust of spring's pollen-laden breeze entered the store. Kate looked up to see Susan Neal walk through the front door. "Mornin', Kate."

Susan was dressed as if she were headed to a photo shoot, lovely and crisp in her grey silk Helmut Lang dress with a trench coat cinched at her waist. Susan had been Kate's employee, mentor, and friend in that exact order. Even at fifty years old, Susan looked younger than Kate's own thirty-five years. That's what Kate thought, anyway.

"What a nice surprise." Kate walked out from behind the counter and hugged Susan. "When did you get in town?"

The Neal family lived in Atlanta, but owned a house twenty minutes away on Hilton Head Island. "This morning. We're only here for a day, so I didn't think I'd stop by, but of course I couldn't resist. I'm trying to take care of some maintenance issues on the house, and I decided to come hug you."

"You looking for anything?"

"Nope, but I wanted to tell you about these two boutiques I saw. One in Atlanta. One in Birmingham. They're similar to ours, but they're doing business hand over fist."

"Hand over fist?" Kate asked, grinning with a teasing smile.

"Bad cliché, sorry." Susan said with a laugh, shooing her hand through the air. "I thought about our store when I visited there. They are doing some innovative things and . . ." She handed two cards to Kate. "You might want to check them out."

"Okay," Kate said. "But more importantly, how is *my* Mimsy?"

Susan grinned. "You forget, she's mine *and* she's a mess."

Before opening the boutique, Kate had been a nanny for Susan's oldest child, Mimsy. Kate had then named the store after the little girl who had brought Kate back to feeling the goodness of life. Led by a small child's laughter and her pure curiosity about life's most mundane moments, Kate had begun to heal while taking care of Mimsy. Kate laughed deeply. "Yes, I imagine. Tell her to come in here and I'll put her back on the straight and narrow."

"Even if Jesus came to visit her with the Holy Mother, I don't think Mimsy would be on the straight and narrow." Susan rolled her eyes, but they both knew she was exaggerating. Mimsy was not only the joy of the family, but also very far away from a mess, at least as far away as any fifteen-year-old girl could be.

They hugged good-bye as Susan reminded Kate to send her any and all new arrivals she thought Susan might like. Her Mimsy partner wanted to be the first to see the best of everything.

The door swished shut and Kate stood in the middle of the boutique, dazed. Although she'd heard every word Susan had said, only one word had stood out.

Birmingham.

A million times Kate had thought about Birmingham, about the city and the name and the ivy-covered house on a hill. But hearing the city's name in Susan's voice—an echo of Kate's innermost memories—caused her to sit in the lounge chair meant for tired husbands waiting on their wives.

Lida blew through the front door of the store the same way the incoming storm would arrive any minute. She carried two coffee cups, and a large tote dangled precariously off her wrist. Her dreadlocks were pulled into a ponytail and the wrist tattoo of a small sacred heart with a sword slashed through its red center was hidden under a cuff bracelet. Her smile, the most beautiful and hard-won aspect of self, was radiant.

"Wow," Lida said, handing Kate the coffee. "You look like you haven't slept all night. What is up with that?"

"So I look that good?" Kate rubbed her forefingers under her eyes.

"You always look good, boss. I'm just sayin', you look tired."

"I am."

"How did the dinner with the parents go last night?"

"Really well," Kate said. "I didn't sleep much, though." She paused. "Listen, can you take over for a bit; I'm running upstairs to try and look more presentable. I'll be right back."

"That's why I'm here," Lida said with no evidence of any bug whatsoever, the kind that came inside a liquor bottle or a virus.

Kate rode the elevator to her loft. Since seeing the ring in Rowan's drawer she'd been gripped with a headache that seemed to dissipate only when she thought of something else, anything else but getting engaged.

"Focus," she told herself out loud. "Think about something else: clothes." She needed to decide what to wear that night for a party at Larson's house. Outfits preoccupied her the way she believed painting or writing occupied others. She could fill her mind with the nuances of color and style, mixing and matching, making something new of something used.

Larson was the one friend left over from her high school days who was also friends with Rowan. His annual St. Patrick's Day party had been cancelled for thunderstorms that shut down the town's electricity. That night, although it was the twenty-first, they would all pretend it was the seventeenth, dressing up in green and listening to too-loud Irish music.

Kate pulled out a bright green Vince sundress and held it up to the light, finally finding her mind somewhere else other than an engagement ring or even worse, a certain man in Birmingham.

The party was too much. Everything about it was amped up to a level that made Kate slink back to the corner of the room. The music's base was cranked too high. The crowd sang along to "Danny Boy" in perfect disharmony. Bodies were slammed between couches and chairs, the food flowed off overcrowded plates, and wine, beer, and liquor bottles were lined up on a bar at the far end of the room, seeming to push each other off the tabletop. And the heat, relentless and grasping, filled whatever space was left.

Why was she the only one bothered by all this too-much? Kate squeezed her eyes shut and took a long soothing swallow of the drink

Rowan had brought her, some concoction made of lemonade, vodka, and ginger. Sweat trickled down her back and into the small space where she'd once threatened to get a tattoo. She never could decide what image was worth being on her skin forever.

"You okay, baby?" Rowan's voice came from far away, and yet when Kate opened her eyes, he was standing right next to her.

"It's ten thousand degrees in here."

"When the rain quits, everyone'll go back out."

Kate nodded. "Can we leave?"

"Are you kidding?"

"No, I don't think I am."

Rowan backed away two steps and wiped his damp hair off his forehead. "Just hang a bit longer, okay?" His green Tommy Bahama shirt clung to his chest. His khaki shorts were secured with a canvas belt decorated with tiny red crabs. This boy from Philadelphia had turned into a South Carolina boy.

These were mostly Rowan's friends, and Kate knew that he desperately wanted them to be "their" friends, combining lives slowly, friend by friend, day by day, then house by house. She knew what he wanted and damn, she wanted to give it to him. She stepped closer to him. "It's not the people; it's how loud and crowded it is."

"When the rain . . ."

"I know. I know." Kate dropped her head back and exhaled. "We'll stay."

Larson and Jimmy came full bore across the room, high-fiving Rowan and greeting Kate. "Hey, y'all. Sucks the rain killed the oyster roast," Larson said.

"It'll stop," Kate said.

Thunder echoed nearby. "Sure it will," Larson said, lifting his grossly green beer high. "And Santa will get me a Red Ryder BB Gun for Christmas."

Kate laughed. "You crack me up," she said.

"Yeah, it's a gift." Larson walked away, waving across the room to someone else.

"See, this is fun, right?" Rowan asked.

Kate looked to him and his smile cracked her heart. Why couldn't she find the generosity to show him that she wanted to be a part of all he was a part of? Just being present couldn't be good enough. It was easy to fake it, right? Then why did she find that so-easy thing so-hard to do? She took Rowan's hand and squeezed.

Norah showed up exactly when Kate thought she'd hit her last minute of party time. Together they stood on the covered back porch. But at least they weren't in the stifling boiler room full of partiers.

"I hate this," Kate said.

"I know." Norah held her hand out from the porch, allowing rain to dance across her palm and drip down her arm. "Good thing you're dating the party boy of Bluffton. I'd bet within a year he could be the mayor."

"You're crazy," Kate said. "A Philly-boy mayor?"

"He's best friends with everyone in town. He's like a hurricane of friend-making."

Kate laughed. "He's charming. People like him."

"Of course they do." Norah shook the rain from her hand. "Everyone loves Rowan."

"I know."

They stood in the silence that best friends stand in; comfortable and knowing that whatever words rested beneath "I know" would be discussed another day and time. They talked about the store and a late shipment, about Charlie's possible job promotion and the never-ending rain, until Rowan burst through the back screen door.

"Ladies, what are you doing? The party is inside." He swept his hand toward the house.

"We're catching up," Kate said.

"Oh, because you don't see each other every day all day?" He smiled and took Kate's hand. "Come on, girl. Becky pulled out Brian's *Cotton-Eyed Joe* CD and you know what that does for Larson."

Kate groaned. "I'm really not sure I can see his version of clogging tonight."

Rowan took her hand to lead her inside as the back door opened and a man walked outside, barely missing Kate with the swinging door. "Whoa," he said. "Sorry."

"It's okay," Kate said, taking a step back. "You missed me."

"Katie? Katie Vaughn?" he asked.

"Hayes?"

"Yep, in the flesh." The guy smiled.

Kate hugged him. "I thought you'd moved out West. Montana, right?"

Hayes nodded. He was tall, a shadow of beard on his chin. "Yep. I'm home for Mama's birthday, and Larson dragged me to his party."

"It's really good to see you," Kate said, and then introduced him to Rowan.

"Nice to meet you. I've heard lots about you," Hayes said. "Welcome to town."

Rowan laughed. "Been here a few years."

"Well, welcome anyway. Guess I'd follow cute Katie anywhere too." Hayes turned to Kate then. "You see much of the old gang?"

"Not really," she said. "Just Larson and Norah."

Hayes turned and saw Norah, laughing. "Hey, you," he said, and hugged Norah, picking her up and putting her gently down. "How you doing?"

"Great."

"Hey," Hayes said, holding his cold beer against his forehead. "Either of you ever see Jack Adams? I thought about him the other day and couldn't find him on Facebook or anywhere else. No one seems to know what happened to him."

Norah looked to Kate and then broke the silence, "Last I heard he was in Alabama somewhere."

"Guess he stayed there after he moved." Hayes took a long swallow of beer.

Rowan pulled at Kate's hand and she took the hint. "Nice seeing you, Hayes, she said."

"You too, darling."

Rowan and Kate entered the living room the same way Kate imagined one might enter a furnace: eyes closed, breath held. The evening passed in a heat-haze. They finally left, hugging friends and then walking outside along the cracked sidewalk. Before they reached Rowan's car a block away, he stopped.

The rain had quit, but the leaves dripped onto Kate's hair and arms, a welcome coolness. A gas streetlight a few feet away cast a glow, causing the Spanish moss to appear as downward curling smoke.

"Gorgeous night. Finally," she said.

"It is," Rowan said. "Did you have fun?"

"Sure. It was nice seeing a lot of people I haven't seen in a while."

"I wasn't too fond of your high school buddy, Hayes."

Kate laughed. "Why? He's totally harmless."

"Calling you Cute Katie and implying I followed you, and then asking about your high school boyfriend. Kinda weird, I thought."

Kate started walking again, making sure Rowan could hear her voice without seeing her face. "That's silly."

"I knew that's what you'd say."

Kate stopped and turned on the sidewalk, wanting to wipe the conversation clean, remove it from the air as surely as the rain had cleared the pollen. "Did you see Jimmy asleep on the hammock?" She laughed and took Rowan's hand, squeezing it. "I almost wish I could see Larson's face in the morning when he finds him out there in the back yard."

Rowan laughed, and leftover rain dripped off the water-drenched leaves into his hair. His quick slip into laughter made her heart unfold toward him, and she pulled him into a kiss. "Take me home," she said. And he did.

He walked her inside, and asked again—as he did almost every night—if she would come home with him because he couldn't stay with her, leaving Dixie home alone to chew through the couch in the middle of the night. And she—as she did almost every night—told him about her early morning. They said goodnight, yawns stifled behind kisses.

She had dismissed the idea as frivolous, yet as Kate stood at her window, staring out over the river and watching the water move, going exactly where it meant to go, its destination already known, she knew too what her destination was.

The idea to visit Jack Adams in Birmingham had crept into her mind and heart. It didn't make any sense, but she was beyond sense now. Life, she believed from living in the wilderness, was tied together by hints, whispers, and unseen fabric-makers. She imagined someone far more knowing than she, sewing together a fragile web that she wouldn't see it until time was done. She could ignore the whispers and threads, everyone could, and she often did, but this time she wouldn't.

If she didn't go then, she wouldn't go at all, and seeing Jack seemed the only cure for *What is wrong with you?*

She understood the dangling corner thread of what was wrong: The first day of spring still possessed mystery not only for the myths, sacraments, and goddesses; not merely for the promise made at thirteen years old under a willow tree; but also because Kate and Jack's lost daughter, Luna, had been born on that day thirteen years before.

She had tried everything to outrun the pain of losing both Jack and her daughter: moving away; coming home; no dating; too much dating: anything to keep her mind away from the memory. People talked about heartbreak, but in Kate's opinion, hearts don't break, they merely ache and throb until you learn to ignore that same heart all together.

She still hadn't read the letter. The one on the side table. The one in the unopened envelope. The one from Jack Adams. She lifted it, staring at the handwriting and the return address, which hadn't changed in the thirteen years the letters had been arriving. Her routine—to read the letter at sunset on the first day of spring—was purposefully broken the night before. She wanted something new. She wanted to really *be* with Rowan without intrusion or memory.

Jack's yearly letters, which were sent on their daughter's birthday, allowed Kate to know Jack in his adult years. And yet, despite these thousands of words, they hadn't spoken. Not once.

Kate settled into her favorite oversized chair in the corner where the side table held not only Jack's letter, but also a small lamp and her bowl of favorite collected feathers. It was still raining, slanted waterfalls hitting the wide panes of glass. A South Carolina spring came this way sometimes: damp with fury and chaos and then just as suddenly quiet. Kate turned the lamp on and slipped her finger under the envelope flap, ripping through the paper to withdraw the letter.

Dear Katie,
   Happy Birthday to Luna.

He always started the letter that way, that exact same way, with a happy birthday wish that neither of them could say directly—to their daughter or each other.

This will be a short letter. I'm sorry, but if I don't mail it today, it won't make it to you by Luna's birthday, so I'm keeping my promise and writing. There's not much to say. Not much has changed. I want

to tell you all the exciting things I'm doing—but they will sound repetitive and dull, as they aren't much different than the year before or
even the year before that.

My work: same. The one new thing: I have opened an art studio.
Not for my work of course, because I don't have any, but for Alabama
artists. It's a small studio in the arts district of Southside. This is my
excuse to indulge in my own addiction without buying everything
I see.

There's a woman running the studio—Mimi Ann—and she is doing a brilliant job. I show up for the bigger events and sneak in when I
need a fix. It's worked out well so far. The studio is called LUNA.

Maybe I should have asked you first or at least told you that I have
a studio named after our daughter, but something held me back. I don't
know what really. Either way, it exists now and I hope one day you get
to see it.

Hope all is well with you.

Jack

Usually the birthday letters were full of information, overflowing
with his year. But this letter was as empty as the one he'd written six
years before to tell of his divorce, which had left him bereft and sharing custody of their two-year-old, Caleb.

Kate understood that most people would think it strange that she
and Jack hadn't talked since the day they'd said good-bye to their
daughter, and yet through yearly letters they both knew the facts about
one another's lives. No blueprint existed for this kind of relationship—
the one between a man and woman who had once been in love and
then placed their child out into the world with a hand-chosen family.

Katie was thirteen when she fell in love with Jack, the day she
made a vow under a willow tree, and yet now she knew nothing,

absolutely nothing, about her own daughter, who was thirteen years old. Did she have copper hair or green eyes? Where did she live? Did she have a best friend? Was she into sports? Did she love her parents?

As Jack had once said in one of his letters: of all the awful parts of missing their daughter, the not-knowing was the absolute worst.

four
. . . .

ARIZONA

1996

When the Arizona heat felt like a cloak she couldn't shake, Tara's words about Jack's date wiggled into Katie's mind, twisting her thoughts with anxiety. That hundred-degree day, preoccupied, Katie was hiking through the shallow trail of a dried river with four young girls when she heard the scream. Dropping her backpack, Katie was at the girl, Anne's, side in one jump. "What?"

Anne was thirteen years old, and so skinny she seemed to be made of the dry sage twigs that covered the desert, her long hair tied with a frayed shoestring. She was bent over, holding her ankle, screaming without words. Anne was a quiet girl, and Katie knew her terrible story: how her mom had tried to raise her alone when Dad left; how her mom found Anne selling pot and drinking bourbon straight from the bottle. The mom had then sold everything they owned to get

Anne into this program and try to save her from the lifestyle that was sucking them both into a black hole of desperation.

"Anne," Katie took the young girl's face in between both her hands. "What is it?"

"Snake." She pointed to the rattlesnake's tail disappearing into the brush.

Katie had been trained for this, and she knew what to do. But she also tasted guilt in the back of her throat. If her thoughts hadn't been braided with anxiety about Jack Adams, about a place she couldn't see, she would've been alert. This was her fault. The one thing Katie was meant to do was keep these girls safe.

Katie tied a tourniquet from the first-aid kit, quieted the other girls and used her satellite radio to call transportation to take Anne to the hospital. The waiting was interminable, but the three other girls rallied and made jokes, trying to keep Anne calm. Katie checked vital signs, secured the tourniquet, and marveled at the other girls' ability to surround Anne. This was a family, an odd and mismatched family sewn together by the threads of abuse and sadness, but together forming something strong. And Katie had failed them.

The crisis passed and Anne was back in the field. Katie told Winsome Wilderness that she needed a few weeks off.

Shawn O'Neal, the owner of Winsome, assured Katie that the snakebite wasn't her fault. *It was nature. It was normal.* But Katie told Shawn it was her fault. She hadn't been alert. She hadn't noticed the danger. It was Shawn who had taught Katie that nature carried messages inside every plant, feather, and animal. Anne's bite wasn't an accident. It was more than the snake and less than the snake. It was what the slithering, biting reptile was telling Katie: something is wrong.

Jack had written to her about the new house he'd bought, a Tudor style home built in the 1920s. He'd told her he loved the way it sat on top of Red Mountain and overlooked downtown Birmingham like a guardian. He bought it for a *steal,* as it needed a total renovation. He spent his limited free time polishing the hardwood floors, painting the trim with a small brush, replacing windows, and chipping away at the rot.

It didn't bother Katie that Jack hadn't consulted her about the house. She believed it showed that he respected her work and her autonomy by seizing the opportunity for both of them, while he could. She'd taken this fact—that he bought a house—as a hint that he was building a life for them, a life that included a house and settling in. And that's where she found him after the long flight to Birmingham.

Jack was expecting her. He stood waiting on the front porch, then hugged her as if she might float away. Inside, he showed her through the partially renovated house. They stood in the living room where his windows, grimy and paint-edged, looked over the city. "Look at that view. Who could resist, right?"

She gazed at the night sky, which dominated the view. Resting underneath the moon, the Birmingham lights faded like a world below opaque glass. "Beautiful," she said.

"The city can look that way from up here, but . . ."

"No, I'm talking about the moon." She pointed to the sliver of light that settled into the night sky like a lopsided, but radiant smile.

"Not much of one tonight," Jack said.

"There will be even less tomorrow night," Katie said and then turned to him. "But then it starts all over again, growing."

"You've become an astronaut in your spare time?"

"Absolutely. Actually, you think I'm in the middle of nowhere Arizona, but I'm working for NASA." She snuggled closer to him, but his subtle move away from her was obvious.

He took a deep breath. "Katie, you can't just walk into my home and pretend you haven't been gone for over a year."

"I'm not pretending anything," she said, taking his hand. "I needed to see you. I only want another few months and I'll be ready to leave."

"You said that eight months ago, and then six months ago, and then again last month."

She cringed again. "I know. But doing what I do, loving what I do, well, that doesn't mean I don't love you, Jack. I know you know that."

"I don't doubt your love, but I doubt your ability to ever stop long enough for us."

"For us to what?"

"To be us. To build a life. For God's sake. We've been together for over eight years and now five of those have been in separate states. One day we'll have to be in the same place to have a life."

She pointed out the window. "You know the first thing I was ever scared of was the moon not being in the sky." She looked at him. "And the second is that you won't be in my life."

"I'm not in your life, Katie."

She wrapped her arms around his waist, pulling herself closer, body on body. "Yes, you are. You're with me every single day. Every second. I want you next to me seeing what I see. Everything. All of it. When a hawk feather floats to the ground, or the moon springs from behind cloud cover, or when I hear—far away—a coyote call. All of it, I think of you. Always."

"Thinking about me doesn't matter if you won't leave."

"Not yet," she said and buried her head into his shoulder. "I'm not ready."

"You've been gone for over a year, and the truth is that you won't leave to be with me."

"I will," she said.

"I'm dating someone," he said quietly.

She pulled back, tripping on a plank of unfinished floor. "What?"

"I told you that in a letter months ago."

"You didn't tell me anything. All you said was that by now we should be dating other people. I thought you meant . . . in theory, not reality."

"Of course you did because you didn't even ask, Katie. You assumed that the way you wanted it was the exact same way I wanted it." He paused. "Her name is Maggie."

"Do you love her?"

He looked away and of all the First Things in her life, this one was the worst: Jack looking away from her as he spoke about another woman. "I don't know."

"How can you *not* know if you love someone?"

"Because the way I love you overshadows everything else, Katie." He did look at her then. "The way I love you blurs all the ways I could love anyone else. But you know what? I want to love her. I *want* to love someone else. Because this is terrible." He waved his palm between the two of them. "Having you and not having you is terrible."

Katie kissed him again. Jack hesitated, somehow giving in and pulling away at the same time, his hand behind her head for a deeper kiss, but his feet taking a step back. Katie held on, sliding closer until the entire length of their bodies touched. She lifted her foot and stepped around him, her leg wound around his. The simple movements of hands sliding beneath fabric, removed shirts and his jeans. Her skirt puddled on the floor. At last she was where she wanted to be, the fleeting and forever moment of skin on skin, legs wound around, her hair a waterfall over his face. The only world that mattered—the one between their touch—returned.

She cried as she left Jack the next morning. She promised to give her three-week notice.

But she didn't because that was when the wounded and twelve-year-old Lida Markinson showed up.

Lida had been living with her aunt outside Chattanooga, Tennessee. She'd been four years old the day her mama dropped her off at Aunt Clara's, and this was the only memory Lida retained of her mama—seeing her walking off in her pale yellow sundress and waving. Mama had told Lida that she was going to do some errands and she'd be back soon. *That's if soon is never,* Lida had told Katie as they sat around a campfire.

Lida's aunt loved and took care of Lida until the whiskey became more important than mostly anything, including Lida, including food, including shelter. Lida soon learned to fend for herself, which sadly and awfully usually included allowing the local boys to do as they pleased so she had a place to sleep and eat. The same whiskey that made her aunt fade into another world allowed Lida to not care what was being done to her or about her. Until her grandmother came to visit from Atlanta and found the conditions in which Clara allowed them to live.

Appalled and scared, Grandmother Garrison made the pleading phone calls to anyone and everyone she knew in the substance-abuse world and found a place for Lida at Winsome Wilderness.

The history, blurry at best, seemed to be that Lida was born to her sixteen-year-old Mama, who believed that of course she could raise a child on her own. Wasn't love all a child needed? Love her and all would be well, that's what Mama also told Aunt Clara.

Well, love, it seems, wasn't all Lida needed. Food, shelter, and safety were up there on the list also. And, in the end, didn't Lida know exactly where to find love? In any shack, corner bedroom, or empty barn available.

Lida arrived with her auburn hair hanging in strands of tangled rope down her back, her freckles fading into her skin, and Katie saw an almost alternate, opposite-world image of her own self, as if Lida was the girl whom she would have been without the love of her family. Shawn had warned all the field guides about identifying with any one child. But who could help it? Who can tell love what to do?

So Katie loved Lida Markinson and wanted, more than she ever had, to find a way to heal a wounded spirit.

Norah was the one who sent a copy of the wedding announcement. Jonathon Gray Adams had married Margaret Lauren Campbell. *Jack and Maggie,* the small print stated at the bottom of the announcement. It had been a small wedding on the bride's parents' farm in central Alabama, no invitations, only announcements after it was all over.

Katie read the card what seemed like a hundred times, and then Lida found Katie throwing up behind a sage bush, and asked the one question that changed everything. "Are you preggers or something?"

It was impossible. *It was impossible,* those were the words Katie told herself, like magic words, like a mantra, like an enchanted wish.

She'd still believed that Jack, as mad as he'd seemed when she'd told him she was staying to see it through with a young girl named Lida, would wait, but he hadn't. He hadn't waited at all.

On an awful and bitterly cold November day, Katie was in Timber for a two-day reprieve. From the crowded apartment, she finally called him. Her resolve had long since dissolved and as soon as he answered, she was already crying. "I miss you so terribly," she said.

He was silent for a long while and Katie thought he'd hung up on her. Then he spoke. "I can't talk to you, Katie. If I do, I'll ruin everything." His voice cracked and, with hope, she jumped into that small space.

"Please talk to me."

"I can't. I just can't. I'm married." He said each word as if it stood alone, as if it explained everything there was to know.

"How did this happen? I mean, I was just there and told you I'd come back. How could you."

"I told you. I did tell you."

"No."

"I did tell you that I was falling in love with Maggie. And when you said for the millionth time that you weren't coming home, I vowed to myself that it would be the last time I heard you say those words. That's when I decided I was never going to beg you again. That's when I decided to ask Maggie to marry me."

"Why didn't you wait? I love you. This is crazy."

"I think I'll always love you, Katie, but I don't want that life of being alone waiting and waiting. I want this life where love is right here, right next to me."

"I don't understand."

"I know, but don't make me say things that will hurt you, Katie. Please. I don't want to think about you hurting."

"Say it," she said. "Say you love her more than me."

"No," he said quietly.

Everything in her that hurt and ached spoke these words. "When you kiss her, when you touch her, when you're with her, you'll only think of me."

"Oh, Katie. Don't do this."

She hung up on him because she didn't have the words she needed—the exact right words that would convince him that he was making a huge mistake. Why couldn't he know what she knew? That they were perfect together. That he was in the absolute wrong place. That he'd needed to wait the littlest bit longer.

As the days stretched forward, Katie's nausea grew worse. She fought through the desperate need for sleep that fell over her like smothering and invisible gauze. Her T-shirts stretched across her swelling breasts. And then came the slim, slow knowing, like a cracked door in a dark room.

five

. . . .

BIRMINGHAM, AL

2010

Phone calls made and suitcase packed, Kate headed for Alabama. She'd told Rowan that she was going to check out a boutique, and her stomach flipped at the half truth, or half lie. The six-hour drive crept through South Carolina, toward Georgia, and then west to Alabama. Except for the Atlanta airport and the snakelike highways through the big city, which would spin her into another direction with one wrong turn, the drive was a view of spring's birth, taking Kate through the dormant cotton fields and farmland. The radio stations faded in and out until Kate finally shut off the radio and rolled down the windows, allowing the passing wind to be the music.

What she didn't tell Rowan was a lie of omission, which according to their Baptist preacher was as large a lie as one of commission. Either way, unannounced, Kate was on her way to Birmingham to see Jack Adams.

Kate knew that if she'd called Jack to tell him she was coming, she wouldn't have gone at all. There was something about overplanning that would have killed the trip before she even put her keys in the ignition. So, she drove with her windows open while her thoughts were as cluttered as the roadside trees drooping with their too-many blossoms. Memories scraped against one another, vying for attention.

When she arrived, Kate smiled at Jack's house as if it were a person—an old friend—which in many ways it was. The last time she'd seen the house, the front door had been a plywood board and the rick-a-rack trim unpainted. The windows had been cracked, their wooden mullions peeling old paint. Now double doors dominated the front, dark, carved oak with wrought iron dividing their bubbled glass into intricate patterns. The windows of the house were wide and long, divided also by thick iron into oversized rectangles, which looked out onto the street with a wide and curious gaze as she parked her car.

Even in the day of Facebook and Twitter, of social networking and cell phones, where everyone knew everything about everybody, Kate knew very little about Jack's life. He worked as a lawyer in downtown Birmingham. He was divorced. He lived with his son.

Kate drove into a parallel parking spot on the street and her body remembered everything: the comfortable ease that nestled next to the jittery desire. All this time, all these years passed, and she'd believed the feelings gone, or at least diminished beyond recognition. Yet there she was within a hundred yards of his house, and the exact desire returned as if it had waited patiently at the end of a long road.

The front door opened. Framed by doorway and sunlight, a young boy emerged with a baseball in his hand, a hat on his head, and a large bag slung over his left shoulder. Kate gripped the steering wheel, holding her breath. The boy—he had dark hair and was small—looked younger than the eight years she knew him to be. He hollered something over his shoulder and his mouth formed a single word, "Dad."

Then there was Jack. He came through the door, placing his hand on top of his son's hat and twisting it straight. Kate took in a quick breath. He still moved with the ease of an athlete. The baseball cap on his head bore the same emblem as his son's, a hornet or bee, Kate thought. Jack grabbed the bag from his son and took two steps down the walkway toward the back driveway.

In her stomach, tiny birds opened their wings and flew up toward her throat. Just because he'd written yearly letters, just because they'd once loved and had a daughter, did this give her the right to show up unannounced in his driveway?

Jack and Caleb were obviously on their way to a game. If she stopped them now, she would make them late and ruin their afternoon. Maybe she'd watch them for a little while. Then decide. Only a little while.

She followed Jack's pickup down the winding roads into Mountain Brook village, an enclave of beautiful homes tucked into the valley. She followed him through the town dominated by old English architecture and brick-lined sidewalks. He turned right into the elementary school, which at first glance Kate thought was a large estate. The field to the left of the school was packed with families. Baseball bags were scattered like litter, spilling bats and gloves, uniforms and Gatorade bottles. Parents sat in clustered groups with folding chairs and blankets.

This world was foreign to Kate, one that she often avoided for fear of turning over the soil of a long-buried ache. Yet, there they were, families doing whatever it was that families did. Jack and Caleb sauntered in almost identical steps as they approached the crowd. Caleb entered a dugout and Jack turned away to unfold a blue canvas chair.

Kate climbed out of the car and locked its doors, although she knew it was completely unnecessary in whatever world she had just fallen into. Staying as far away as possible from the field, but still able to see, she leaned against a metal light pole and watched the unfamiliar movements of school-age sports. Jack sat in his chair, scribbling in a notebook: stats, she assumed. His full attention was on the game and she didn't fear him turning to see her.

Jack seemed content—happy, even—as he hollered encouragement toward the field, writing in his notebook. Every once in a while he checked his cell. A girlfriend maybe? A business deal?

Birmingham was showing off in its spring finery, an overdressed woman wearing too many colors and bright jewelry. The azaleas and camellias, the dogwoods and the daffodils burst from the ground. Kate glanced around the fields and surrounding homes, feeling as though she'd fallen into a Disney movie. She knew it wasn't perfect, nothing was, but this town sure looked like it on that spring afternoon. She watched Jack, content to be an observer. Maybe she wouldn't tell him she'd been there at all. Maybe she'd get back in her car and leave him to his perfectly nice life without her interference.

The baseball game was into the second inning when Jack stood to walk to the concession stand. He spoke on his cell phone and meanwhile glanced toward Kate, still leaning against the light post. She held her breath and averted her eyes, as if this would make her invisible. Kate counted to ten and then glanced back toward the concession stand, but he was gone.

"Katie?" Jack said her name.

When she heard his voice, she felt her heart expand and reach for him, but it was when she turned and saw his eyes that the need returned in full. In the middle of a bright baseball park, surrounded by families, she saw only Jack. It was propriety and fears that kept her arms straight and her hands from touching him at all. She smiled. "Hey, Jack."

They stood, face to face, inches apart as unsaid words filled the cracks of distance and time. Finally he spoke. "It's really you. What are you doing here?"

She bit the right side of her lip in a childhood nervous gesture. She'd hoped she wouldn't want exactly what she wanted at the moment—to kiss him, and more than once. She would not ruin this moment with her need. She would not chase him away with her old desire. "Would you believe me if I said I just happened to be in the neighborhood?"

He laughed and it was a lovely sound—deep and freeing and full of life. He hugged her and she fell against his chest, into the hollow cleft where she'd once so casually settled her body. He let go and stepped back. "Let me look at you and then you can explain yourself."

She blushed. Warmth traveled through her body and settled in her face. She covered her face with her hands, and he took her fingers and pulled her hands into his grasp. "You," he said.

"You," she said in return, staring once again into those green and unsettling eyes.

"So, you're a big baseball fan?" he asked.

She smiled. "Really, I'm not positive about the difference between a run and a touchdown. I came to see you. I guess, maybe, I should have called."

"How did you find us?"

"Well, I went to the house and you were leaving, so I followed."

"Were you going to tell me you were here or just spy on me?"

"Tell you, of course. I sort of felt like I was interrupting and I wanted to wait until the game was over."

"This is amazing, Katie."

"I go by Kate now," she said.

"Well, that's nice. But to me, you're Katie." He tipped his hat. "With all due respect." He took a deep breath. "I don't really know what to say because I'm a little stunned."

"I know. I wanted to see you and talk."

He smiled. "Can all those things wait until after Caleb bats?"

"Absolutely. They can wait until he bats ten times."

He laughed—that lovely sound again—and shook his head. "This is wild. But come sit. Watch baseball with me."

"Watch baseball with you." She smiled. "Nice."

They walked together toward the baseball diamond and Jack offered Katie his chair. Number 17 was at bat.

"That's Caleb. He's the shortest on the team, but he's the fastest," Jack said, talking in a low whisper. "His coach is obnoxious, but Caleb loves the game. He's obsessed. Knows every stat of every player in the majors."

"There are worse things to be obsessed with," Kate said and leaned forward, her elbows on her knees,

Caleb swung the bat and missed the ball, which landed with a *thwump* in the catcher's mitt.

"Strike One," the ump hollered, making a motion with his hands.

"Does he have to scream it like that?" Kate asked.

Jack smiled at her and shook his head. "You don't go to many games do you?"

"I think the last baseball game I went to, I was with my dad and he took me to Atlanta. I was about ten years old. I whined the entire game about being bored and he never took me again."

"When you meet Caleb, do not tell him that story," Jack said. He was speaking to her, smiling, but his gaze was on the field.

"Ball," the ump hollered as the pitch went far right and hit the fence. Caleb stepped back from the plate and looked over his shoulder at his dad.

Jack gave his son a thumbs-up and said, "Wait on the ball."

Caleb nodded and stepped back, facing the pitcher. A ball came across the plate and Caleb swung, making contact with a *thunk* that sent the ball flying over the second baseman's head. Kate jumped up with a holler before she even understood what she was doing. Caleb was safe at first base.

"Looks like you're good luck," Jack said.

Chatting about the weather and the rules of a game she didn't understand, Kate enjoyed watching eight-year-old boys running around. They were all so earnest.

"They all look like they're playing the most important game of their life," she said.

"They are. Today is always the most important when you're eight years old," Jack said and squatted down next to her chair. "Always."

She nodded. "Good way to live, I think."

They sat through the remainder of the game and watched Caleb's Hornets lose by one run. While Jack folded up the chair and waited for Caleb, Kate wandered over to the concession stand and bought a fountain Coke. She sipped from the vintage-looking red-striped straw as Jack and Caleb walked toward her.

They reached Kate's side, and Jack stopped as Caleb kept walking.

"Son," Jack said. "Stop. I want you to meet an old friend."

Caleb turned around to look at Kate. His baseball cap partially shaded his face but his green eyes and the cleft in his chin were obvious statements of his father's imprint.

"Hello, Ma'am," Caleb said in a voice that was young and quiet.

"Hi, Caleb. I'm Kate Vaughn."

"Miss Vaughn to you," Jack said and came to his son's side. "I think we can take her to our postgame pizza, don't you?"

Caleb nodded. "I think so too."

"Well, I'm honored," Kate said. "I love pizza."

Caleb looked up toward his dad. "When is Gram picking me up?"

"After pizza. I have your bag in the car." Jack turned to Kate. "Do you want to ride with us?"

"I'll follow," Kate said, pointing toward the parking lot. "I've got my car."

In the parking lot, Caleb and Jack threw bags into the truck's bed before walking to opposite sides of the vehicle and climbing into their seats. Caleb looked so like Jack, and questions she rarely allowed to surface rose with a furious roar.

Yes, it was the damn un-knowing.

six

. . . .

BLUFFTON, SC

1996

The first telling had been the worst: her parents. Katie had said the words, "I'm pregnant," and then hid her face behind her hands. Molly was a senior in high school, and her questions were simple and yet completely complicated: Would the baby have a dad? Where would the baby live? These were, of course, unanswerable.

After the family tears had been shed, Katie left to tell Jack. Yes, he needed to at least know that their last time together had been much more than a simple last time.

The road between Bluffton and Birmingham seemed formed of a flimsy connection like the lines drawn on the astronomy chart that hung in her childhood room. She was five months along and could no longer put off the inevitable. *We are pregnant.*

If she had ever imagined this moment, which of course she had, she was carrying Jack's child, yes, but they'd be married and living in a two-bedroom house with a front porch. They'd do laundry together and match socks while watching a movie in the living room. They'd talk about whether to have a holiday party; they'd argue over whose family was more annoying. They'd plan the pool for the backyard and argue over bills. Then one day, together they'd visit the doctor to hear the news, "You're going to have a baby."

Instead, Katie had been alone on the day she'd heard the news from a nurse at the doctor's office in Bluffton. The earth had opened wide and her Planned Life fell in. She'd held a protective hand over her belly and known that decisions needed to be made. She could no longer deny that a child, already five months along, was growing inside her body. Her child. Jack's child.

An hour into the drive, anger arrived as an unwelcome guest: boisterous, raging, and red-faced.

Katie thought about Lida and how the young girl would believe that Katie had deserted her—exactly as her mama had, just as her aunt Clara had. Lida had been the girl Katie wanted to heal more than any other and now she was causing more pain by leaving the wilderness early. Moving her hand over her stomach, Katie felt as if Lida and her own child were somehow one, as if she were being given a chance to do *right* and *well* by this child. How could she ever bring a child into this world that wouldn't be totally loved? Completely adored by both parents? Completely wanted? Yes, that was the word—*wanted*. Katie had seen—first- and lasthand—what could happen when a child wasn't completely wanted. It seemed ridiculous to even think that this child wasn't loved and in so many ways wanted, but was that enough?

Katie banged her fists on the steering wheel. *Now? Seriously, now when he's married?* She pulled the car to the side of the road, to the emergency lane (if there was ever an emergency, this was one) and ranted at the sky and the gods and all she'd believed. Bent over the steering wheel, she fought tears that came without regard for her need to stay calm.

Flashing, pulsing blue lights surrounded the car, bouncing off the rearview and side mirrors. Kate wiped at her face, embarrassed at her own tirade and at the emotions that had ripped through her like razors.

The policeman came to the car and Katie rolled down the window.

"You okay, Ma'am?"

Katie nodded.

"Have you been drinking?"

Katie protested, holding up her hand. "No, Sir." And then the oddest thing happened. She began to laugh. It was a giggle at first, the kind a child would emit in the middle of Sunday school when the teacher spoke of Adam *knowing* Eve. Then she was into full-blown laughter, bent over the steering wheel. Sobs and laughter mixed in a combination of opposites that made an animal-like sound.

Sunglasses covered the policeman's eyes, but his smirk told her that he didn't believe she was sober. "Will you please get out of the car?"

Katie opened the door and stepped out. The winter chill swept over her.

"I need you to walk a straight line, toe to toe." The cop explained in slow words as if speaking to a toddler.

"Seriously?" Katie asked. "You think I've been drinking? It's noon."

"Just do it."

Her feet firmly planted, she placed one foot in front of the other and then did a cartwheel, landing on the same line. High school cheerleading finally became resourceful. She twirled around and bowed to the cop.

He shook his head, but the hint of a smile pulled on the corners of his mouth. "That's not what I asked you to do."

"I'm sorry, Sir. I'm trying to prove a point."

"Okay, then. Why are you parked in the emergency lane? Are you in trouble?"

"I needed to cry. I don't usually need to cry and so I thought it best if I wasn't operating heavy machinery while I did so." She smiled at the policeman.

He nodded and took off his sunglasses. "You okay to drive now?"

"Yes, I think I am."

Katie returned to the car. The cop walked with her and placed his hands on the roof, staring into her driver's-side window as she started the engine. "Are you really okay? If you're not, you can take a little time here. I'll park behind you."

"Thanks, but I really do think I'm good for now."

He nodded. "I hope that whatever made you cry gets better soon."

"It won't," she said. "But I'll be okay."

Katie rolled up the window, put the shift into drive. "I'll be okay," she repeated to herself, but the words fell hollow into the empty car.

"Are you okay?" Jack asked. He greeted her without hello, preamble, or hug.

He stood on his front doorstep, the shadow on his face from more than the setting sun. She wanted to touch him, to wrap her body around his until they both found peace, until they could be together for good and all. No one moved her this way. And she knew no one ever would.

"No, really, I'm not okay. I need to talk to you. I promise it won't take long."

She'd called to tell him she was coming, and yet he stared at her as if she'd shown up unannounced. "Come in," he finally said. Together they walked into his house, and then to the living room she hadn't seen since *that* night.

"Sit down, please. I can't stand up and tell you this," Katie said. She glanced around the room. Only one wall had been painted. Closed paint cans were piled in the corner waiting to be used again. A hole gaped open on the top right corner of the ceiling where she could see into the attic. Everything was half-finished, almost done.

But only almost.

"Okay." He sat and they faced each other on opposite ends of the couch.

"We." She took in a breath that shook with fear and truth. "You and me. We're pregnant."

Emotions she was never able to label worked their way across his face. Like fast-action photography it was morning and then noon and then twilight and then darkest night and then morning again. It ended in agony.

She fell into him. "I'm sorry," she said into his chest.

He pulled her back. "My God," he said.

"I know, Jack. I know. I'm not asking for anything and I don't expect you to run away with me. You don't have to say it. But I needed to tell you. It's not a secret thing I could keep from you."

"Oh, Katie." He dropped his face.

Sunlight filled the living room as if it had been poured on the couch and floors; the aroma of coffee filled the lightness, thrusting its smell into Katie's nostrils. "I think I'm going to throw up," Katie said, closing her eyes.

He touched her back, gently, tentative.

"I'm sorry. It's the coffee smell—all my favorite things now make me sick. It's like an opposite world."

His face crumbled, a puzzle undoing. "I needed to move on and I did. And now you're telling me that we are going to have a child?" He paused, struggling for the words she didn't want to hear. "I'm married. I love . . ."

"Please don't say how much you love her. I can't have the words in my head for the rest of my life. I know you don't love me anymore. I'm only here to tell you so that . . . well, I thought you should know." Katie said.

He knelt before her, taking her hands into his. He admitted that he'd always love her, but that he'd made a vow to someone else and that promise had to be kept. He didn't want to leave his life or his wife; that much was clear. And yet he cried out, "What now? This is our child."

Katie didn't have the answers and yet she knew that if she begged Jack to leave, it would ruin them both. He seemed far away, as if the life of him had gone deep inside where Katie would never again find him.

"We could try to find a way to split the parenting . . . or," he said.

"Raising a child isn't something you *just* try, Jack. Being married isn't something you *just* try. Seeing what I've seen, knowing what I now know, even the best parents, even with love and resources and family, parenting is not something you *try*. You do it all the way or you don't do it all, and even when you think you're doing it right . . . still . . ."

He held out his hand to stop her flow of words. "Let's not decide anything right now. I can't. I can't breathe."

"I know you don't want Maggie to know I came here, so I'm going to leave. We'll talk and figure this out. We have months."

They didn't cry, either of them, but their bodies shook with the three words that changed everything: *we are pregnant*. He took her in his arms, held her until she couldn't tell where he began and she ended. Someone had to let go and it was Jack who did so first.

Time heals all wounds. That was the old adage, but for Katie Vaughn, these were hollow words. A decision needed to be made and time wasn't helping at all. In fact, it was rushing by too fast.

The final choice to place her baby for adoption wasn't made in a single day or even a month, but like the tributaries that fed into Katie's beloved river, the facts joined in a raging and moving body of one tear-drenched choice.

Katie was never alone. She was surrounded by her family and

Norah. But it was Jack's absence she felt, wider and deeper than anyone's presence. And it was that loneliness that ached the most. Katie had always thought herself strong and sure, but now she found herself weak and unable to make the slightest decision. Her wildness and strong will seeped out, leaving her hollow.

In the end, she wanted to offer this baby, her child, every chance in life she could have. And she questioned—every day she questioned—whether or not she could give that child her every chance. It was with those very questions that she found herself in an adoption agency in downtown Savannah, her heart almost dead inside, seeming to beat as little and as slowly as possible.

The small blond counselor, Barbara, leaned forward on her desk. "Kate, I know it's incredibly difficult to talk about this. We can move as slowly as you'd like. I am here to listen and I'm here to help you answer all of the questions you have to help you decide whether parenting or adoption is the right plan for you and your baby. You want to consider adoption?"

Katie nodded and with that acknowledgment, she began to weep, bent over with the force of her own admission. "Yes," she stuttered. "I need to talk about it . . . consider it . . ."

For what seemed like hours, but was probably much less, Barbara talked to Katie, going through "parenting plans" and "adoption plans." The counselor asked questions Katie could barely answer. "What does parenting look like to you?" "What does adoption look like to you?" "What is the life you envision for your child?"

Confusion blurred her mind, and Katie finally said. "I want to keep this baby. I want to . . . keep it. That's what my heart says."

Barbara smiled. "I know. I know what you want to do. Of course you want to keep this baby. I can tell how much you love her already. But are you prepared to parent this precious baby, to give this baby the life you so desperately want her to have? Sometimes, just sometimes, being a 'good mother' means choosing adoption."

For the first time since she'd entered the office, Katie's tears stopped. She exhaled and saw as clearly as she did the moon on a cloudless night—there was a difference between *keeping* and *parenting*. What she wanted to keep was this part of Jack, to *keep* what remained of their love. But could she actually be a parent?

"What are my choices?" Katie asked, dry-eyed, staunch, her voice not sounding like her own. "What happens if I choose adoption? What kinds of adoption are there?"

She returned home that afternoon, and it was Katie's mother who set her mind in direct opposition to adoption. "We can raise this baby, Katie. Your dad and I can do it. Please don't give her away. It's not nineteen sixty. We don't have to hide."

The words—*give her away*—tore every last piece of fragile flesh in Katie's soul. "Mom, you know that can't be—my child in your house thinking that I don't want her. I could never do that. You have no idea what it does to a young girl if she thinks she's not wanted. It is by far one of the most devastating beliefs in the world." Katie fought for control.

"Don't use your wilderness-therapy psychology speech to explain what you want to do."

"What I *want* to do? For God's sake, Mom. Jack is married. I'm twenty-two years old and hiding in my parents' house. I'm pregnant and alone. At this moment, I'm not doing a damn thing I *want* to do. I can now only do what is best. . . ."

"I'm sorry, baby. I'm sorry. . . ."

"Mom, I'm begging you to stop and see what I see. To know what I know. . . . I'm not giving up, and I'm not giving her away. You can't ever say that again. It's a choice, mom. I'm choosing not to focus on everything in me that is screaming, 'keep her,' so that I can focus on what I want to give my child. I'm choosing. I'm offering. It's a gift to another family, to my child."

"So you could give her to a stranger but not to us?"

The conversations ended this way every time, and often in weakness Katie agreed to allow her parents to raise her child, her and Jack's child, until her strength returned. Always underneath the tension and arguments and deathly silent days and nights while her child grew within her, Katie's decision remained the same: she would offer her child the gift of a beautiful, hand-chosen family.

Katie began to show, her belly forcing its way past the buttons and zippers of her clothing. She had to make a decision. At the very least, she had to buy herself some time. Kate knew that if she brought the knowledge of this child into her hometown, she'd need to bring the child itself. And she wasn't prepared for the questions or the well-meaning advice that was bound to come her way. That's why, when she asked her dad to rent a small cottage on the lake an hour away, Katie felt she was protecting her child and herself, not hiding her pregnancy. Norah and Katie's family were the only visitors, and they often spent the night, watching movies and reading books.

Katie walked through the paths and hiking trails around the small lake, and she continued to collect feathers. Wherever she went or walked or sat, there seemed to be a feather floating beneath her feet or at her side. She placed them in a bowl. She mixed the wilderness feathers with the new ones until the individual was indistinguishable region from region.

She found feathers so blue they shimmered, the red ones and brown, the soft down and the coarse bristly ones. Her favorite was all white, so white it seemed bleached and yet had a single dot: a freckle. Blue-bird, raven, hawk, chickadee, cardinal—and then she found some that she couldn't identify, ones she hadn't yet found a name for. She became obsessed with the nameless ones. She checked Audubon books out of the library and they were piled on the dining room table. Engrossed in discovering what bird had lost a piece of self, she tied tiny labels to the quills. She didn't have any plans for the feathers, and maybe that was the best part—they existed for beauty only.

She brought something wild to the tame and rational. She brought heart into a place where she must soon give away her heart.

Jack shut down, or that was the best way Katie knew to describe what happened to the man she once knew. He disappeared and another man, a married man who wanted to get on with his life, took his place. She felt it wasn't true, that deep down Jack still existed, but the facts proved otherwise. He left her alone to go through family profiles until she decided on a closed and confidential adoption.

Through terrible phone calls and months of agony, Katie chose a mother and father who had been trying for nine years to have a child and were unable: a couple with a large extended family and a seemingly solid (as solid as one could look on paper) background.

Still and yet, through all this agony, Jack never told his wife, Maggie.

seven

. . . .

BLUFFTON, SC

1997

The cramps weren't bad. Really, they were little more than a stomachache or muscle spasm. Katie still had another week and anyway, the agony she'd heard about—head-spinning pain that tore women in half—would be much more severe than this. She wouldn't panic over muscle aches. It wasn't time yet.

Katie sat back against the tub and let the warm water soothe her. Twilight was turning into night, and the bathroom was dusky and serene as the first knife-searing stab thrust itself through the middle of her body. She bent over with its force and lost her breath into the darkness.

"Mom . . ." she called, tentatively at first, then louder, then loudest of all. "MOM!"

Nicole ran into the bathroom where Katie stood in the middle of a puddle, naked and round, doubled over and dripping water onto the tile floor. "Are you okay?" Her mom placed her hand on Katie's bare back.

Katie looked up. "I think . . . it's time."

"Get dressed. I'll get the bag and start the car."

Another knife ripped through Katie's body, a searing heat that she'd never felt before. "Oh . . ."

Her mom uttered the same soothing sounds she'd used when Katie was sick as a child, the sounds a mother uses with any child in any world, rubbing her hand up and down Katie's spine until the pain dissipated.

Nicole rushed into the bedroom and grabbed the prepacked bag as Katie wobbled, wet and bent, into the room to pull on sweatpants and a T-shirt. Within two minutes, they were on their way to the hospital.

Fluid gushed from Katie's body, drenching the towel that had been placed on the passenger seat. She knew from her classes that her water had broken, meaning that the baby would come quickly now. "Mom." Katie uttered the name, feeling its shape change with each contraction. She would be a mother soon. And then she would relinquish the right to be called by that same name.

Nicole gunned the car, placing her hand on Katie's leg. "You are going to be okay. This will be fine."

"I'm scared."

"Of course you are." Tears dripped off Nicole's chin and Katie turned away.

"We forgot to call Jack. I promised . . ." Katie's words were stopped short by a quick contraction, her body disobeying her commands to be still. Her body's unrelenting defiance left her breathless.

"I'll call him as soon as I get there. Shhh . . . be still. Focus on your breathing."

Tears blurred Katie's eyesight and as they drove, the Spanish moss hanging off the live oak trees blurred into winged birds.

"Katie, I will take care of everything. Focus only on your body. On the birth. Let go of everything else."

And she did. Closing her eyes, Katie went inside her body, talking to the baby she had named Luna, moving with the pain and the stirrings and the shifting of her bones. When they arrived at the hospital, the nurse told Katie that she was five centimeters dilated and moving fast.

In her last birthing class, Katie had decided she would not have a single medication, and she stuck with that choice. Using every technique she'd ever learned, she took control of her body, allowing the reckless spasms to move through her, crying when needed and screaming when something begged to be released.

There was, she found, a tunnel of darkness that she willingly entered as she pushed Luna from her body and into the world. Only the two of them existed—the crush of body cooperating outside time and space, allowing life to endure. The doctor, the nurse, and her mom were all in the room, yet they seemed somehow outside the world, another dimension.

Bearing down one final time, Katie was silent and resolute as Luna was born. For the briefest moment, the baby was simultaneously attached to Katie and in the world. The doctor cut the umbilical cord, releasing Luna from Katie's body. It would be Katie who would have to release Luna from her life.

The nurse walked around the bed and placed a wide-eyed Luna into Katie's arms. Katie looked down into her daughter's face. "Oh, she's the most perfect. Most perfect." Luna's hair was dark and thick, poking out in wet clumps after her journey. Her eyes were green, clear: Jack's eyes. If grief had a sound, it was the silence of that birthing room.

Nicole walked over and took Luna from Katie's arms, and the room filled with the deepest and most awful knowing: They would hold Luna this once and then she would be gone. Somewhere in the same hospital, a family waited to hold their new daughter.

Nicole held Luna and stroked her face, staring into her eyes. "We love you, baby Luna. We will, from this day forward, pray for you every day." Nicole handed Luna to Katie. Pictures were taken as if it was a normal birth—a day of celebration even—and then it was time to say good-bye.

"How do I do this?" Katie looked to her mom.

"I don't know."

Katie held her daughter, her heart yielded to the good-bye she hadn't yet spoken. "I can't go through this pain if there isn't peace at the end. I can't. Please promise me there is peace at the end of this."

Nicole placed her hand on Katie's forehead, but didn't promise anything at all. The nurse entered the room with her own tears. The social worker stood at her side with papers and a sad smile. "Are you ready?"

Katie pulled back the blanket, memorizing every bend and curve and sinew of Luna's body. Touching her. Kissing her.

Jack was there, at the hospital, waiting in a separate room to both meet and then say good-bye to his daughter. If a last living piece of Katie's heart existed (which she wasn't sure about) seeing Jack would have killed it.

"You, Luna, are beautiful and special and you are going to have a wonderful mother and dad. I want you to grow up to know your God, and be surrounded in and by love. Be a good girl. I love you with every piece of me." Katie kissed her daughter's forehead as a tear dropped on Luna's wild hair.

In a motion she would have thought impossible, Katie handed her child to the social worker and then reached into her bag. "I have something I want to send with her," Katie said in a voice suffused with sorrow. She handed the social worker a small feather.

"It will be up to the parents whether they will take this," the social worker said softly.

"I found it the first day I thought I might be pregnant. It's my only gift."

Nicole laid her head on the pillow next to her daughter. "Life is your gift, Katie."

"Kate," Katie said to her mom. "Now, from now on, call me Kate."

Kate handed Luna to the nurse, and something felt torn away, a hollow feeling like her insides had been scooped out. A great wind could blow through her without hitting resistance.

Kate's words echoed across the empty hospital room. "What will fill the place where you were?" The question was meant for her daughter, who was now someone else's child.

eight

. . . .

BRONXVILLE, NY

2010

Science was Emily's favorite class. She sat at the long black table with a plastic DNA helix at each place. The model was constructed of colored plastic bubbles attached by thick straws in a winding helix. Emily thought it beautiful. She was awed that every body had miles and miles of these microscopic and twisted ropes inside. Human bodies were so much more interesting than trying to decipher words.

Words made her crazy really—the way the letters moved around and changed their sounds just by being next to each other. The teachers and testers called the moving letters "dyslexia" but Emily called it obnoxious. Now she needed to have one more tutor and one more hour of school and one more sheet of homework.

Emily raised her hand.

"Yes?" Mrs. Graceland, the teacher, asked.

"Is dyslexia on DNA?" Emily held up the plastic molecule.

"Wow. That is a great question, Emily. But sadly, I don't know. I will look that up and tell you as soon as I find out. But usually attributes like that are on DNA; they don't know where yet." She touched the helix as if trying to find the exact spot where dyslexia would dwell.

Mrs. Graceland turned back to the board, holding chalk like a cigarette above her head before drawing a chart that would explain how DNA bestowed someone eye color or hair color or height. "Every attribute in or on your body is coded into this strand."

Two seats over from Emily, Chaz Ross laughed in that confident way that only athletic, good-looking boys could laugh, the way that meant they didn't care what anyone thought because only what they thought mattered. Emily looked at him and he smiled at her. "Guess that means that nice butt was coded before I was born."

"Gross," Emily said. "You're disgusting." But of course that was the last thing she thought he was. She turned back to her DNA strand and ran her finger across the plastic and then down to the base.

Sailor Kessler, Emily's best friend, whispered. "I got my dad's brown eyes and Mother's curly hair. What parts did you get?"

Emily stared at Sailor, who was so confident where every part of her had come from and why. "I don't know," Emily said, lowering her eyes to the desk.

"Don't know? I mean, are your pretty green eyes from your Mom or dad?"

"I don't know because I don't know." Emily looked up at her friend. "I'm adopted."

"Really?" Sailor paused as if swallowing a long sip of lemonade and waiting to decide how it tasted. Then she smiled. "Wow. How cool. How come you never told me?"

"I don't think about it much," Emily lied.

Sailor, whose parents not only gave her good looks, but all the money a thirteen-year-old girl could possibly need, hugged Emily with one arm, almost tipping over their metal chairs. "Just think, *you* have four parents. I mean that's something I can't have, right?"

"But not really. The other two—well one really—gave birth. Birth parents are what they are. So whatever."

"Not whatever. It's like a mystery. Like that book we loved when we were little."

"Harriet the Spy?"

"Yeah, like that. We could go try and find them. We'd be good at that."

"I don't want to find them." A half truth, which Emily continually convinced herself was a full truth.

Sailor looked up to the ceiling and sighed. "Oh, you are so lucky. I have my two boring parents and you have *mystery* parents."

Mrs. Graceland stopped her lecture on the X and Y chromosomes with her funny chart. "Sailor, please stop moving your lips and making noise come out."

The class laughed and Sailor apologized with her batting eyelashes. Class resumed, but Emily's thoughts were in the land they often were: Far-Away-Emily-World, her parents called it.

Mystery Parents. Emily had never thought of it that way—she'd only believed someone "gave her away." Now her adoption took on a mystique it hadn't before.

After school, Sailor and Emily sat on the back steps of the junior high.

Sailor pulled out a pad of paper. "Here, we are going to make a list. I mean, we have to find out, Emily. What if you finally kiss Chaz and then find out he's your brother or something gross like that? Maybe you were saved from a horrible situation or war, like all those kids Angelina Jolie adopted."

"You're wack-a-doodle," Emily said, smiling through her favorite word.

"Yes, I am, and that's why you're my best friend."

The two girls put their heads together and made a list of all the mysterious reasons her birth parents couldn't keep her.

- They were spies on the lam.
- The dad was the President of the United States and needed to hide her.
- The mother was a famous actress and she didn't want people to know.
- Both parents had to leave the country because they robbed the biggest bank in New York.

There they sat, Sailor and Emily, designing parents out of nothing, out of imagination and dust.

Finally Emily folded the paper with the mystery parent list, and tucked it into the side pocket of her backpack. Together they walked into the village, stopping for a shaved ice from Brinson's Pharmacy. When they reached Emily's home, Sailor looked up at the brick house. "You are so lucky."

"Yes, I am." Emily waved good-bye and walked into the front door, inhaling the smell of her mother's cooking in the back of the house. It smelled like pot roast—her least favorite, but her dad's very favorite.

Home.

Emiy walked down the back hall, dropping her backpack onto the hardwood floor by the basement door. "Mom?" she called out, tasting the word as if it were new and fresh, something she'd never thought about before although she was told it was the first word she ever said.

"Back here," her Mom's voice called from the laundry room.

A bowl of grapes sat on the counter and Emily grabbed a handful before walking to the laundry room and hugging her mother. "I love you."

"Well, that's good," Elena said, throwing clothes into the dryer. "Because I love you too."

. . .

Emily's homework that night was to write a paragraph about the fa-vorite parts of her DNA and add a pedigree chart showing where those attributes came from: X for mother. Y for father. The blank sheet stared at Emily until she began to wrap the words around what she wanted to say.

My DNA gave me green eyes with a few brown freckles inside. My DNA gave me wavy coppery hair that isn't really red or brown, but a little of both. My DNA made me short and strong. My DNA gave me ugly nail beds that go all flat on the sides. My DNA lets me roll my tongue upside down. There are lots of things my DNA gave me, but my parents gave me love. I can't make a chart out of love because there is no such thing. My parents made me out of love and not a molecule.

Emily 13 years old
Born on March 20, 1997

nine

. . . .

BIRMINGHAM, AL

2010

Walking into the pizza parlor with Jack and Caleb, Kate felt as if only days had passed, not years. The restaurant was dim and loud—the perfect combination for boys. Baseball players tumbled into the restaurant one after the other, taking over the middle section. Parents clustered around satellite tables.

"Jack," a man called from across the room. "We're over here."

Jack made a motion to indicate he would stay at the corner table where he sat with Kate. He looked to her. "Unless of course you want to eat with the team parents and talk about game strategy and batting order."

"No, really," she said. "I'm good here with you."

They ordered a pizza and salad to share. Caleb sat with his teammates, leaving Jack and Kate to face one another across a cracked linoleum table. "So," Jack said. "What brings you to Birmingham after all these years?"

"Well, you know I own that clothing store in Bluffton? My favorite client wanted me to check out this boutique in Birmingham that won some design award. So, here I am."

"Really?"

"Yes, really."

"So that's why you're here."

"No, that's my excuse for being here."

He smiled. "Good then."

The pizza and salads arrived, and the combined noise of boys' voices and rock music over the speakers filled the silence until Jack finally leaned forward. "Okay, I'm really glad to see you and I can't wait to catch up, but is there something . . . specific?"

"Yes." She nodded at him and wiped the pizza grease from the corner of her mouth. "I want to talk about some . . . old stuff."

"Caleb is going to his grandparents' farm for the rest of the weekend, so we can talk later, okay?"

"When did your parents get a farm?"

"No, Maggie's parents."

"Maggie," Kate said quietly.

Jack nodded, but changed the subject. "So, tell me, how are things in Bluffton? How's the family?"

"All is well in South Carolina. I ran into Hayes at a party the other night. He asked about you."

"Wow. I'm surprised anyone even remembers me. It's been a long time."

"You're memorable," Kate said, smiling.

"I'm not sure for all the right reasons."

"Well, Larson asks about you. And Norah says hello."

Jack shook his head. "Sometimes I forget about South Carolina, like I never lived there. But then, if I close my eyes, I can see the river. . . ."

"Yes, the river."

The years melted away and for a breath in and out, they weren't Jack and Kate in a pizza parlor, but Jack and Katie on the edge of a river on the first day of spring, making promises. Then the moment was gone, a passing cloud or whisper.

"So," Jack said. "Tell me about your clothing store."

Yes, they would do their very best to avoid the past, the river, and the vows. Kate dove into his question with relief. "My store." She smiled. "I've written to you about it. It's called Mimsy. I named it after a little girl I took care of for a few years."

He shrugged. "I pictured you doing a lot of things, but owning a boutique wasn't on the list."

"You pictured me?" She teased, smiling across the table.

He laughed loudly enough for the next table to smile at them. "Yes, I picture you sometimes. Now go . . . tell me about it."

"Well, while I was being a nanny during the summer for this family, the mom, Susan Neal, noticed my eye for detail. She started asking me to shop for her, pick things out. Next thing I knew I was flying to New York with her, talking about opening a boutique, and obsessing about new styles and designers. I fell into it like I fall into most things—accidentally."

She heard the word slip from her mouth at the same time that she wanted to stop it—*accident*. It wasn't what she meant to say and its meaning nudged too close to something else, to all they needed to avoid.

"So this Susan woman started the store with you?" Jack asked.

Kate exhaled. She was being way too sensitive, weighing every word like that. "Yes," she said. "Yes. She put up the seed money and is majority owner. I run it and do all the buying. But you're right; I never saw myself doing this either. But now that I'm doing it, I can't imagine another way. I love it. I really do."

"You run it alone?" he asked.

"No. Norah works with me part time and a girl named Lida, also."

"Lida," Jack said, leaning back in his chair. "How do I know that name?"

Kate looked up to the ceiling. Damn. Minefields existed in every word she spoke. "Lida," she said. "Is the girl who was in the wilderness with me right before I left. The one I stayed for . . ."

Jack held up his hand. "Yep, I remember." His eyes closed and for the first time since he'd seen her on the baseball field, his smile dissipated. Then he opened his eyes. "So, tell me about your sisters. How are they?"

For the remainder of the meal, they talked about families and siblings, about jobs and cities, until Grandma came to pick up Caleb. Kate stayed at the table as Jack walked his son outside.

Alone at the table, Kate realized she'd never told Jack about Lida coming to South Carolina. How the girl she'd stayed with in the wilderness for all those years ago was still with her now.

Mimsy Clothing had been open for three years when Lida had shown up at the front door with a duffel bag. Considering that Kate had thought about Lida almost every day since leaving her in the wilderness with the new field guide, it took Kate longer to recognize Lida than it should have. She blamed the complete surprise, like seeing a desert cactus in Key West.

"Hi, Katie," Lida said and dropped her filthy bag onto the white slipcovered chair.

In an instinctual movement, Kate picked up the bag and placed it on the floor. "May I help you?"

"I think you already have," Lida said, and then laughed that deep, raspy sound that came from smoking since she was eleven years old.

The remembering came in a sudden wave, and Kate embraced the young girl, hugging her hard and holding tight. "Oh! I've thought about you every day." She stepped back and took the girl's face in her hands. "I tried to find you. I called Winsome, but they weren't allowed to give me your information. I've wondered . . ."

"Well, no more wondering." Lida shrugged her shoulders. "Here I am."

"How are you? Where have you been? What are you doing here?"

"How many of those do you want me to answer?"

"All, but not at once." Kate took Lida's hands. "Sit, tell me everything."

It took the afternoon to catch up on the previous nine years of Lida's nomadic life, in which she'd somehow finished high school and was at that moment trying to enroll in community college, thinking that South Carolina might just be the right place for such a thing.

Kate hired Lida, helping her find a small garage apartment. Exactly as Kate had put her hand over her unborn child all those years ago, and somehow connected Lida and Luna, this seemed a second chance to do at least one thing right. Lida had seemed a symbol of hope and Kate grabbed onto it as a life raft with a flag of faith.

Months after Lida began working at Mimsy, she'd learned to run the store as well as, and sometimes better than, Kate. Natural and comfortable in her own skin, her dreadlocks pulled into a ponytail, her face fresh and consistently smiling, all the customers loved her. She had a knack for knowing what outfit would work on what woman and they all grew to trust her, often asking for her on the days she wasn't there.

While Kate thought about Lida, Jack startled her by returning and holding out his hand for her to stand. She looked up to him in absolute wonder. Yes, he was real.

Standing outside the restaurant, feeling as if she'd come out of a movie theater in the middle of the day, Kate put on her sunglasses, shielding the evening sunlight.

"Should we go back to my house or is there somewhere else you wanted to go?" Jack asked.

"I remembered this time you took me to Vulcan and we had a picnic and . . ."

Jack smiled. "Yep, he's still there." He motioned toward his truck. "Come on. I'll drive."

Birmingham had the largest iron statue in the country and this Roman god, Vulcan, stared over the city with his bare bottom and a raised fist, proclaiming the power of steel and its ability to form a city out of the deep iron ore in the red dirt. The Magic City.

Jack parked and Kate looked up at the iron edifice, remembering the first time he'd brought her here and how she'd believed that love itself was a god, that it could conquer anything. But obviously lesser gods had conquered.

With evening fading to night, Kate and Jack sat at a picnic table facing one another. "So, Katie, tell me why you're here."

"I don't really know how I want to say what I want to say."

"Just start," he said.

"It's so messed up and confusing, so I'm not sure it will come out right. But here's the thing. I've been dating this guy, Rowan, for four years now and I still . . . doubt. And I know this is crazy, but I felt like if I talked to you I could get to the other side of that doubt. I mean, you found a way to . . . move on, and I'm hoping I can do the same. Something is . . . stopping me."

"You think I'm stopping you?" He leaned back, as if moving away from her words, from her.

"No, not you. It's something in me." She sighed, digging for the right words. "You moved on and had a child and made a life. I haven't been able to do that. I've been running and avoiding and denying, and now I've finally met this amazing guy. I found an engagement ring in his bedside drawer . . . and I want to commit. I do. But I needed to see you. I want to ask the terrible questions. I want to understand. Is that okay?"

"It's okay, but why do you feel like you need to see me after all this time? I don't get it." He took off his sunglasses and those green eyes, the same ones that had been on their daughter's sweet face, stared back at Kate.

"When I look back on those days, I see that I was such a mess. I know we made the decision about Luna together. I know that we talked until we both couldn't stand it any longer, but to do what I did I had to shut my heart completely. I slammed it shut."

"I'm sorry. I am. I don't know how to go back and change things."

"I don't either. I think that's the point. I want to know—what happened? I've gone from hating you to loving you at least a million times. I want to know. It might help. I mean, why did you marry Maggie and not wait for me to finish with my job?"

Her words seemed a weight, slumping his shoulders and head forward. "I did wait. I've gone over this in my head, too. What could I have done differently? How could I have changed things?" He sat straighter as if shaking off the past. "I asked you to come home. I loved you. I waited. And then I waited some more. You didn't come home. You wrote letters about all the fabulous things you were doing and seeing. Then you came to visit me and promised you'd give your notice, but you didn't."

"Lida . . ." she said.

"And then I waited some more."

"I know." Her explanations and reasons and rationales no longer mattered even as they begged to again be spoken.

"When I finally mattered to you, it was too late. Sometimes, Katie, it's too late for something. And by the time you came home pregnant, it was too damn late."

She nodded.

"So, to answer your question—I didn't stop loving you. Not once. But I did stop believing. *There* is the difference."

"I get it," she said and stood. "God, I'm so stupid. I knew all this. You were always clear about it. I don't know why I thought that coming here might help. I shouldn't have come. I shouldn't have . . ." Kate backed away. "This was a really bad idea."

He stood also and then took her by the shoulders with both hands. "I'm being honest."

"I've made us both feel all that old terribleness again. I'm sorry." Tears came before she felt them rising, salty puddles in the corners of her eyes. "I'm so sorry. I'm making everything worse."

"You know, when I first saw you standing at the game, I thought you might be coming to tell me you found Luna. Or that you knew something about her. That's what I was hoping for."

Kate dropped her head into her hands. "I should go. I've completely screwed this up."

Why couldn't she have kept it light? Talked about Bluffton and Birmingham. About old friends and jobs. Why the hell had she ruined what had been a perfectly nice afternoon?

Jack's face was obscured from Kate as he spoke. "I have no idea why doing the right thing can feel so wrong and awful. But that's what it felt like after we had Luna. And I don't want to *ever* feel that way again." He paused and then stepped into the circle of lamppost light. "Come on, I'll take you to your car." His voice was distant, as if it came from the past to reach the place they were.

Somewhere in the middle of their conversation, evening had turned to night, and they drove down the twisting road back to the village where Kate's car was the only one remaining in the baseball field parking lot. He finally spoke. "I'm glad you came. Of course I wonder about you and how you are. But the truth is that as good as it is to see you, being near you brings up all the awful feelings. I've never tried to forget anything like I've tried to forget that time."

"I shouldn't have come here. Maybe I should have let us send yearly letters for the rest of our lives, but something in me wanted to talk about it, to see you."

"I understand," Jack said, staring through the windshield.

Katie pushed her thumbs into the inside corners of her eyes, trying to stay the tears. She would not cry in front of him. She would not make this any worse than it was. Visiting Jack was an incredibly stupid idea. The sight of an engagement ring had obviously made her lose all sense.

She stepped out of the truck and dug into her purse for keys. She wanted to say good-bye, some kind of parting words that mattered, but she couldn't find her voice. She shut the passenger door, turning away to walk to her car, and then she spun around to return. She opened the passenger door and placed her hands on the truck's roof, glancing into the cab. "I came here because I wanted to see you again, to heal whatever could be healed." She again shut the door and walked away.

She didn't look over her shoulder or glance backward as the tears had come and she wanted to get in her car, safely in her car. Her head dropped onto the steering wheel and she groaned. She couldn't reform the past with words and apologies and explanations.

Long minutes passed as Kate sat in her car, waiting for her tears to stop, waiting for her mind to calm. She finally turned the key in the ignition, tuning the radio to a country station where Rodney Atkins sang about his son, saying, *"He's mine, that one."*

Backing out of the parking spot, Kate drove toward the stop sign at the end of the street before she realized that she didn't know where she was going. She'd followed Jack and now she was lost. She hadn't seen the boutique. She didn't have a hotel reservation. She slammed her hand on the steering wheel. She'd made the usual mess of things.

A honk startled her, and she glanced in the rearview mirror. A black truck was on her bumper and a man was waving at her from the driver's seat. "I'm going. I'm going," she hollered, and then glanced one more time. She twisted her head and looked at Jack through the back window as he got out of the truck and walked to her car. He had the grin, that adorable shy grin she'd loved for her whole life. He approached her driver's-side window. She rolled down the window, and he leaned down.

"You know where you're going?"

"A little, yes," she said and then laughed. "No, not at all."

He reached into her car and touched her cheek, wiping off a tear. "Katie, I'm sorry. I'm acting like an ass."

"I shouldn't have shown up here like this." She sighed. "I don't think things all the way through . . . sometimes."

"No, sometimes you don't." He shook his head, but that astonishing grin never left his face. "Thirteen years ago, I let you leave. Not this time. I don't really understand why you're here or why I'm asking you to stay. But I am."

Kate smiled at him. "Really?"

He nodded. "Just a little while. We can talk and catch up. Caleb is gone all weekend and it would be nice to spend some time together."

"Yes," Kate said. "Really nice."

March 20th, 1998

Dear Katie,

   Happy First Birthday to Luna.

   Thank you so much for writing to me. Yearly letters are a great idea: we can't wish our daughter a happy birthday, but we can say it to each other. It seems terrible for us to never talk again, but we've also got to move on with our lives, and this is a nice in-between.

   I've been wondering where you are and how you are. I admit though that I haven't tried very hard to find you. Right away, I will be honest and answer your first question—do I hate you? Of course not. It was deeply terrible, but we agreed. You asked, in your letter, for forgiveness, but you don't have to ask because I gave it to you a long time ago. I gave it before you asked. And of course I must ask for your forgiveness also. I know we both did the best we could do, but I also know that I hurt you.

The pain had to go somewhere and for a while I tried to hate you, but I just couldn't. Like you, I wonder about Luna and where she is. I hope she's safe. It's the not-knowing that is the hardest. Don't you agree? All that not-knowing. There is so much of it.

You asked what I'm doing now: I'm a lawyer at my father's firm in Birmingham, watching my life turn into something I never thought it would. Soon I'll probably do something ridiculous and become an artist living in Bali. (Not really, but does that make me sound more exciting than I am?)

Maggie is doing great and really loves Birmingham. I thought it would be hard for her because she's always lived on acreage (her family farm), but she's already made a million friends and she loves the convenience of being so close to downtown.

I hope your family is well.

So, I'll stop writing now because really I'm terrible at it.

Jack

ten

. . . .

BRONXVILLE, NEW YORK

2010

Bronxville was small. Small enough for almost any kid to walk from the junior high school to almost any house. That's what Emily wished she was doing that particular afternoon. Walking home. Instead she was walking with Chaz, Sissy, Mattie, and Lisa—the group she had been assigned for her volunteer work. It was also the group designated The Cool Crowd by the other kids, the ones who stood outside it. The cool crowd was part of an old familiar ritual of teen deference, the same one their parents performed and their parents before them. As if some bloodline picked the character and coolness of any child in Bronxville or anywhere else for that matter.

Lisa and Sissy were the ringleaders and they were as interchangeable as their names. Blond and slender, they were overly sexy for their age as if they'd watched too many music videos. Mattie was the quiet one, part of the group because she was Sissy's cousin and that made it difficult for Sissy to leave Mattie aside. And then there was Chaz, who was the cutest boy God had ever made into human flesh. And yet, he defied any definition of junior high cool. He didn't play football. He was shorter than the average boy. He had acne that flared at the worst times. And yet . . . something about him drew everyone in. Everyone, including Emily.

Usually this crowd ignored her, and Emily was proud as she was walking with them in the spring afternoon, discussing their volunteer work for the afternoon: cleaning out the storage shed at First Presbyterian. They walked toward the church and Chaz picked up a stone from Mr. Forester's front yard, throwing it toward the flowerbed. "Mean old man," he hollered.

"He's not mean. Just crazy. Wack-a-doodle," Emily said in a rush. Words often went from her mind to her mouth, crossing a bridge that shouldn't have been built (at least that's what her dad told her). Right before she'd left for the afternoon, she'd looked at her mirror-self and said, *think before you speak*. And there she was doing the exact opposite.

The group stopped. Lisa was the leader, and if it were possible, she would wear a crown or tiara to prove it. "What?" Lisa asked.

Emily attempted to keep walking, moving along the sidewalk as if she'd never spoken, as if she didn't need to answer Lisa, which of course she did.

"Oh, you know." Emily lifted her finger and made a swirling motion at her temple. "He's crazy like a worm on hot pavement."

"Now that's funny. Worm on hot pavement," Chaz said and laughed with that low, vibrating sound that made Emily's insides expand and reach for something unnamed.

"No, she's not funny at all," Lisa said.

"Like you get to decide who I think is funny?" Chaz stepped closer to Lisa.

"Let's go," Mattie said. "This is stupid."

"How do you know old Mr. Forester?" Chaz asked Emily.

"I don't really," Emily said. "I hear my aunt Mitzi talk about him. She feels all sorry for him, so I know it's not that he's mean, but 'not right.'"

"Sad," Chaz said as they walked toward the church where some grown-ups were waiting to show the kids what to do with the storage shed.

After the adults had vacated and left the five kids their instructions—empty the storage shed, sweep it out, then put everything back in a very organized manner—they all stood staring into the dusty space.

"This sucks," Lisa said.

Chaz stepped inside, pulling on a string that turned on a bright overhead light bulb. "Let's get this over with."

They split up, each taking a small corner of the shed.

Sissy stood next to Chaz as he swept the back corner, twirling her hair around her fingers. He pointed the broom toward the ceiling, poking at the corner. Dust, cobwebs, and dirt fell, raining down on them. "Ew, gross," Sissy screamed, backing up.

"That's what you get for flirting instead of working," Mattie called out from the center of the room, where she was stacking plastic chairs.

"I'm working," Sissy said. "See?" She lifted a sewing machine from the corner and set it on a table.

"Whatever," Mattie said.

Emily handed a roll of packing tape to Lisa. "Let's tape these boxes and we're almost done."

"I have an idea," Lisa said. "Why don't *you* tape up those boxes and we'll be almost done."

Chaz threw a deflated basketball toward Lisa. "Throw that in the trash, Lisa, along with your meanness."

"Ha, ha," Lisa said. "You're just so funny, Chaz." She flipped on a light in the back corner. "Oh, cool, everyone look at this." Together they stopped to stare at a disheveled manger scene with the big spotlight shining down like a dim star of Bethlehem.

Manger scenes were something of a competitive sport in Bronx-ville, *which of course is the last thing a manger scene should ever be,* Emily thought. There were the wooden carved ones, the plastic ones, and the live-animal ones (which always had a disastrous outcome one way or the other). This particular manger scene was definitely on the list of *most pitiful* and yet it was Emily's favorite. Emily was the girl who'd pick the runt of the litter, the girl who felt sorry for the losing team, so her affection for this mismatched manger was to be expected. Something sad and beautiful filled the faded faces of the plastic kings, Mary's bowed head with her now-yellowed but once-white veil hanging over her face so you could see only her chin and half smile. Not to mention the crouched, cracked animals (the donkey was miss-ing a hind leg).

There'd been a scandal of manger donkey–stealing the previous year. Every ass from every manger scene in town had been taken, and then on Christmas eve they'd all appeared on the high school princi-pal's lawn—a statement not one person missed.

"So we get to clean the holy family," Chaz said.

"I have an idea," Sissy said in a whisper that sounded more like a hiss.

"No," Mattie said. "No more ideas from you."

Chaz laughed. "I love your ideas. What is it?"

"Let's start our own manger tradition."

Emily's stomach flipped over. She wanted to speak, to avert what-ever idiot thing was about to happen. But she stalled.

"The Marys. We'll steal all the Marys this year. I mean, really, every year it should be someone or something from the manger scene right? Last year, the donkeys, this year Mary, next year Joseph."

"But never the baby Jesus," Tara said. "We would never do that, right?"

"Of course not. Stop being so scared of everything. Really."

Chaz laughed. "You up for it, Emily?"

"Only after we do the cleanup. We can take her then, I guess. But won't they know it's us who took her?"

If Emily told them this was her favorite manger scene, if she told them it made her want to cry to think about taking Mary away from baby Jesus, if she told them they were idiots, they'd make fun of her.

Glancing out the door, Lisa grabbed Mary around the waist.

"What are we going to do with her?" Lisa asked, holding Mary without lifting.

"Hide her in the back woods until I can carry her home and put her in my daddy's shed," Chaz said. With that he took the five-foot Mary, slung the plastic statue over his shoulder, and ran out the door. The girls ran after him, disappearing into the dark shadows. Emily was stuck in the storage shed as firmly as if she were a figurine, as if someone had to take Mary's place and she was chosen. The teens didn't miss Emily as they ran into the woods, hiding Mary amongst the tangled ivy.

Emily stood under the spotlight of the now-clean First Presbyterian storage shed. She didn't understand the need to take baby Jesus from his wooden trough, but she knew she couldn't leave him without a mother. Emily closed and locked the storage doors. With Jesus wrapped in a moldy tarp, she walked away

She'd walked halfway home by the time she wondered what she would do with the baby Jesus. Guilt tasted like metal in the back of her throat and instead of home, Emily ran to Sailor's house.

It was Sailor who saved the day. It was Sailor who went with Emily into the poison-ivy infested woods and retrieved Mary, delivering both to the storage shed before anyone knew they were gone, reuniting mother and child. And it was Sailor who whispered, "Now we have to get you and your mom together."

March 20, 1999

Dear Katie,

Happy Second Birthday to Luna.

I wonder how you are. I can't wait to read your letter and find out where you've been in this wide world.

Oh, you ask, the places I've been? That should take about fifteen seconds to tell you. Birmingham. Atlanta. New Orleans for Mardi Gras. And the thrilling convention in Cincinnati where I thought I lost my nose to frostbite. The hours I'm working are insane, truthfully. Dad wants me to take over the firm in the next two years, and I'm not sure how to tell him it might not be in the cards. I do love the job, but running the firm? I don't know. On top of it, Maggie wants us to move to her family farm. Between Dad and Maggie, I should be two people.

Well, that's more than you probably want to know, but it's something anyway. I think about what it must be like for you on this day, on this day that you're opening this letter. What do you think about all day? Do you think about saying good-bye? Do you get drunk? (I do.)

Every single day, at least once, I wonder where Luna is. I believe she's doing great. I think, or I hope, that I'd feel it if she weren't.

Tell me about you. Something. Anything. A story.

eleven

. . . .

BIRMINGHAM, ALABAMA

2010

Jack's house was warm and spacious, the living room filled with scattered pillows and sports magazines. Kate looked up at the coffered ceiling, at the carved woodwork and limestone fireplace, at the buffed hardwood floors and the plank walls painted dove grey. Baseball cards sat in piles on the coffee table. "Welcome," Jack said and held out his hands. "You never did see the house finished."

"It's gorgeous," Kate said. "Really. Have you ever thought about doing this for someone else?"

He laughed and held up his hand. "No way. I could never do this for someone else."

"I like the colors."

"Maggie chose those," he said. "She wanted to be an interior designer for a little while. That was before she wanted to be a photographer and then before she wanted to work on her family farm, forming a gourmet goat cheese business." Jack smiled and Kate followed him toward the archway she remembered would take them to the kitchen. The hallway walls had the same plank board. Framed photos of Birmingham landmarks hung on the wall.

"These are hers?" Kate asked.

"Yep." Jack said without turning around. "I've always loved them. Great photos. She was good at it."

Kate reached forward and touched his shoulder. "I'm sorry you went through that terrible time," she said.

"Thanks, that's sweet," he answered softly.

They walked into the kitchen with the stainless appliances, the stone countertops, and vintage lamps hanging over the island.

"Wow. This is amazing." Kate touched the countertop.

Jack pulled a bottle of wine from a small refrigerator under the counter and poured Pinot Grigio into oval stemless glasses, handing one to Kate. "You know, I never told Maggie about Luna, or about you. I meant to. A million times I meant to. Even when we had Caleb, or I snuck off to mail those letters to you, I promised myself I'd tell her. I've never forgiven myself for that deception. But I was afraid that it would change everything."

"I don't think there's anything to forgive and I don't think there's a right way to do these things. She still doesn't know?"

"No."

Katie took a long sip of wine. "I haven't told Rowan."

"Rowan?"

"The guy. The guy I'm dating. The guy who has an engagement ring in his bedside drawer. The guy I love, but panic every time I think about anything that sounds like 'forever.'"

He nodded. "Ah, that guy." He smiled. "Yes. Forever has always tangled you up."

"That's not true," Kate said, following him out.

He ignored her comment and they entered the living room, holding their wineglasses and sitting on opposite chairs. They faced one another over the baseball card–laden coffee table and thirteen years. Comfortable, Jack prodded Kate forward with questions about her life.

"Enough about me," she finally said. "I mean, aren't you tired of hearing about me? Don't you want to change the subject?"

Jack leaned forward. "I've wondered about you for years. So no, I don't want to change the subject."

She smiled, warming inside as if the sun had just risen instead of fallen. "Do you want to go get dinner?"

"Good idea." Jack stood. "Come on. I'll take you to my favorite restaurant."

Highlands Bar and Grill overflowed with people on a spring night, spilling out onto the sidewalk in Southside Birmingham and then into the bar where not a single barstool sat empty. Jack greeted the maître d' with a firm handshake. "Burt, I know I didn't make reservations and it's a Saturday night, but my dear friend surprised me and of course I want to show off my favorite restaurant. Any chance you could find us a table?" Jack introduced Kate.

Burt, in his crisp white shirt and skinny black tie, looked like he was in a Frank Sinatra cover band in his spare time. He nodded. "Nice to meet you, Kate. Let me show off Birmingham's finest." He motioned to a table snuggled in the back corner by a window. "That should be available within fifteen minutes. Why don't you two go get a drink and I'll come get you in a few."

"Thanks, Burt. Seriously. I so appreciate this," Jack said.

Burt smiled. "It's not for you." He nodded at Kate. "For the lovely lady."

Jack placed his hand on Kate's lower back and guided her to the bar. She'd changed into a summer dress, one of her favorites from the new Show Me Your MuMu line. It was made of the finest pale blue linen, and fell slightly off her left shoulder to form a low V down her back where Jack's hand now touched skin. Warmth spread from his hand in every direction. She wondered, did he feel the heat also? Or was she conjuring the old magic on her own?

"What would you like?" Jack asked.

"What do you usually get here?"

"They have a drink called the Orange Thing. It's made with fresh-squeezed orange juice, vodka, and some secret ingredient that causes addiction."

"Sounds perfect," Kate said.

To the bartender, Jack made a motion with his hand, which must have been sign language that only the two of them understood because within a minute, two drinks appeared. "You must come here a lot," Kate said.

"Yes," Jack said, and then stared at her. Kate turned away with heat rushing, a river, underneath her skin. "You are really beautiful, Katie. I remembered you that way, and it's nice to see I was right."

"That's so sweet. Thanks. You're making me blush, and I don't blush easily."

He lifted his glass and she did hers. They clinked their drinks together in a toast. "To renewed friendships," she said.

Jack smiled and they both took a long sip.

Kate leaned against the bar and dug into her purse for her cell phone. "I need to make a hotel reservation. I decided quickly to come here and didn't know where I'd stay, or if I would stay, so I need to do that. Any ideas?"

"You can stay with me. Caleb is at Grandma's. I have two guest rooms and an empty house. It's silly for you to get a hotel."

Without hesitation, something she only later noticed, she placed her phone back into her purse. "That would be nice."

Men and women stopped by the bar, shaking hands with Jack, greeting him and meeting Kate. Half an hour later, Burt came to seat them, and Kate asked, "Do you know everyone in town?"

He laughed and pulled her chair out for her as she sat. "I've lived here for fifteen years. It's not a big town. It has nothing to do with popularity, just familiarity."

Finally settled at their table with fig appetizers between them, Kate lifted her fork to hold across the table. "You have to have a bite of this. I've never tasted anything this good anywhere."

He took a bite. "Amazing, I know. It's the chef's favorite."

"I want to tell you something," she said.

"Anything."

She laughed. "I doubt that, but I do want to tell you how much those yearly letters meant to me. I always waited until the end of the day to read it."

"I loved writing them," Jack said. "Sometimes I felt guilty writing to you without telling Maggie, but it somehow seemed so separate. And important."

"It was important. I don't think I would have gotten through some of her birthdays without those letters," she said.

"I'm glad," he said. "I'd hoped that was true. And of course I loved getting yours at the office. Thanks for . . . being thoughtful about that and not sending to the house. I mean, I never asked, but—"

"I know," she said. "New subject?"

"Your favorite vacation the past few years. Good one?"

"Absolutely." She laughed and the cadence of their friendship resumed as if thirteen years had never passed, as if the birth of their child and then his marriage and divorce had never happened, as if Kate's life had never been broken.

But it had.

. . .

In the spill of light from Jack's table lamp, they sat in the living room facing one another across the couch. Kate curled her legs beneath her bottom. With the comfort that had arrived, Kate asked the question that had niggled below the surface of all her other questions. "Were you and Maggie happy at all? I mean, I know you must have been, but . . ."

He leaned into the cushions. "We were. The last time I really remember it, though, was a trip to Mexico."

"Tell me about it."

"My stories are boring." He waved his hand across the room. "Look at me. While you've worked different jobs and opened a store, I've been right here."

"I want to hear about all of it. I want to hear about Caleb and your job. And your art studio. And your friends. And life. All of it."

"Well, all that will take a lifetime to tell you."

"We've got that—a lifetime." It wasn't until Kate spoke the words that she understood how they sounded—as if *they* had a lifetime together. Just the two of them. "Oh," she said. "I mean, I mean that we have all our lives ahead of us. I didn't mean . . ."

He laughed and reached forward to touch her knee. "I knew what you meant."

"Tell me about your last happy time with her."

He closed his eyes and then opened them with a smile. "Okay."

"Good."

"So there we were on vacation for the first time in two years. Caleb was a year old and neither of us felt like we'd slept since the day he was born. The colic. The crying. The diapers. My God, we were past exhausted. So, we decided that we needed a few days: sleep, drink, eat. Repeat. We stayed in this tiny family-owned resort in Cozumel. There was a private and tiny beach. A tiki bar. And the most amazing guacamole I've ever tasted. I still think about that guacamole.

"We were well into our second day when we decided to go snorkeling. The hotel owners told us that if we walked a half mile up the beach and then jumped in, the current would carry us right back to our beach. We did this a few times and it was our third time when we realized we'd floated too far down, way past our hotel. We ended up at a hopping singles' resort about a quarter mile down the beach. Now we'd heard the parties at night and laughed at how old we must be that we didn't even care that there was a party in walking distance down the beach.

"We climbed out of the water and thought we'd walk back to our resort, but a mariachi band was playing and the next thing we knew we were dancing and putting margaritas on the tab of someone named "Burris." It all seemed funny and fun until Mr. Burris heard me put one last margarita on his bill.

"Now this Mr. Burris wasn't just any guy. He was drunk. He was huge, and if he wasn't a professional bodybuilder, he should have been. When I tried to explain that we were just having fun, that I would go back to my hotel around the corner and get him some cash, that I had every intention of paying him back but I had nothing on me but a bathing suit and a mask with a snorkel, he didn't think I was funny.

"So that is how I ended up in the back of a police car."

"My God," Kate said through bubbled laughter. "Seriously?"

"A fight ensued. Then there was a bouncer. And a policeman. And yep, handcuffs and a cop car."

"Did Maggie freak out?"

"Absolutely. In the end the local police were a little too busy with some drug cartel to give a shit about some half-drunk, fully sunburned tourist. They dropped me off at the hotel, where Maggie and I swore that being up all night with Caleb was safer than partying. We never left the country again."

"Really?"

"Not on purpose, actually. I wanted to take her to Scotland. That was her dream. Her husband is taking her next year." Jack looked directly at Kate. "Is it okay if we don't talk about that?"

"Of course."

He stood then and held out his hand. "Lights out for me. I'm used to sharing the house with an eight-year-old who has an eight-thirty bedtime."

"Yeah, I'm pretty wiped out too," Kate said and stood. "I'll leave in the morning and head home. So don't feel like you have to entertain me or anything."

"I thought you came to see the boutique," he said.

"I'll go by in the morning on my way out."

"I'd love to show you the studio," he said.

She smiled. "I'd like that."

She followed Jack down the hall where the bedrooms hid behind closed doors. He had already showed her to the guest bedroom where her suitcase sat on the end of the bed. She stopped in the doorway and Jack turned before he entered his bedroom next to hers. "Sleep well," he said.

"You also," she said.

They both shut their doors, and yet Kate stood with her forehead against the doorframe until she heard the sink run, and then the soft sound of his feet moving across the room. Then she lay in bed, the sheets pulled tightly around her body, which hummed with the utterly true, but perfectly impossible fact that Jack Adams was on the other side of the wall.

March 20th, 2004

Dear Katie,

Happy Seventh Birthday to Luna.

I think in many ways writing this letter every March has become a cornerstone for my year. You know, sometimes it takes me a week or more to write the entire thing. But it is here in this letter that I look backward and forward, like some people must do on New Year's Eve.

This is a difficult letter to write. I don't know how to say this gently, but Maggie and I divorced. Maybe you've already heard or maybe this is a shock; I have no way to know really until I get your letter in return.

I thought maybe I'd write to you of the details, but I can't.

Caleb wakes in the middle of the night hollering for her, and I have to go to him and explain that he will see her tomorrow or the next day. He isn't taking this well. No hollering or calling or wishing or praying or being good will make her come back to this house. She's moved to her family's farm where she wanted to go all along.

I'm not sure I've fully felt the awfulness of it all yet. I feel very separate from life; free-floating almost.

I hope that this is the most terrible yearly letter I will ever have to write to you. And that you will never have to write one like it to me.

Love,

Jack

P.S. I saw this poem a long time ago and copied it. I thought you might like it, but now I don't remember who wrote it or even its title. But here it is anyway.

It's hard to believe
we're looking at the same moon.

But if what they say is true—
then you are there and I am here
while that lazy moon floats high between us,
as if she doesn't care.
Or worse, as if she doesn't know.

twelve

· · · · · · · · · · · · ·

BIRMINGHAM, AL

2010

Morning came with a sudden gasp. Kate sat upright, briefly disori-
ented. Sunlight streamed onto her face, into her eyes. She shouldn't
have spent the night at Jack's house. Everything that needed to be said
had been said and now she would have to go make small talk over
cereal or eggs. It would have been best to have a nice good-bye the
night before and move on with their lives.

The clock read 5:30A.M.—it was still early and she didn't want to
wake Jack. How awful would it be to sneak out?

They'd talked. They'd summarized the past. What was left? The
truth of course. She'd only told him the best parts, leaving out the
pain and disorientation of those years. Like how that first year after
the adoption, she'd folded into herself like a flower that was too fragile and too complicated to ever open. How she'd dipped into a deep
darkness, a place where she'd wondered what there was about her

aimless life that was so important that she couldn't have raised her little girl. How only one vow had helped her get through that year—to never love again. All that romance, fairy tale, love forever and ever was crap. Loss: it was the period at the end of every sentence.

She hadn't told him how, during that year, she'd taken a job at the marina in Hilton Head, cleaning yachts, babysitting kids, and serving at cocktail parties. It was a job, pay and busywork. She'd tried not to think about Jack living his life in Birmingham and loving his wife as if nothing had ever happened. She'd hated him. She'd loved him. She'd missed him. She'd then hated him. All in a never-ending cycle.

She didn't tell Jack how much—how deeply—she'd hurt her parents. Luna was the first-born grandchild, one they held and then let go. Kate had known it was their fervent prayer that Luna would be restored to their lives. In her worst moments Kate was annoyed with their hopes for "one day." She felt that her parents yearned and pushed into the future, into the day they would see Luna again as if this day wasn't good enough, because this day didn't have Luna.

She'd understood, of course. Didn't she feel the same? And yet she'd been frustrated again and again when her parents brought Luna into the conversation. "Oh, we planted a tree for her, darling." "We found those pictures last night and looked at them again. She is so beautiful." "Did you fill out that paperwork that will allow her to find us when she's twenty-one?" And the worst of all the comments was from her dad. "I hope I live long enough to see her again."

And why would Jack want to know how Molly and Tara had had opposite reactions, as if they'd sat down and Tara said to Molly, "Okay, you talk about it almost every time you can and I'll never ever bring it up. Okay? Good. Now we're balanced." It wasn't because Tara cared less and Molly cared more. No, it was because of who they were. The sisters shared the same hurt. They just showed it in very different ways.

She skipped the part where on Luna's first birthday, she'd sat alone at the large restaurant table, staring out over the water, wondering what her one-year-old daughter was doing at that very moment. Sitting in a highchair with a little piece of pink cake? Ripping wrapping paper off a doll?

Was she really supposed to tell Jack all of that? Kate groaned, cuddling up further into the pillows, wishing for sleep. She'd told him the best parts, erasing the harder truths. He'd probably done the same. What good was there in reliving it all?

They both wanted to know that Luna was well and happy. They both wondered and lived with the what-ifs and the could-have and the should-haves. It didn't matter what they said or did.

Somewhere down the hallway, a door clicked open. Kate rose from bed and slipped on her jeans and white tank top. She entered the living room; it was awash in morning light that simultaneously softened the edges and exposed every flaw in the glass and furnishings. She walked to the windows.

"Spring is such a show-off." Jack's voice came from behind.

Kate turned and smiled. There he was—in his jeans and black T-shirt, the same Hornets baseball cap on his head. And the smile, the impossible smile.

"Good morning," Kate said.

"How'd you sleep?"

"Great. So much that I had no idea where I was when I woke up."

"Coffee?" he asked.

"Of course."

And then the nervousness disappeared as they walked into the kitchen. A calm cadence of conversation reappeared and Kate sat on the barstool waiting on her coffee and watching Jack move around his kitchen.

"So," he said with his back to her. "Which first, studio or boutique?"

"Studio," she said. "Because I'll drive back to Bluffton after the boutique. I left a message with the owner that I'd be there late morning."

He turned and handed her a mug of coffee. "I've wondered about Norah. So, she works with you?"

"Yep. When the boutique really took off, I needed a partner. We expanded and now we co-own. She came after she quit her yacht stewardess job and married this great guy, Charlie." Kate shook her head. "It's weird how fast time can go."

"I know." Jack sat across the bar. "There are things I say I'm going to do every year and then the year is over. Just done."

She nodded. "The only times a year seemed like more than a year and not less than one was the couple of years after Luna. Maybe time moves slow when you feel awful and time moves fast when you feel good."

He laughed. "Or something."

"I really shouldn't spout philosophy before I finish my first cup of coffee," Kate said and smiled. "Maybe keep some thoughts to myself."

"Your thoughts are nice," he said.

They sat in silence until they both stood simultaneously, as if on cue, as if a bell or whistle had signaled their leaving time.

LUNA STUDIO. The sign was made of a ten-foot-high piece of dark wood and the letters were fashioned of bright zinc reflecting the morning sun in sharp swords. Kate glanced up at Luna's name high and bright on the signage, and shivered.

"You okay?" Jack asked.

She nodded. "Yes. It's quite something to see her name up there like that. All big and proud."

He opened the thick glass door to let Kate walk in first. The foyer was brightly lit with tiny sconces sending indirect light onto canvas and wood. Kate walked through the small studio while Jack told her about it.

"The idea of this started seven years ago. Maggie wanted to have a place to show her photography and the art of some friends she'd come to know. After the divorce, I dismissed the idea. But then it wouldn't leave me alone, so even though she has nothing to do with it now, it was Maggie's idea."

Kate stopped in front of an angel painting so misty and surreal she thought the angel should be able to fly. "She never asked about the name?"

He shook his head. "I thought that when we opened the studio I would tell her, but now I don't feel any need to explain."

The desire came over her too fast. To touch Jack. To kiss him. To reach behind his head and rest her head on his shoulder. Kate averted her eyes.

"Only Alabama artists," he continued. "We have shows about every eight weeks or so."

"Who takes care of all this while you're working your real job?"

"Mimi Ann," he said, and then stopped and called out the same name.

A woman came from the back room, smiling and full of energy. She was all blond and platinum, all smiley and crisp. "Hi, y'all," Mimi Ann said as she walked toward them.

Jack hugged her and then introduced Kate. "This is Mimi Ann Davolt. Luna Studio is nothing without her."

"No," Mimi Ann said, "Jack has that backwards." She smiled at him. "I keep it going. Jack *is* Luna Studio." Mimi Ann looked at Kate then, and it seemed as if this was a terribly hard thing for Mimi Ann to do, as if it hurt to look away from Jack. "He has a fantastic reputation for finding the newest geniuses and showcasing their work first."

"Nice," Kate said.

A silence fell over the three of them, an uncomfortable emptiness that made Kate turn away, pretending to look at other work. Her heart was up underneath her throat, beating against her collarbone, an old and devastating feeling she'd avoided.

The studio was too warm. Or the name *Luna* in bright letters had caused alarm. Either way, Kate felt light and dizzy, off balance. She sat on a bench at the end of a short hallway and stared at a coastal scene painting. Jack and Mimi Ann's voices were murmured and light, coming down the hallway like music turned low, laughter as punctuation.

Kate pulled out her cell phone, which she'd turned off at dinner the night before. The phone's light flashed back on, and she saw that Rowan had called six times. Lida had called four. Text messages and voice mails had arrived from both of them.

Without checking the voice mails and with a single click, Kate called Rowan back. He answered on the first ring.

"Are you okay?" he answered without preamble.

"I'm totally fine. What's going on?"

"I've been trying to call you since yesterday afternoon. Where the hell have you been? Why aren't you answering?"

"I'm fine. I told you, I'm in Birmingham. I'm about to go by the boutique and then come home. Is something wrong there?"

"Where were you last night? What did you do all day?"

"I drove around. I looked at Birmingham. I ate. I slept."

"Where did you stay?" he asked.

Kate's heartbeat doubled knowing she must again tell an untruth. She had no way to explain the situation in a brief phone conversation, never mind in Jack's studio, which was named after their lost daughter. "The Regency," she said. "I stayed at the Regency."

"I wish you would've called."

"I'm sorry," Kate whispered, sinking into herself. And she was.

Sorry for the lie. Sorry for her inability to explain her story. Sorry that only seconds before she'd wanted to touch Jack Adams.

"It's okay," he said. "I just worry."

"Don't. I promise I'm fine."

"Call me on your way home this afternoon and maybe we can figure out a way to meet for a late dinner."

"I will."

Kate hung up and scrolled through Lida's texts, each one a short question about something that needed to be handled at the boutique. She answered and then looked up to see Jack walking toward her. She stood to face him, embarrassed that she had thought to reach for his hand, or touch his face, anything to have her skin on his.

"You ready to go?" he asked.

She nodded without finding her voice.

Wisteria boutique sat nestled in the middle of Mountain Brook Village. The old English architecture matched stonewalls where ivy crawled in random patterns of its own making. Kate sat on a large white couch in front of an iron-framed mirror large enough to cover the entire wall. The owner, Colleen, sat across from Kate. "So, how did you hear about us?"

"My friend, Susan Neal, was recently here and she told me I must see what you're doing. Susan thinks you have some secret you won't tell anyone."

"Secret? Ha. I wish. Really, if I had a secret I'd duplicate this store all over. But the only secret I have is that I'm in a great location surrounded by great people and we've become a sort of gathering place." She stretched out her hands. "That's why I have the couches and chairs. Sometimes the women come here to hang out, and that's okay, because eventually they buy something."

"And great taste," Kate said. "I mean you carry lines no one else does. And Susan says you're always the first."

"Yes." Colleen nodded. "No one had ever heard of Flaming Torch or Haute Hippie until I brought them here, but I can explain that." Colleen smiled and leaned forward as if she were about to divulge a world secret. "I am obsessive about clothes, new lines, designers, and style. I'm preoccupied by it all, completely to the detriment of my life. And you can't teach obsession." She grinned.

"I get it. I know," Kate said.

As Colleen and Kate talked about their mutual passion, about New York buying trips and fashion designers changing houses, Jack signaled that he was going next door for coffee. The front door shut and Colleen asked. "How do you know Jack Adams?"

Kate stared at Colleen for longer than comfortable as she had no idea how to answer. *Oh, we had a baby together thirteen years ago.* Finally she spoke. "I knew him years ago, and then ran into him yesterday when I came to town."

"Can't believe that man is still a bachelor," Colleen said. "Lucky girl who nabs him."

"Do you mind showing me around and talking a little bit about your layout?"

Together Colleen and Kate wandered the store and back rooms. When they'd finished, Kate looked toward the front door to see that Jack had returned and was leaning against a large table covered with shoes and belts. Kate turned to Colleen, grateful. "Thanks for everything. I'll stay in touch," she said, hugging Colleen good-bye.

Kate reached Jack's side, smiled. "Was that torture?"

He shook his head. "Nope. I loved hearing you talk about your work. Who knew you were so crazy about fashion?"

"I'm *not* going to take that as an insult." Kate opened the door, waving over her shoulder to Colleen.

"Not an insult at all," Jack said, handing her a cup of coffee. "This is a new part of you, that's all."

"Life changes us, doesn't it?" Kate asked, lifting her face to the afternoon sun.

Cherry blossom snow fell around them, and the sidewalk appeared like a forest floor. Tulips burst from the ground in gatherings of bright faces. Dogwood trees bloomed white from green, an umbrella.

"This is the most beautiful time of year here," Jack said, stopping in the middle of the sidewalk, oblivious to the people walking past who halted and walked around him.

"It must be," Kate said.

He stared at her and then touched her cheek with the palm of his hand. She didn't move. She didn't breathe. Then, in the middle of a spring afternoon, outside a boutique in Alabama, Jack leaned forward and kissed her. She tasted coffee and warmth. It was a soft and short kiss, almost as if he merely wanted to brush against her lips, not stay to rest. Kate leaned forward, an instinct of wanting more.

Jack took a step back and Kate looked away, embarrassment and need combining in tender combination. He took her chin to make her look at him. "I've been wanting to do that since I saw you at the concession stand."

"I think I've been wanting you to do that since I decided to drive here," she whispered.

"But it was not a good idea," he said.

"No, it probably was not."

"I'd really like to do it again, but I promise I won't."

She stepped forward and dropped her head onto his shoulder. He placed his hand on the back of her head. "Don't go. Just stay one more night."

"I can't."

"Why not?"

She lifted her head and looked at him. "I told Rowan that I'd leave as soon as I was finished at the boutique. I've already lied to him once." She cringed, squeezing shut her eyes.

"You don't have to lie. Tell him the truth. You ran into an old friend and you want to stay one more night."

"You make it sound so simple," she said.

"There's nothing about this or us that's simple. But hell, I don't know when I'll ever get to see you again, so don't leave."

"Okay," Kate said, nodding. "Okay."

thirteen

· · · · · · · · · · · · ·

BRONXVILLE, NEW YORK

2010

Of course desire grows. That's what desire does. Thirteen-year-old Emily Jackson was finding that out.

"I don't know," Elena said to her daughter. "This might not be a good idea. Not yet anyway."

"Mom, it's just some lady. That's all. Let's see what she looks like."

Elena closed her eyes. She knew this day would come. All adoptive mothers know there is always the chance their child (and this was her child, make no mistake) would ask, "Who is my *real* mother?" As if the word *real* meant that Elena was a fake, a replacement, an imposter.

It had only been that morning that Emily had rifled through her father's office looking for the adoption papers. It was Sailor's fault really, because she kept pushing and asking, and when Emily had finally kissed Chaz during a spin the bottle game at Sailor's birthday party, Sailor had whispered. "Gross, what if he's your brother?"

Elena had found Emily with the adoption papers in hand. They were original documents, and the names and dates could be read through the thin coat of aging whiteout. Maybe the secretary had been too busy to use the second coat of Liquid Paper or maybe she'd been distracted by a phone call or had reached the bottom of the bottle and couldn't be bothered to open another. No matter all the possibilities, when Emily held it up to the light, she could read the name of the birth mother.

"Will you look for her with me?" Emily asked her mom in the quietest whisper.

What is a mother supposed to say then? *No, I'm too scared. Please God, don't let anything ever take you away from me?* Or does she say, as Elena did, "I love you and yes, let's look together."

Elena stood behind Emily, staring at the computer screen where the search bar said KATHRYN VAUGHN. Emily's finger poised over the enter button while Elena stared at the back of her daughter's head, not needing to see her face to know that Emily's green eyes would be carrying her exact expression of need.

So there they were and a cold sweat covered Elena's body, yet she was the one who reached over Emily's shoulder and pushed "enter."

A list of Vaughn women popped onto the screen, but not one Kathryn. With an exhale of relief, Elena squeezed Emily's shoulder. "When you're twenty-one, the records are open for you to find her. We can wait."

"This lady—Tara Vaughn—keeps coming up over and over." Emily clicked on the journalist's name and a Web site popped up: Mothering Heights. From the information they quickly read they discovered that Tara Vaughn was a journalist specializing in parenting magazine pieces: *O, The Oprah Magazine, MORE* magazine, and others like it. Tara looked out of the screen with her wide smile and auburn hair falling over her shoulders. She sat on a chair leaning forward with her glasses in her hand and her elbows on her knees in a casual look that suggested she was in the middle of a conversation.

Emily reached for the screen and touched the smile of the un-known journalist. "I'm related to her," she whispered.

"You don't know that. Let's let this go," Elena said.

Emily then clicked on the small *f*, which designated Tara's Face-book page. The page popped up, and Elena and Emily both took a simultaneous deep breath, a quick intake that would almost prove they were mother and daughter.

Without asking, Emily clicked the friend request button and waited. It was late afternoon and homework waited, but Emily sat in front of the computer with her mother until Tara's approval arrived. *You are now friends with Tara Vaughn,* the message said.

Elena whispered. "What are we doing?"

Emily turned in the swivel chair, her large eyes full of tears. "Will you do it, Mom?"

"Do what, darling?"

"Search her friends? See if there's a Kathryn? I can't do it. I might throw up."

"I got it," Elena said and Emily stood to allow her mother to take her seat.

"Mom. You're my *mom.* Just look."

Elena sat and typed the name KATHRYN into the friend search bar. Nothing.

"Try Kate or Katie or something like that," Emily said. "Or only the last name."

Elena typed "Vaughn" and two women's photos popped up—Kate and Molly.

"It's her," Emily said.

"Yes, honey, I think you're right." Elena clicked on Kate's photo. And then she spoke the truth. "Now you know. You look just like her."

fourteen

. . . .

BIRMINGHAM, ALABAMA

2010

Jack and Kate sat at an outdoor café table, and he ordered wine.

"French café in Birmingham. Weird," Kate said.

"What? You think Alabama is backward?" He smiled at her, warmly.

"No . . ." she laughed. "Well, maybe. And I'm warning you," Kate said. "I know you want to go to the museum, but if I drink this, I might not make it. I could easily fall into some sunshiney afternoon nap."

"Is *sunshiney* a word?" Jack said.

"It is now." Kate pulled her sunglasses from the top of her head to cover her eyes. "You know, that's the word that actually came to mind when I met Mimi Ann. She seems so . . . sunny and all. And very smitten with Jack Adams."

He laughed. "Not true. Now how are things at the store and home?"

"I called Norah and told her I'd have a full report. So, she's happy.

I called Lida and told her that I had some great new ideas for the store. So, she's happy. I called Rowan and told him I'd run into an old friend and I was staying one more night, so he's not happy."

"Sorry about that," he said.

"Be quiet. It's not your fault."

The surprise of their kiss on the sidewalk had faded. Guilt replaced that warm place. Kate resolved, right there at the table, to enjoy Jack without again touching him. That's how all the trouble had begun and that is not how it would end.

A waitress approached with their wineglasses and salads. Jack reached for the saltshaker across the table and bumped the vase, spilling water as a small wildflower fell into Kate's lap. Jack threw napkins over the water as Kate picked up the flower. "This is beautiful." She stared into its center, a place where brilliant yellow mixed in a pattern of intricate lines and swirls. "I wish I knew its name," she said.

"We can look it up," he said. "There's nothing Google can't tell us." He smiled and again those eyes and the green that changed with the light.

"I wish I knew what they'd named *her*," Kate said, wine loosening her thoughts.

Jack tilted his head. "We aren't talking about the flower anymore are we?"

"No, not the flower at all."

"I wish I knew too, but that's not something we can look up on Google."

"No," her voice cracked.

"I wonder if they kept Luna as any part of her name," Jack said, lifting his wine.

"It would be nice if they had. But Luna isn't a usual name, and probably not one a parent is likely to keep." She shrugged. "I bet if we had . . . if we'd kept . . . if we'd been her parents we wouldn't have named her Luna. I did that because of my love for the moon, not because I thought she should be called that name."

Jack reached across the table and took her hand. "I like it. I would've kept it."

"I'm sorry," she said. "I shouldn't have brought her name up. We were having such a nice day. I don't know when to shut up and I don't ever, ever talk about her and . . ."

Jack looked over his shoulder. Sunlight glared into his face like a spotlight so Kate couldn't tell if he was upset or wincing against vivid light. "I like talking about her. It's okay. I like it. I've never been able to."

Kate lifted her wineglass to the sun, changing the subject. "This looks like a red wine that someone watered down."

"It's a rosé."

"Ah," Kate said.

"Reminds me of the time my brother watered down Dad's Talisker, as if he wouldn't notice that." Jack shook his head. "Fool."

"Water in the Talisker? Isn't that like a mortal sin or something?"

Jack stretched back. "Probably. But if it was, my dad beat the devil out of him and saved his soul. So tell me about your family. I wonder about your dad sometimes. I'm sure he's not my biggest fan."

"Oh? You wonder about my family?"

"Yes, I do."

"Dad never blamed you. So stop there. But my parents are great. They live only a few miles away from me."

"So you all ended up right there near each other. Still all wound up together."

"You make that sound like a bad thing," she said.

"No, not at all. It's great. I know how much your family means to you. You've never been one to have a horde of friends, you like your close family and best friends near you."

"Yes," she said, her voice breaking in the middle of the word.

"Did I make you upset?"

"No. It's this thing that Rowan and I sometimes argue about. Not fight really. He can't seem to understand why I don't want to be part of some never-ending party line of dinners and large groups. They unsettle me."

"I know," Jack said. "You feel like you're going to come out of your skin."

"Exactly . . ."

"I know."

I know.

Kate wanted to defend Rowan even as she reached across the table to Jack. "It's not his fault. I mean, he likes to be around a ton of people. It's like crowds feed him, but drain me. It's not a big deal," she said, waving her hand across the air.

Jack nodded, but didn't answer.

"He understands." Kate's words were coming too fast. "Our parents met a couple days ago."

"Nice."

"It was Luna's birthday. Isn't that crazy?"

"Those coincidences happen all the time, don't they."

They sat silent under that warm sun, Luna's memory between them. Kate kept her thoughts locked inside, wanting to tell him that there were some things she'd miss for her entire life. Forever probably. Some people you stop missing. Some things you stop wondering about. But not Luna. Not him. Not this.

Instead she smiled at him. "You're not making me sad."

Lazy light fell over them, silence comfortable until Kate asked. "Do you date?"

"What?"

"Colleen says you are the most sought-after bachelor."

"She's lying."

"You never wrote about girls or dating. Always and only your job, Caleb, and Birmingham. A restaurant opening, a new artist, or whatever, but never a girl." She smiled at him. "Surely you date, Jack."

"Nothing to write about."

"Miss Mimi Ann Davolt?" she asked, smiling.

"Yes. But it's tricky. She runs the studio and I've been alone for a while now with just Caleb."

"You're a dad," she said, a simple statement that carried a million others.

"Yes, I am. Caleb is amazing. He really is."

In the honesty and simplicity of the moment, she spoke the truth. "I'm afraid I wouldn't be able to love another child; I'd close up or something terrible."

"You wouldn't. I don' t know how to explain why. But you'll be able to . . ."

"When the time is right," Kate whispered.

" 'Time does not bring relief.' "

"Huh?"

"That's part of my favorite poem," he said.

"Poem? You've turned into such a Renaissance man."

"Yeah, right, Katie." His laugh was soft.

"Yep," Kate said as it became impossible to make any more words that made any more sense.

The day passed with stories, but no touching. Saturday night turned into Sunday morning. Sunday afternoon turned into Sunday evening and Kate still hadn't left. The day and night passed with hours spent in conversation and quietness.

While Jack cooked dinner, Kate finally brought up the one subject she'd avoided all weekend. "Do you still see Maggie? I mean, how are things between you?"

"I do see her. We have Caleb and we live twenty minutes away from each other, so yes."

"Do you still . . . love her?"

"That's a complicated question,"

"It always was," Kate allowed.

"I don't know what to say. The answer seems tangled."

"Try," she said.

"No, I don't love her like I want her back. I loved her the best I knew, but she was right when she left me—I didn't love her enough or the way she needed. I thought I did. I wasn't trying to be duplicitous or fool her. But in looking back, I see how I married her when everything was unsteady and, as my Brit friend says, mucked up. You were gone and she was here. She loved me. I loved her. Simple, right?"

"Sounds so."

"Until you look back and realize that you loved someone as part of an answer to a question."

"What was the question?"

"What am I going to do without the only person I loved my whole life?" His voice soft.

Kate wanted to stand, stomp her foot, argue that his one decision had ruined all their years. She wanted to unravel the past days, wind them into a tight ball of yarn and start again. Begin again. "So you married her because I was gone?"

"I didn't marry her *only* because you were gone, but it was part of it."

The silence lengthened to the inevitable conclusion: Kate needed to go home. "I really do have to go," she said. "I've said that at least five times." She laughed and shook her head. "But this time, I'm leaving. I've got to go."

"I know, and Caleb will be home in about an hour." Jack stood from the table and carried their dishes to the sink.

"I'll be gone by then," she said, feeling the weekend's end seep into her with sadness. "I should have been gone a long time ago." She stood. "I'm going to get my stuff together real quick." She walked away, her heart directly behind her feet.

The doorbell rang, and Kate startled as she zipped her suitcase. She heard voices: deep and familiar. She walked out of the bedroom to the front hallway to find Rowan Irving, in his khakis and white button-down, standing in the doorway, talking to Jack Adams.

This fact was so impossible that Kate could only stare. Rowan walked to her and put his hands on her shoulders. "Kate."

"Rowan," she said, her arms loose and seeming unattached. Tingling formed at the back of her brain and moved forward.

Rowan stepped back and looked first at Jack and then at Kate. "Does anyone want to explain this?"

"What are you doing here?" Kate asked.

"I was worried as hell. You said you were coming home last night and you didn't. You won't answer the phone. You won't call back. You had this crazy explanation about an old friend and how you'd explain all of it to me when you got home. Is this your friend?" He pointed to Jack.

"Yes, this is Jack Adams." Kate didn't look at Jack, not even a glance or she would've been unable to speak.

"And Jack is an old friend? Or is this the old boyfriend?"

"Seriously. How did you get here? I am so confused," Kate said.

"You're confused? I thought you were here to look at a boutique and then coming home. And now you're here snuggled up with an old boyfriend? Coming out of a bedroom? What the hell is going on?"

"I promised I'd explain everything when I got home. How did you find me?"

"Lida."

"What?"

"I asked her if you were visiting anyone here."

Lida was one of the very few who knew where Kate was. But why would she tell Rowan? "I don't get it."

"Does that part even matter right now?"

"Yes, yes it does," Kate said.

Jack stepped toward them now. "Would you all like to come out of the hallway? Inside?" His voice was a broken robotic sound, uneven.

"No," Rowan said. "We'd like to leave, but before we do, would you two like to tell me anything?" He waved his hand between them. "Is there anything I need to know?"

"There's lots you need to know," Kate said. "And if you'd waited for me to get home, I would've been able to tell you."

"Are you two . . . ." Rowan's face crumbled with his next words. "Together?"

"No." Kate stepped forward and took Rowan's hand. "Nothing like that is going on here. We went through something together a long time ago and haven't seen each other for a very, very long time. Please believe me. I came here to close a chapter, not start a new one. I wanted to begin my life with you and I had to see Jack to do that."

Kate then looked at Jack and his face was blank, cold.

"I flew here," Rowan said. "And I'm going to drive you home. Let's go."

In movements as slow as walking through water, Kate went to the back guest bedroom and grabbed her suitcase. Her toothbrush was still on the sink's edge as if waiting for her to spend one more night. Just one more night.

Jack and Kate said good-bye without a touch. Kate climbed into the passenger seat of her own car, and the words tumbled out in a mangled mess of explanation.

"Rowan, you've got to listen."

"Go for it. Explain."

"This is hard for me."

"Hard for you?"

Kate took in the longest breath and turned toward Rowan. His face was hard and sad, a combination she'd never seen on him before. Compassion rose. "Jack and I dated all through high school and college."

"I know that part, Kate. It seems I've missed out on the part after that . . ."

The story of Luna took an hour to tell, and there remained five hours to argue and understand.

The word *pregnant* dropped into the car and into their life.

He pressed his body hard into the back seat; his fists clenched the steering wheel, turning his knuckles a grim bluish white. "Oh, dear God. You have a daughter."

"Yes," she answered.

"Why didn't you ever tell me? You have a child living out there in the world somewhere and you never, ever told me? Who else knows? Why did you keep this a secret? Who is she?"

The questions pelted her. She focused, trying to answer each one truthfully. "I never told you because I was happy with our life and I didn't want to remember the pain. I didn't want that darkness to enter our lives. I've meant to tell you, but . . . when I want to forget something, I don't talk about it. And I wanted to forget."

"Did you forget? Obviously not."

"No, of course I didn't. No. She's this part of me that's not with me."

"Stop. I get it." He stared through the windshield, his voice a metronome, measured and slow. "Who knows about her?"

"My parents, my sisters, Lida, Norah, and Jack. That's all. That's it. I've never told anyone else."

"What is this some vast conspiracy to make sure I'm not part of the family or close friends?"

"No," she cried out the word. "My family wanted me to tell you.

Especially Tara—she can't stand that you don't know. They begged me, but I was scared."

"Why did you have to come see him?"

"I haven't seen him in over thirteen years. I haven't seen him since the day I told him I was pregnant. There are things Jack and I never talked about, and I felt like there was this unfinished conversation or something. I wanted to put 'The End' on the story. I don't know, Rowan. I'm confused."

"Confused," he said. "Yeah, I bet. Now I know why you acted so weird when that guy Hayes brought up Jack's name at the party."

"Stop." Kate closed her eyes. "Tell me how you got Lida to tell you where I was. I don't understand."

"I told her you were sick and that I couldn't get a hold of you and you had told me the name, but I couldn't hear you and—"

"You lied," Kate said, opening her eyes and looking at Rowan's clenched profile.

"And you didn't?"

"You're making it into something it's not."

"I'm afraid the only reason you're telling me now is because I found you at his house. You're not telling me because you trust me or love me or want me to be part of your secret life, but because I found you and there's really no other choice."

"Please don't be so mad. I've wanted to tell you so many times, but maybe I was waiting for the right time."

"What right time, Kate?"

"I'm embarrassed, Rowan. Can't you even see that a little bit? How was I supposed to explain it all? There I was, this girl with everything in the world and still I felt like I couldn't be a mom?" She paused, feeling the unraveling begin again, shame undoing the resolute decisions. "Mom. It's the name that haunts me everywhere I go. Even my sister writes about it, the most sacred of all jobs in the world, right? And I gave it up? I didn't want you to think less of me."

"Less of you?"

She was crying and she didn't try to stop. What was there left to hide? "I wanted to do the right thing. And I believe I did. He was married, Rowan. When I found out I was pregnant, he was married. It was a mess. I did the best I knew to do. I still wonder if it was the best thing. I didn't want you to think badly of me. I was wrong to hide it. I did everything wrong with you. I'm so sorry."

"Did you ever, even once, think that maybe the girl I love is all the parts of you and not only the parts that you've decided to tell and show me?"

Kate's only response was a sharp intake of breath.

"Kate?" Rowan prodded.

"I don't deserve . . . to be loved like that," she said.

"You could have told me and it wouldn't have changed how I feel about you at all."

"I don't think that's possible," she said.

"It is. So, tell me. Where is she? How old is she?" he asked.

"She's thirteen, and I have no idea where she is at all or with who. I chose the family from an adoption agency. I spent months going through family profiles . . . and I chose. But no names. She could be anywhere at all."

"That must be so hard."

"Yes, it is."

"I'm sorry for all of this. I am. But you need to know that this kills me, it destroys me to think that you would keep something so important from me."

"I told you." Kate's heart skipped over her words, tripping, falling and then righting. "Yes, I told you everything. It's all awful and wonderful because I believe somewhere she has a good life that I could've never given her."

He reached for her and then pulled her close as he drove with his left hand. "Well, can we let it go now?"

"I hope so. I really hope so." Kate moved closer to Rowan's body, wanting to feel the solid warmth and sweetness. She closed her eyes and pretended to sleep as Rowan hummed to the country music. She'd never told him that she'd seen the engagement ring, and she wondered what he'd done with it, if it still sat alone in the drawer. A silent hour passed as Kate realized that if Jack and she kept up their regular letter-writing routine, it would be a full year before she heard from him again.

She remembered once when she and Tara as children had been on the beach (this was before Molly arrived to rock their world with laughter). They'd spent an entire afternoon building a sand castle with towers and moats, with white coral windows and seashell-covered walkways.

The Cooper Clan was the royal family. There was a princess named Tiffany who slept in a pink room at the top of the castle with her white cat named Fluffy. All day, Tara and Katie built a world until dusk arrived, and their parents told them it was time to leave and get cleaned up for dinner. The sand glowed with otherworldly pink twilight. Katie and Tara stared at the castle with deep respect for the world they had created. That night, lying in bed, they'd whispered about how they would add to the castle, and to the family.

But the next morning, the hard lesson arrived: Nothing lasts. Nothing. Especially when built on sand below the incoming tide line.

March 20, 2005

Dear Katie,
 Happy Birthday to Luna.
 I hope you're doing great. All is well here. Caleb is now three years old and I'm watching him grow right before my eyes.

Before I tell you about work and such, I want to tell you a story.

I was on a plane to Philadelphia last month when I swore I saw Luna. I know it sounds impossible, too coincidental like I made it up, but I think I did. There was this little girl about seven years old, begging her mom for candy at the newsstand. She had your color hair that curled under her chin and on her forehead above her green eyes. She stood there with her hands on her hips (like you did that day you stood up to Principal Proctor), and demanded the Sour Patch Kids she held in her little fist. The mother was blond, pretty, and had two little boys in a double stroller. She leaned over and said. "Emily, you may not have any more candy today. You will throw up."

I wanted to grab that lady and ask questions, take a picture—anything, but instead I just stood there like the damn Vulcan statue made of iron. I couldn't move at all. This Emily pursed out her lips and blew air up into her bangs—just like you do when you're thinking—and put the Sour Patch package back on the shelf and stalked off with her hands never leaving her hips.

The weird thing is that I bought that bag of candy.

Now I know it probably wasn't our Luna. That would be too perfect. I get it. But in case it was, I bought that stupid bag and have it hidden in my desk drawer.

Have you ever thought you saw her? You know—in a crowd or anywhere at all?

fifteen

· · · · · · · · · · · · · ·

BRONXVILLE, NEW YORK

2010

"You have to tell him," Sailor whispered, using her elbow to nudge Emily into Chaz. Emily tripped sideways, her left foot catching on the boardwalk. Chaz grabbed her arm to steady her. She might be mad at Sailor for tripping her, but it was worth it to have Chaz touch her arm.

"What'd you say?" He turned around to walk backward and face Sailor. "Tell me what?"

"Nothing." Sailor gave him a little push, but he skipped and kept pace with them.

"Liar," he said, stopping so that Emily and Sailor had to walk around him or stop also.

The beach boardwalk was overcrowded, full of teenagers on the first warm weekend. The air had the taste of summer at its edges. Watermelon. Ice cream. Sand in her lemonade. School wouldn't be out for another month, but Emily was already inside the laziness of it all. Then Sailor had to go and ruin it all by bringing up the "mom" thing again.

Sometimes, no, a lot of times, it seemed like Sailor was more obsessed than Emily with finding the birth mom. Emily held up her hand. "It's nothing. I want to stop and get cotton candy."

Chaz ran his left hand through his wind-snarled hair, caught it and then let go. "Really? Like that's some big thing to tell me?"

Sailor made a noise that was halfway between a huff and a laugh, her way of telling Chaz that Emily was bluffing. Emily walked around Chaz and shot her best friend a look that she hoped said "shut up."

They reached the steps to the beach. To Emily, the haze of sunshine made the towels and blankets that were spread across the sand look like jellybeans. "Let's go," she said. "You two are being annoying."

"Annoying?" Chaz asked, laughing. He jumped off the boardwalk, over the steps and into the sand, his weight denting the surface. He pulled off his T-shirt and held it in his hand. "Me, annoying?"

"Absolutely," Sailor said. She stepped carefully onto the sand, crouching down so she wouldn't slip from wood to beach.

Emily looked down at both of them, only a step below her. "You're not annoying," she said, a quietness winding into her voice.

Sailor threw her arms in the air. "First one in the water wins," she hollered.

"Wins what?" Emily asked. She jumped to join them, and the beach bag bounced off her hip.

"Doesn't win anything. Just wins," Sailor said.

"You can win then. The water is freezing. No way I'm going in," Emily said.

Someone, a girl from the left, called Chaz's name and he answered, walking away. The voice belonged to Sissy, who was wearing her too-small yellow bikini. Sailor shrugged as if to say, well, there he goes.

Emily shook her head. "Sissy wins and she didn't even have to jump in the water," Emily said, smiling.

Sailor's laughter seemed to be part of the surf sounds beating against the shoreline, and then Emily and Sailor ran toward the water. They set their towels next to each other and then began the process of lathering sunblock on their winter-white skin.

"You should tell him, you know." Sailor handed Emily the lotion.

"Why? It really doesn't matter."

"Have you heard back yet?"

Emily shook her head. The hope-thing inside her sank again, a quick drop inside her chest. "I guess I shouldn't have even friended her. I mean, she gave me away so why would she want to hear from me? It was stupid. I shouldn't have done it." Emily sat on the towel and stared out to that place where water and sky met and turned into one shadowy blue line. "If I got rid of something I didn't want, I wouldn't want that something to show up again."

"You're not a something, Emily." Sailor's voice was kinder than usual. The mystery-solving voice turning soft. "You're a some-body."

"Yeah, but maybe to her I was a something." Emily shrugged. "I just wanted to see what she looked like. And now I know."

"She's pretty," Sailor said, sitting down and facing Emily. "But of course she is because you are."

"Now you're only trying to be nice because you feel sorry for me," Emily said, but smiled.

Sailor shook her head, her brown curls moving like smoke around her face. "I don't feel sorry for you. I know I'm annoying about it. I'll stop. I wish I had other parents. . . ."

Emily wanted to have something smart to say, something that would make Sailor feel better, but she couldn't. If she had Sailor's parents, she'd be looking for new ones too. But Emily loved her parents; she didn't want new ones.

So then why did she feel so terrible and empty just because the Kate woman hadn't answered her friend request?

Kate's sister, Tara, had accepted her friendship. Did she know? Did the sister know who Emily was? Emily imagined them talking about her, wondering why she was bugging them. Sailor and Emily had spent an entire Sunday afternoon going through Tara's page, looking at photos and identifying people. Cousins. Uncle. Grandparents. But really none more important than the only one they wanted to identify: birth mom.

They'd zoomed in on Kate's hair, curly and copper like Emily's. They commented on Kate's great clothes, and how Emily must have her birth dad's chin because Kate didn't have a cleft. Sailor said that Emily's smile was an exact copy of Kate's, like the kind from the dentist when you got your retainer.

But as much as the friends talked—and talked and talked and talked—Emily kept a great many thoughts to herself. She wondered, as she had always wondered, where she came from and why? Why did her stomach flip upside down when she was sad? Why did pollen make her sneeze? Why did her nose turn up on the very end?

And the biggest wonder, a wonder so big that it was a universe: Why did her birth mother give her away?

Emily sat forward, curling her arms around her bent legs. She rested her head on her knees and turned to look at Sailor. "Let's not talk about it anymore. Okay?"

Sailor nodded. "Okay, if that's what you want."

"That's what I want," Emily said.

sixteen

· · · · · · · · · · · · · ·

BLUFFTON, SOUTH CAROLINA

2010

Kate dropped onto the slipcovered couch at Mimsy, groaning. "That's enough for today," she said.

Lida laughed. "No way. Let's set the boots up on the front table before we open tomorrow."

On an April evening Norah, Lida, and Kate moved furniture and display shelves as they remodeled Mimsy, emulating Wisteria in Birmingham. The couches had been re-covered in white sailcloth, and they were placed in the middle of the room facing a long mirror. Lida sat next to Kate. "Is everything okay with you and Rowan now?"

Kate smiled. "Yes, of course."

"I'm so sorry. Again, I'm sorry if I got you in trouble."

"Stop it, Lida. There's nothing to be sorry about. I made my own mess and you got caught up in it."

Lida leaned forward and shifted the handbags on the coffee table into an organized pattern. "It's crazy with a capital *F*."

"You are so bad." Kate gently swatted Lida's leg.

"I want you to be happy, Kate. It's like you run into it and then away from it as fast as you can."

"Well, it's all good now. I don't know why I waited so long to tell him."

Norah called from the other side of the boutique. "Kate, Lida, how does this look?" They stood and walked to the scarf display.

"Perfect," Kate said. "I think that we've set up a more social scene now, one that'll make women want to stay and not only shop, but talk and hang out."

Her phone buzzed in her jeans and she lifted it out, glancing at the screen. And there, in the middle of finally *not-thinking* about Jack, he called.

The preacher who had once told Kate that she had free will didn't understand love at all, or at least the thought-life of love. It had been a full month since she'd left Alabama, a full month in which Jack entered her thoughts—unbidden and unwelcome—again and again. Jack preoccupied her in ways that made her miss meetings, run red lights, and wake at three AM with no hope of returning to sleep.

Kate looked down at her cell phone and smiled. "I'll be right back," she said, walking to the rear room where boxes cluttered the space.

"Hey, you," she answered.

"Hi, you. I'm sorry it took me so long to call you back."

Kate had called Jack several times. She couldn't bear to leave their last words as *the* last words.

She took in a deep breath. "You're mad at me."

"I'm not mad," he said, quietly.

"I called you because I really want to talk. I didn't want to leave things like I did—running off. I'm sorry Rowan busted in like that. It's not his usual way. He was worried."

"I understand. And you were right—we have to finish some things before we start new things. I understand now, that's what you were doing."

"I don't think that's all I was doing."

"Listen, let's let this go. Isn't that why you were here? To let it all go? Begin again?"

"It's all mixed up now."

"Kate, there's not much more to talk about."

"Then why do I feel like there's so much left to talk about?"

"Probably because you need to talk about them with Rowan. Not me."

"Oh." Kate closed her eyes and dropped her forehead onto the doorframe of the storage room. "Okay."

"Take care of yourself, Katie."

Then he was gone.

Lida ambled into the storage room, dodging packages of folded clothes and boxes of hangers. "You okay?" she asked.

Kate looked up. "I don't know."

"Who was that?"

"Jack."

"And?"

"He was cold and short."

"What else do you want him to be?"

"Mine," Kate said as she sat in an office chair shoved in the corner. "I want him to be mine."

"What?"

"It's insane, but so true. And sad. And terrible. And impossible."

"Damn," Lida said, leaning against the wall. "What are you going to do?"

"I have absolutely no idea." Kate glanced at her cell phone as if it held answers. " 'Patience is wider than one once imagined . . .' "

"Huh?"

"A poem . . . never mind." Kate stood. "Right now let's get this store just right. Let's finish."

"You're a mess," Lida said, and hugged Kate before they walked out into the boutique.

They emerged, and Kate's mom stood in the middle of the store talking to Norah. "Mom," Kate said. "What a nice surprise."

"Oh, the store looks so great. I was talking to Norah about having a cocktail party here with some of my friend, maybe a fundraiser for my friend, the mayor, Lisa Sulka."

"You love saying, my friend, the mayor, don't you?" Kate teased her mom.

"Shush. But don't you think that's a good idea? I mean, if you're trying to make it more social, why not have events?"

Together, the four women talked about parties and displays, about clothing lines and artwork, until Norah yawned and ended the evening.

Left alone with her mom, Kate asked. "Okay, Mom, really why did you stop by?"

"To see you."

Kate smiled and placed her hands under her chin as if framing her face. "Here I am."

Her mom sat on the couch and motioned for Kate to do the same. "Darling, I really want to hear about how it went when you saw Jack. You won't talk about it and you know how Dad and I care about all of it. We do."

"I know you care. Jack is doing well. And I'm glad I finally told Rowan. But that's all over now. Really, there's nothing to talk about."

"He hasn't heard anything from Luna, has he?"

Kate exhaled through her mouth, blowing her hair off her forehead. "Don't you think that's something I would have told you?"

Her mom nodded. "Yes, I guess it is. I just . . ."

"I want to know about her also, Mom. But guess what? I can't. And neither can you. So, let's get on with our lives until we can, okay?"

"Okay, I get it."

"I'm glad you do," Kate said and smiled. "Because I sure don't."

Mom and daughter sat in silence, quiet and sure of their place in each other's world. The sad knowing that her own daughter was out there in the world settled right next to Kate's need for Jack, knotted and aching.

seventeen

. . . .

BLUFFTON, SOUTH CAROLINA

2010

That last day in April started as ordinary. It was five A.M. and Kate once again stared at the ceiling as dawn unfolded through the cracks of her curtains. Ever since Alabama, sleep had been slippery and stubborn, never arriving when she needed it most. She rose in frustration, read e-mails, browsed through Tara's blog, Mothering Heights, and checked on the dark and quiet boutique. On the storeroom's computer, Kate decided to check her Facebook. It had been over a month since she'd browsed the site. She wasn't anything like a Facebook regular. She was bored reading about what her "friends" cooked for dinner that night, or seeing photos of yet another party she'd declined to attend.

The Facebook page opened slowly. Kate imagined the Internet signal trying to find its way through the oak branches crowded around the building. On the top left corner of the page, there was a single notice: *Emily Jackson wants to be friends.*

Kate clicked on the friend request. Emily Jackson's photo was not of her face, but a kitten curled in a lap. Kate couldn't get to any of the young girl's information as it was blocked with the words *You aren't friends with Emily Jackson.* Emily and Kate had only one friend in common: *Tara.*

Mothering Heights had a following on Facebook and often those "friends" would see that Kate was Tara's sister and assume it was okay to friend her. But Kate was more protective of her site: only friends and family. Not cyber friends.

With a quick e-mail to Tara—*Who is Emily Jackson?*—Kate turned on the coffee pot. The rest of the morning was the definition of typical, a regular world spinning on its usual axis of work. An entire shipment of clothes to be unpacked, steamed, tagged, and hung. A briefing with Lida. Phone calls to be returned. *Women's Wear Daily* to go through, not to mention her favorite fashion blogs. Were her clients ready for the bright orange that was dominating the runway?

By the time Kate looked at her cell phone, she saw that Tara had called five times.

"Hey, Tara," Kate returned her sister's call, pouring more coffee into a mug.

"Kate, I can't believe this." Tara's words were garbled. She was drowning in tears. Kate felt the panic rise to the surface. Tara rarely cried, and if she was sobbing like this then something was terribly wrong.

"Oh, God, what is it?" Kate set her mug on the counter, readying herself for the worst news. Their parents. One of Tara's children.

"She found us," Tara said slowly, pronouncing each word as if English were her fourth language, as if she'd never spoken those three words in a row.

"Who?"

"Luna. She found us."

"What?" Kate's soul unmoored, rising with hope. Dare she believe? She closed her eyes and waited because only one thing was worse than not hoping and that was believing and then allowing despair to wash inland.

For all these years, Katie had been telling herself, *Maybe one day. Not today, but maybe one day in the future.*

Was it too much to hope that today was *that* day?

"The girl, Emily Jackson. The one you e-mailed me about this morning. I went to her Facebook page. It's her. Same birthday. If you get to her information page, her full name is Emily Luna Jackson." Tara waited while her breath caught up with her words. "Kate, she looks like you!"

Relief began to tear open the closed and scarred places inside Kate. "Are you sure? I mean that's impossible, right?"

"Go look. Now."

"Oh, if this is true . . . the poor girl friended me over a month ago and I just hadn't checked my Facebook."

"Go," Tara again demanded.

"I'll call you back," Kate said.

There hadn't been a day in thirteen years when Katie had read or heard the word "Luna" and hope hadn't leapt toward her daughter. And this time was no different, although she knew, as she did every other time, that it was nearly impossible that Luna was *her* Luna. No, totally impossible.

This wasn't how the lost became found—in an early morning e-mail on a typical day. Kate took the back staircase to her loft. Tara's tears, which Kate had thought meant the most terrible news, were sobs of joy, a preamble to the only news Kate had prayed for every single day for the last thirteen years. Every day. *Please let her be okay.*

"She found me," Kate said out loud in her kitchen as her soul fell to its knees.

The extraordinary happens in the exact middle of ordinary, she thought clearly and permanently.

No trumpet blast to announce the moment, no parting of clouds or Hallelujah chorus. Just the simple miracle (as if any miracle is simple) between an in-breath and an out-breath, the wide-open space where the unknown was known, the lost found, and the unseen seen.

Moving as if in slow motion, she opened her Facebook screen and clicked "accept" on Emily Jackson's request. In incremental understanding, she flipped through this girl's photos, saying her name out loud.

"Emily. Her name is Emily."

Kate's chest expanded with the beautiful and overwhelming knowledge that she was staring at her daughter's photos. To maintain her breath and her sanity, Kate read Emily's profile out loud.

The facts became surreal, blurred, and too coincidental, as if someone were playing a prank on her, as if someone were taking all the ways to connect Kate and Emily and drawing lines between those dots as an example of universal synchronicity.

Her last name is almost Jack's first name.
She is the oldest of three siblings.
She looks like Tara's middle school photo.

Kate finished looking at the photos for the fifth time and then paced the kitchen. The phone hadn't stopped ringing, but she'd ignored it, needing only the silence and these photos. Her cell phone screen flashed six missed calls combining only two names: Tara and Molly.

Yes, Tara would've called Molly by now.

The news would soon explode, changing the world. Kate wanted to be alone with the knowledge that Luna had found her. She wanted to taste the truth, to bask in the in-between of what was and what would be. Before the world knew, before her family descended with vigor and tears and gratitude, she wanted to hold Luna to herself.

Her daughter.

An hour later Tara called again, and Kate answered without greeting, but with a question. "Now what?"

"Send her a message. I mean, for God's sake, Kate. If she had enough nerve to 'friend' you, answer her." Her words were skipping and rough like an old record with scratches.

"Did you tell Molly?" Kate asked.

"I did. She is freaking out. Freaking. This is a miracle."

"Isn't there a word that is past a miracle?"

Tara laughed. "What do you mean?"

"You're the writer. You're the girl with words. What is better and bigger than a miracle?" Kate asked.

"I have no idea, but whatever it is, this is it. Now e-mail her."

"What do I say? Tell me what to say."

"Exactly what you feel."

Dear Emily, for thirteen years I have loved you and been waiting to see your beautiful face.

Of course there was so much more to say, but who could prepare for that moment?

What next?

Kate picked up the phone and dialed Jack's number. His heart, of all the hearts involved in these tangled lives, would be the most relieved. Kate didn't think he'd answer after their phone conversation the night before, but he did. He had barely finished the word "hello" before she spoke.

"She found us," Kate said.

"What?"

"Luna. She found us."

"Luna . . ."

"Yes." Kate wanted to see Jack's face, to see his green eyes fill with knowing.

"Oh, God. Tell me. Where?"

Even in the retelling of this conversation a hundred times, Kate wouldn't be able to remember the order or way in which she told Jack that their daughter had found them. The truth tumbled out like champagne poured, bubbly and unruly.

"Tell me what you know," he said.

Kate laughed. "I don't think she meant to talk to me, or even anyone at all. I think she was messing around on her Facebook. She hasn't even answered me yet. I feel terrible, because she's been waiting a month. God, I hope she doesn't wait a month. She's only thirteen. I'm sure her mother has some say in this."

"And you're positive it's her? Absolutely positive."

"Yes."

"Send me her photo. Right now."

Jack rattled off his e-mail and Kate sat down at the computer, dragging Emily's photo onto her desktop and e-mailing it to Jack as they talked on the phone. She rattled off facts. "She lives in Bronxville, New York. From the photos, I think she's always lived there."

There were, she imagined, a million rooms in every woman's heart. Oh, how many doors had she shut when she handed her child to the social worker, when she closed her eyes as her daughter left the room? Those doors were now flung open, light pouring in.

"Call me as soon as she writes back to you. Promise?" Jack asked. "I don't have a Facebook account."

"Of course."

The hours were eternal and timeless as Kate, Tara, and Molly waited for a response from Emily Luna Jackson, daughter of Kate and Jack, yet daughter of another family. Hours passed and phone calls were made and the world stood still and spun out of control. The sisters agreed—Kate would tell their parents in person. But not until they had heard back from Emily.

Later, when the day was relived as all miraculous days are, the sisters would talk about what each one did during the delay.

Tara wrote to Emily, "We have loved you since the day you were born." She paced the house, cleaning her children's rooms as if acknowledging their existence and being grateful even in their mess.

Molly searched the Internet for information and cut and pasted photos, forming a scrapbook of pictures. She made a list of Emily's facts, one after the other, as if they could add up to someone she knew.

Kate browsed through every single photo on Emily's page, looking for signs of Jack, for symbols with as much import as a feather or snake in the wilderness.

Deductions and assumptions were made. Emily had two younger brothers (But Kate had thought the mother couldn't get pregnant? Had they adopted more kids?). They lived in Bronxville, New York. She had strawberry blond hair. Her parents were married still.

During the chaos, Kate's Facebook message in-box finally glowed with a *1*. Kate held her breath, and clicked to read the note.

Hi, I'm happy that I found you. I have always wondered what you look like and where you were. You have a beautiful family and your sisters already wrote to me. Love, Emily Luna Jackson. P.S. This is really weird and wonderful and I'm a little bit nervous, but my mom said I could write back.

Kate read the e-mail over and over, trying to find a hidden code, a Fibonacci sequence of words. What did Emily really mean? Was she okay? Did she want to meet her birth mother or was she merely curious? The questions rattled loose and dangling like wind chimes in a storm, dissonant and unnerving.

Fingers poised over the keyboard, Kate finally found the sentences she needed.

Most Beautiful Emily, I would love to meet you and your precious family, but I will leave this up to you and your family. Love, Kate Vaughn.

Notes and messages flew between South Carolina and New York. Emotions were tangled inside words read over the hours, every syllable analyzed. Phone calls crisscrossed between the Vaughn sisters. And inside this disorder, a new order slowly unfolded.

eighteen

. . . .

BRONXVILLE, NEW YORK

2010

Voices echoed from the playroom down the hall as Emily's brothers played Xbox and screamed at the screen as if it were a living thing. Emily and her parents—Elena and Larry—sat on the couch ready to talk.

"Mom, I didn't want to make you upset. I just wanted to see what she looked like. That's all. I've always wondered."

"I wanted to love you enough that you never wondered."

Elena's legs were curled up underneath her bottom. A tissue crumpled and wet in her hand was the only sign of her tears. Emily scooted across the couch and hugged her mom, throwing one leg over Elena's lap as if she were a toddler. "You love me more than anything. For sure this has everything to do with me and wondering where I got my looks from and stupid stuff like that. I mean, really, Mom, wouldn't you be curious?"

Elena nodded. "Maybe so, yes. But now she knows you. She knows where you live and who you are. Her sisters know too."

"So?"

"They'll want to meet you. Who wouldn't want to meet you? I hate Facebook." Elena dropped her head into her hands. "I told you Facebook was nothing but trouble."

Larry hugged his wife and laughed. "Nothing but trouble."

Fighting over a remote control, Emily's brothers tumbled into the room to find their mom, dad, and sister huddled together on the couch as if a tornado had rattled the home. "What did Emily do now?" Steve, her littlest brother, asked.

Emily looked up at her brother while reaching for a magazine off the coffee table, which she promptly and accurately threw at his head. Steve ducked and the papers crashed into the wall, knocking a botanical sketch crooked.

"I didn't do anything. We were just talking," Emily said.

"You made Mom cry."

Elena stood and faced her sons with a smile. "No, she didn't. Come here, I want to tell you something."

The boys glanced at each other finally forgetting who really "owned" the remote. "What?" They asked in unison.

Elena glanced at Emily and then to the boys. "Emily found some photos of her birth mother and we were talking about that."

"And her sisters and family," Emily said, glancing over the back of the couch to make faces at her brothers behind her mother's back.

Ethan, the older brother pointed at Emily. "Does she look like Emily? Does she look like a mushroom?"

Emily jumped off the couch and ran toward Ethan, who knew that if he didn't escape, an Indian burn would appear on his arm.

"You're dead," she hollered after him.

"I love you, Sissy," his voice echoed from the back hallway.

Emily shook her head. "See, Mom. We're real family. Nothing can change that."

Elena looked up to the ceiling with a smile on her face. "Oh, Dear Lord, where oh where did I go wrong?"

Laughter filled the room and Elena walked to the kitchen to begin preparations for dinner. Emily plopped next to her dad. "What do you think? Should I meet her?"

"I think you and your mom should discuss this."

"Cop-out." Emily smiled at her dad and poked his arm.

He leaned forward and placed his hand on Emily's knee. "Baby, you know we're your parents. You know how much we love you. If you want to meet the woman who gave birth to you, then you should. I trust you. This is hard on your mom because deep down she's always been worried about losing you and this brings up all those fears."

"Lose me? That's crazy."

"Not to your mother." He winked. "And I suggest that you don't even think about using that word with her."

"I won't." Emily leaned back on the couch cushions. "It would be interesting, I think, to meet her. Just see what she's like. It's not like I want to hang out with her and be best friends."

"Like a country you heard about, but never visited."

"Exactly." Emily said, taking her dad's hand. "Exactly. I don't want to live there. I just want to see what it looks like."

He nodded. "Then you should."

Emily settled into her dad's shoulder for a hug. How could they ever believe that they could lose her?

nineteen

. . . .

BLUFFTON, SOUTH CAROLINA

2010

The pier was empty that next evening as Rowan and Kate walked to its edge. Rowan carried a shrimp net and a bucket as twilight flirted with the river. Kate was nervous. After telling her parents and watching them weep with their own relief, it was time to tell Rowan.

They sat on a bench as Rowan untied the net. "Hell, I don't understand how this damn thing gets knotted when all I do is put it in the bucket. It's like someone comes in and tangles it up when I'm not looking."

"Necklaces do that in a drawer too," Kate said and took his hand.

He stopped his movements and looked at her. "Is something wrong?"

"I have to tell you something."

"Why do I feel like this something is a thing I don't want to hear?"

Kate tried to smile. "Oh, it's good."

"Okay, what is it?"

"Yesterday Luna found me. On Facebook. A month ago, she'd sent a friend request, but you know I never check."

Rowan dropped the net and took both Kate's hands in his. "This must be a relief for you."

"It is," she said. "But, it's so much more than a relief. I want to scream it from the mountains. I want to fly to New York right now. I want to kiss her face. She's beautiful." Kate took in a deep breath and exhaled everything she knew about her daughter: her name and age, where she lived, and how many siblings.

Rowan was quiet during this word-torrent, untangling his net while still keeping his eyes focused on her. "Wow," he said quietly.

"Isn't that crazy? I mean; you can't make up stuff like that. There are all these weird coincidences. Her last name is Jackson."

Rowan looked away. "Her last name is Jackson." He shook his head. "And you aren't making that up?"

"No."

"Sounds like this was all very meant to be."

"Oh, I hope so. I mean, since the awful day I said good-bye to her, I've survived knowing that I did the right thing. And all the littlest things—like her name—are little God-hints that I did the right thing, that all is well even when it doesn't feel well."

"Have you told Jack?"

"Yes, of course."

"So, you told him before you told me?"

"He's . . . the dad."

"I know that part."

"I'm so sorry this hurts you. Right here is the reason I waited so long to tell you. I didn't want this thing between us."

"What thing between us?" he asked.

"The sad thing I see all over your face."

"I want you to have *our* child in our lives. I'm not mad. But yes, it's a little sad for me."

Kate placed her arms around his neck and held him close, wanting to want him, needing to need him. Her feelings twisted and pulled. She was unsure of anything but the need to see her daughter.

"I know this is awful and hard for you," she said.

"This means you'll be seeing Jack again."

"Probably at some point, but that's okay, right?"

"I hope. I sure damn hope so."

"It's not about him. This is about Luna."

"No, it's also and most definitely about him." Rowan looked directly at her. "I love you, Kate Vaughn, but this *is* about Jack Adams." Rowan stood and shook the net. "It really is amazing how one thing can change everything." He walked to the edge of the pier. "One damn thing."

"I'm sorry," Kate said.

"What are you sorry for?"

"Everything."

He glanced over his shoulder as he gathered the net into his hands, readying it to toss. "Go find your way in this, Kate. I'll be here for you, but this is yours and Jack's. I hate it, but it's true."

"I'm sorry."

"Yes, you've already said that." He turned his back to her and tossed the net in a pearl-tinted circle that hovered in the air before splashing. "Go on, Kate. Do what you need to do, we'll talk later."

She kissed his cheek, but by the time Rowan had pulled the weight of his net out of the water and dumped the shrimp into a bucket, Kate was halfway down the pier with her back to the water, to Rowan.

Kate bent over the Mimsy computer in the back storage room and clicked on the refresh button of her in-box. Nothing.

Lida came from behind, laughing. "You gonna check that every five minutes?"

"Probably." Kate stood and smiled. "Yep, probably. Maybe every two minutes."

Lida smiled. "I would, too." Then she held up a gray silk shirt. "Mrs. Plinson brought this back. She said it itched in the back." Lida rolled her eyes. "Whatever. She probably wore it to a party and didn't get enough compliments." Lida held up a sleeve. "This right here." She pointed to a small spot that looked wet. "That's where she tried to clean off a stain, probably bourbon if I know her."

Kate exhaled. "So how many times do we let her get away with this?"

Lida shrugged. "That's your call."

"The last thing I need right now is to argue with Mrs. Plinson. She's been a great customer for six years."

"You are too damn nice, you know that don't you?" Lida asked.

"I think I'm too damn preoccupied." Kate turned back to the computer. "Finding Luna—it's like those first days after you fall in love."

"I wouldn't know. . . ."

Kate looked over her shoulder. "You will, and when you do, you'll check your e-mail every five minutes. You'll call me to talk about it over and over. You'll rearrange your spices in alphabetical order just to have something else to think about. You'll start ten things and not finish one."

"Um," Lida said. "I doubt it."

"Just you wait."

Lida handed the shirt to Kate. "Here. This will give you something to do." She smiled. "You know I'm kidding, right? I mean, I totally get why you're all scattered. This is a big deal. She's not even my daughter and I want to know everything."

Kate sat and clicked on her e-mail again. Nothing.

She turned to Lida. "I wonder if she walks to school or takes the bus. I wonder if her mom wakes her up or if she has an alarm clock.

I wonder—who is her best friend? What's her favorite food? Does she like one brother better?" Kate took a breath.

Lida reached down and touched Kate's shoulder. "You're going to make yourself crazy."

"Yes, crazy." Rowan's voice filled the room.

"Hey," Kate said and jumped up, hugging him. It was an awkward embrace, the kind given to a stranger, or a new friend, not a lover. Kate felt remorse seep into the edges of her happiness. "I'm so glad you're here. What's up?"

He shrugged. "I wanted to say hello. . . ."

"Hello," she said, smiling.

"You want to go get lunch together?" he asked.

Lida slipped out of the room to leave Rowan and Kate alone. "I can't," she said, pointing out at the store. "It's really busy and Norah couldn't come in today."

He nodded. "Okay."

Kate's cell phone, sitting on the desk, face up, buzzed. JACK—only four letters—flashed on the screen. Four letters that could hurt Rowan more than a hundred sentences combined.

Rowan cringed and turned away. "Later, Kate. I'll see you later."

Kate put her hand over the phone, as if hiding JACK made any difference at all. "No, it's okay. I can call him back."

Rowan stood still, quietly looking at her. The only sound in the room was the buzz of the phone against the desk. When it quieted, Kate lifted her hand.

"Do you want to go to Rich's tonight?" Rowan asked. "He caught a ton of redfish yesterday and he's having a big fish fry. You in?"

Kate shook her head. "I promised Tara I'd watch the monsters so she and Kyle could go to some parenting seminar at church."

He nodded. "Got it." He was halfway out the door when Kate grabbed his hand.

"Rowan. Don't be mad."

He kissed her on the cheek, as if she were a child. "I'm not mad." Then he was gone.

Kate thought to follow him, to run after him and soothe him. But she didn't know how, and the helplessness only made her feel worse. How long had it been since they'd been alone? A week? Two?

Since Emily found her weeks before, time had become odd and sporadic—moving too fast and then too slow as the days unfolded and e-mails were sent, slowly unraveling the years of not-knowing. Kate forwarded every e-mail to Jack and to her sisters. Through the years, while they'd been living their life, Emily's world had run parallel, and now it was as if train tracks were finally converging.

During these days Kate had gone to her closet and dug out the hidden box containing pictures, feathers, and journals from the days of her pregnancy. She read her own entries almost as if they were someone else's words. Had she really felt that way? The days after the adoption seemed distant and foreign, and then suddenly immediate and familiar.

Kate still held the phone in her hand, and when she was sure that Rowan had reached his car and driven away, she hit "return call" for JACK.

"Hey," his voice was quick and tight; it always was. He answered every call and e-mail, but never wanted to talk about anything but the facts. Every time Kate drew near to any subject other than Luna, from his art studio to his law office, he steered the conversation away or said he had to go for something urgent.

"What's up?" Kate asked, forcing lightness into her voice.

"Did you check your e-mail?" he asked.

"Only every five minutes. Why?"

"Check again."

Kate bent over and clicked refresh. "Oh . . ." she said. "An e-mail from her."

"Yep," Jack said. "You gonna go?"

"Let me read it," Kate said.

My mom and dad said that maybe we can see each other at the end of this semester. What do you think? Love, Emily.

Maybe? Was she serious? Kate would have been on a plane within five seconds of the first Facebook request if she'd been asked. "Oh, Jack. Oh, this is amazing. Of course I'll go. Will you go with me?"

"She isn't asking me. She's asking you. Her mom copied me."

"I want you to go."

"Not this time, Katie."

"You don't want to meet her?"

"I didn't say that."

"How are you feeling about all this?" Kate asked quietly. "You won't tell me."

He didn't answer and the silence became long and uncomfortable. Kate closed her eyes and forced her mouth to be still, not fill the empty spaces he wouldn't.

"So, I gotta go. Caleb is home. Have a good weekend, Kate."

She didn't say good-bye because she didn't need to say good-bye. He was already gone.

Her hands poised over the keyboard, she typed six different responses with varying tones of positive agreement until finally she typed, *Yes! You give me dates and times and I'll be there.*

twenty

· · · · · · · · · · · · · ·

BRONXVILLE, NEW YORK

2010

The clouds below the plane were meringue, whipped above the un-seen world below and seeming thick enough to walk on. Staring out the window at the twilight-tinged earth, Kate marveled how time wasn't linear, how it didn't move in a straight line, but made sporadic lurches forward to destiny. If she tried, she couldn't tell this story in a straightaway manner, from Jack to the wilderness, to his marriage, to her jobs, to the birth and adoption, and then to now when she would meet her daughter. No, not meet, reunite.

Kate's mom had also come along, but she was two rows behind, reading an advance copy of Tara's new article for *MORE* magazine. At first, Kate had decided she would go alone and then knowing that not everything turned out just like some made-for-TV movie, she thought she might need some help along the way. Nicole was already packed when Kate asked, knowing her daughter as well as she knew anyone in the world.

It was Rowan who had driven them both to the airport. Kate knew what this must have cost him, such chivalry, as if driving your girl-friend to the airport so she could be reunited with the daughter she had placed for adoption was the most natural thing in the world. He had even rolled the suitcases to the curbside check-in, where he hugged Nicole and then Kate. "Have a great time," he had said. "And call me, okay?"

"I love you," Kate said as she hugged him back tightly. She meant it. She did love him.

For the past two months, Rowan had kept his distance, sometimes not calling for days and yet attentive and quiet when he was with her. Only the night before he'd told her "I want to be thrilled that you're going to meet her tomorrow. I do. But this is tearing me to pieces."

"What's tearing you to pieces?"

"It's selfish and it's terrible, I know that, but I can barely stand thinking of you and Jack with a child, of you and Jack talking and e-mailing, of you and Jack all together."

"This is about Emily."

But the conversation was stale and repetitive, something neither of them wanted to repeat, but seemed to every time they got together.

They assured each other that after Kate met Emily, normalcy would resume. He kissed her good-bye, and Kate didn't tell him that what he thought was "normal" was far gone, if there ever had been.

The closer the plane came to New York, the faster Kate's pulse tapped against her throat and wrist. Images of her daughter had once been made of fantasy, and now were fashioned from photos, a cut-and-paste of a girl in situ, nothing moving.

When the flight attendant offered Kate a glass of wine, she almost took it but decided that reuniting with her daughter with the smell of cheap chardonnay on her breath was not the best way to begin.

She'd always believed this day would come. Even when her family pushed her to look for Luna, she knew she needed to wait. They hadn't understood her reasons, her desperate and crawling need to give her child everything: the mom, the dad, the possible brother and sisters, a full and complete family.

The family's unspoken and hidden emotions exploded only once—on Luna's first birthday when her family had quietly and deliberately planned a dinner party at their favorite outdoor restaurant.

Tara arrived first wearing her flowing skirt and tank top; her new baby, Colin, sat in his stroller looking up at Kate with eyes as round and blue as new planets. Tara's husband, Kyle, held onto bags and blankets, looking confused and exhausted as if he'd been dropped into baby world without any warning. Molly had been on spring break and just shy of her twenty-first birthday and was a junior at University of South Carolina. She ran up behind Tara, draped in a sundress of such bright yellow, as if she was honoring the thick yellow pollen of a Low Country spring. Her hug was the longest. "I miss you, sissy," Molly said.

Kate's mom and dad arrived dressed in almost-matching pressed khakis and white button-down shirts: Nicole's frilly; Stuart's starched. They hugged Kate simultaneously, stumbling over the end of the gangplank and laughing. Sitting at a round table, Molly reached down into a bag she carried and pulled out what Kate first thought was a stuffed animal and then realized was a real, live Shitzu, white and fluffy with a black-dot nose.

"You can't bring a dog into a restaurant," Kate said, irritation already rising above the calm.

Molly pointed at their Dad. "Don't tell me. Tell Dad. I told him it wasn't a good idea, but he won't go anywhere without Mister, his new love."

"Dad?" Kate looked to her dad who was trying, unsuccessfully, to look innocent and preoccupied.

"Huh? I didn't think it would be a problem."

"That's why you didn't say anything?"

Nicole interrupted, changing the conversation to Molly's outfit, and soon the family was talking over each other and somehow carrying on a conversation in the way any family in any world was probably able to do with half-finished sentences and incomplete sounds, and silent meanings running underneath.

They talked about Molly's first boyfriend, and Tara's column for *Savannah Parenting*, along with her new Web site called Mothering Heights. They discussed Kyle's possible job change.

The waitress came by to pour the wine and Molly held out her hand for a glass. "No way," Nicole said.

"Give her a break," Stuart said. "She's twenty-one next week."

Mister started to bark from his blue and white dotted bag and somewhere inside the restaurant someone turned up the jazz music. Soon the world faded into a buzzing distant image. The rhythm of Vaughnness that defined them as a singular unit took over.

"So," Nicole finally said, holding up her hand to silence the family. "Kate, really, how are you?"

She didn't know how she was, really, the world a buffered and distant thing going on outside a thick wall of fog. But she didn't want to say this, so she waited too long to answer and her dad saw an opening to say what he must have wanted to say all night. "Today is our first granddaughter's birthday."

"Dad, I know that," Kate whispered. "I know it's her birthday. You don't have to tell me."

"I wasn't being informative as much as I was telling you that I remembered."

Mister yapped in earnest, as if trapped at the bottom of a well; Molly swayed across the table; baby Colin began to cry with a high mewling sound. Kate ignored the Vaughn chaos to look her dad in the eyes. "It's okay to talk about it. I think about her all the time."

Nicole made a noise, a whimper, and Kate turned to face her mother. "What, Mom?"

"We just wish we could find her. You know—just know that she's okay. Isn't there a way?"

"Of course not. You saw the legal papers. You know. Please don't do this."

Molly leaned forward, clearly drunk, a shrimp bobbing off the end of her fork as if dancing. "I have a niece out in the world somewhere. A girl. Today is her birthday."

"Enough," Kate said.

It was then that Mister's barks became intolerable and Kate spun around in her chair. "Dad, take the damn dog out of his silly bag and let him breathe so he shuts up."

"It's not a damn dog," Stuart said, leaning down to free Mister. "I just want to see her—my first grandchild," Stuart said as he unzipped the dog bag.

"Stop," Kate said, and her single word became a detonator that exploded the evening.

It all happened at once, but Kate could later recount each event as if they occurred one after the other in perfect synchrony. Mister shot out from his imprisonment and crapped on the deck of the restaurant while Molly pitched forward, grabbing Kyle as she threw up, trying to catch it with her wineglass. Her dad cursed, a litany of many curses strung together as one. The baby screamed as if Granddad had insulted him about his grandchild status, and Tara jumped from the table while Kate dropped her face into her hands and groaned.

In the pause, in the aftermath, in the moment when no one should have said anything, they all heard Kate say, "Sometimes the future is just further away than we want it to be."

When they arrived home, somber and silent, Molly curled up in the corner of the couch and pulled her knees up under her chin.

"Sorry," she said. "I guess I drank too much. But when the dog pooped, I just couldn't hold it in."

Stuart stared at Molly but spoke to Kate. "What you said at the table is hard to hear. You're so factual about it, like this is happening to someone else."

"What *I* said?" Kate asked.

"About the future being further away than we'd like for it to be."

"It's terrible and it's true, Dad. If I could find out where Luna is and be able to call her and say happy birthday, if I could see her photo or hold her and tell her how much we all love her, I would. But I can't and you can't and we aren't able to change anything about it."

"How can you be so resolute about this as if it isn't the saddest thing in the whole world?" he asked.

"I'm not resolute, Dad." Kate's voice cracked open on the truth. "I can't *do* anything about it. What do you want me to do? Make the present turn into some imagined future? You want me to be a magician and change the past? I don't know what you want from me."

Nicole came to Kate's side. "Stuart, stop." She hugged her daughter. "Baby, we don't want anything from you. We just . . ."

"I know you hate what I did. I know I didn't do it the way you would have. But it's done. Done. Done." Her last word vibrated, anger finally arriving.

"It's not done," Tara said quietly. "There will be a wonderful day in all this. I know it."

Kate spun around and faced her sister. "You do?"

"Don't be mad at me, Katey-Latey. I'm just saying that I believe in good coming from this birthday." She turned to her dad. "I know you don't mean to be hurtful, but just think about what you're saying before you say it."

"He knows what he's saying," Kate's anger gained speed, as if knowing it was late to the party and bursting through the door. "He knows exactly what he's saying. He's telling me, and all of you, that he cares more about Luna than I do. Oh, how he misses her. How much he wants to see her. He wants all of us to know that he has a bigger and better heart than I do."

"No," Stuart's voice shook. "No."

"But you all have no idea what I carry around with me. No idea." Kate spread her arms wide. "It's something you can't know. It is a missing so deep that it feels like a canyon. It's a thing I can't change no matter where I go or who I'm with or how I wish or want or pray. The only thing I can do is wait. Nothing." Kate's body shook with sentiments she'd kept inside. "I miss her more than you can imagine. I miss everything I know about her and everything I don't know about her."

Stuart dropped his head and mumbled. "I'm sorry."

Tara handed the baby to her husband and took Kate's hand. "We all know, Katey-Latey. We know."

"We didn't mean to make you upset. I thought it would make you feel better, not worse, to know how much we thought of her and cared," Nicole said.

Molly's voice, quiet and fragile, ended the night. "She's right, you know. No matter what we do or say, sometimes the future is farther away than we want it to be."

And now, on this plane to New York, the future had finally arrived. Yes, she'd always imagined this day, but it seemed that the word *imagine* was what made it *impossible,* the two words inextricably linked.

Kate leaned back on the seat and looked out the window to the growing skyscraper skyline, to the gaping lost-tooth hole where the twin towers had once been, and to the state where her daughter lived.

Nicole and Kate rented a car at LaGuardia airport. It was brown, dingy, and smelled like acrid air freshener sprayed over cigarette smoke.

"I feel like I should have a limousine or chariot for this trip. Not some smelly brown car." Kate said, throwing her luggage into the backseat.

Her mom placed her hand on Kate's shoulder. "Dear, not everything has to go perfect today. Get that part out of your mind. It's a miracle, but not a perfect miracle."

Kate rolled her eyes. "Such a mother thing to say."

They climbed into the car and hooked up the GPS system, plugging the Jackson's Bronxville address into the system. Neon green numbers flashed *THIRTY-TWO MINUTES*.

"Thirty-two minutes. Wow." Kate pressed the bottom of her palms into her eyes and stayed the tears. "Now I've messed up my makeup." She reached for her makeup bag in the backseat, knocking over her purse.

"You don't need makeup. You'll just cry it off when you see her," Nicole said.

"Nope. I'm going to remain calm. I don't want her to think she was born with some psycho heredity that makes her an emotional basket case."

"Oh, good, then let her think you're an ice queen."

"There's no right way to do this, is there?" Kate asked in exhale.

"If there is, I don't know it."

The car moving off the exit, Kate took in a deep long breathe. "Whatever happens, happens. That's that." She turned on the radio, and finding only static, she turned it off. Glancing over at her mom, Kate saw that her eyes were closed. "Are you seriously sleeping, Mom?"

"Of course not. I'm praying."

Kate navigated the New York City highway system before exiting into a quaint town that could be painted and hung over a mantel. They passed the dry cleaner, the boutique, the bagel shop, and the bookstore, all snuggled next to each other and wrapped under the blanket of ancient brick. The evenly spaced trees were crowded with new summer leaves, sunlight falling through to make ragged lit patterns on the cobblestone sidewalks.

The GPS instructed, "Turn right now." And then, in a robotic voice announced, "You have reached your destination."

Kate looked up. The Jackson house looked down from atop a hill, white-painted brick with ivy crawling up the sides and around the front door. Stone steps led from the sidewalk to the double front door where two iron urns spilled over with flowers and ferns. "I have reached my destination."

"Do you want me to go to the door with you?" Nicole asked, softly.

"I think I should go alone and then . . ."

Nicole took Kate's hand. "I'll wait right here."

Together they climbed out of the car. "Do you think they're looking at me?" Kate asked.

"I'm sure they are." Nicole kissed her daughter's cheek and Kate started up the stairs. A breeze, full of cherry blossoms, flew across the yard. Pink petals fell to the ground and scattered in extravagant waste along the steps. Kate glanced down and on the front steps she saw a feather, freckled with brown and brushed with red. She squatted down and picked it up, placing it into her purse and whispering, "thank you" to the God who sent feathers and Facebook requests.

Kate was calmer than she imagined she'd be. Emily opened the door with a half smile. In the briefest crack of time before she took Emily in her arms, Kate took in these details: copper hair catching light, a nose sprinkled with freckles, and the green of Jack's eyes.

For all the practicing and the imagining of the first words to her daughter, this is what she said. "Oh, look at you. Beautiful you," Kate's voice broke over the last word.

Emily smiled fully. A gale-force of unnamed emotions arrived, and Kate took Emily in her arms and held her as if, once again, someone were going to take her away. Mother breathed in as daughter breathed out.

"Welcome to our home," said a soft voice from inside.

Kate released Emily to see her daughter's mother. "Hi, I'm Kate Vaughn." She held out her hand to shake Elena's hand.

"Hi." Elena reached for Kate's hand and then pulled her into a hug. "Thank you for the gift of my daughter." It sounded like a practiced line from a play or a production, yet Elena's voice shook with its realness, with its honesty.

Kate felt the slight shake of a shifting world. "Nice to finally meet you too," she said.

Emily giggled, a nervous resonance that broke them free to move. "Okay," Elena said. "Come on in."

Kate glanced over her shoulder and Elena followed her gaze. "Is that your mom?"

"Yes, she came with me and she didn't want to . . . interrupt or anything."

"Please tell her to come in." Elena made sweeping hand motions to Nicole.

Soon they'd all gathered in the living room: Dad, Larry, and the brothers came out as if they'd been hiding behind a corner, which maybe they had been. Introductions were made and everything felt so normal that Kate felt as if she were just meeting another family, any other family in the world, until she looked at Emily.

Instead of the feared silence, words and explanations and stories overlapped one another like too many simultaneous songs. Everyone tried to speak at once while telling his or her side of the passed years.

Sitting in the Jackson living room with family photos and the knickknacks of family life, they went around the room, slowly unfolding an intricate storyline and overlapping years where coincidences were synchronicities, when similarities were profound, and where ordinary days were magical, and they all added up to that moment. "Whoa," Larry finally said. "I'm lost." He smiled. "Kate, you first. Tell us all about your family."

At one moment, Emily left the room to grab a photo album and Elena leaned toward Kate. "I know you must wonder about her brothers. I know you chose us because we said we couldn't have kids. I don't want you to think I was lying or trying to . . ."

"I don't think that," Kate said. "Not one bit."

"I know this story happens all the time, but we tried for nine years to have a child and nothing worked." Elena looked to her husband. "Three miscarriages and then the miracle of Emily. Two years later, when I was late, I thought I might be going through the early change. But the change was Steven. And then Ethan. It's like Emily coming to us began the miracle that kept going."

Kate smiled at Elena across the room, wanting to take her hand and kiss her cheek. But Emily bounded back into the room, dropping the photo album on the coffee table and then settling next to Kate on the couch. Emily held out her hand, waving it back and forth as if it was underwater. "I used to stare at my hands, or my feet, or my eyes and wonder where things came from. Like who gave me this or that? Now I never have to wonder. I never have to . . . not know."

"You have Jack's exact eye color," Kate said. "Like green glass that lets you think you can see inside your soul. Like everything green in the world at the same time."

Emily grinned, a shy smile. "I've always wanted to look like someone."

Kate took that same hand into her own. "Ask anything. Anything you want to know."

"Did you . . . love him? My birth dad. Did you love him?"

"Yes, and I still do. Greatly. I loved you from the minute I knew about you. I loved you more the minute I saw you. And my family too—all of us have loved you and prayed for you since the second we knew you'd been . . . formed."

Emily looked around the room, surprisingly dry-eyed and clear. "I think my 'I'm-not-wanted' button just turned off."

Laughter filled the room the same way the universe fills the sky: with pure delight.

In a stark hotel room outside Bronxville, Kate sat on the edge of the bed with her cell phone in her hand. The simplest of all things to do—hit one button that dialed the seven numbers for Rowan—she couldn't do. She couldn't explain to him what it felt like to walk into Emily's bedroom and see her bright apple-green bedspread, her bulletin board covered in photos, dried flowers, and cutouts from fashion magazines. She couldn't tell him how they held hands while Emily talked about her best friend, Sailor, pushing her to find them.

Kate wanted to call Jack, tell him every feeling, every moment, every sparkling sentence that had passed between the families. This wanting—the one of needing Jack more than Rowan—felt more betraying than even the lie she'd told about Birmingham all those months ago.

Nicole came out of the bathroom and sat on the hotel bed across from Kate. "You okay?"

Kate nodded. "I want to call Jack. I want to tell him everything about everything. Her freckles. The way she covers her lips with her fingertips when she laughs. The way her bulletin board looks like mine did at thirteen years old. The cleft in her chin. Her greenest eyes. How happy she is. So good and so happy."

"Then tell him, darling." Nicole glanced around the room, as if looking for escape. "You'd kill me if I lit a cigarette. So, I'm going outside." She stood and grabbed her purse from the side table.

"Mom?"

"Yes?"

"I did the right thing, right? I mean, now that we see her and know. I did the right thing."

Nicole nodded. "I don't know if there's a right thing here. But yes, it was a good thing. A great thing."

"What now?"

Nicole smiled. "Just like you couldn't know back then, I don't think you can know now."

The hotel room door slammed its metal weight with a startling pop as Nicole left the room. Kate again looked at her phone contacts and scrolled to Jack's name, touching his number with the tip of her finger.

twenty-one

· · · · · · · · · · · · ·

BRONXVILLE, NEW YORK

2010

"Tell me again," Sailor asked.

"Seriously? Can't we talk about something else?" Emily pushed her feet against the grass, sending the tire swing higher so she looked down at Sailor, close and then far, a kaleidoscope. "I told you every single thing."

"Maybe you forgot one thing."

Emily stopped the swing with the jolt of her heel into the dirt. "It's been like a month and I can't think of anything I haven't told you."

"Liar," Sailor said. "I don't know why you are so super-secret about it all. I mean, really, if it wasn't for me you might not have even looked for her. You'd still have that stupid notebook full of fake mom stuff."

Sailor was right, and Emily took a deep breath. "Something I haven't told you . . . let me think." Emily sat in the grass and plucked clover—the green stem with the tiny white flower edged in pink—from the dirt, making a pile. "I want to meet Mr. Jack."

"Mr. Jack?" Sailor plopped down next to Emily, joining in the flower collection.

"Yes, that's what we all decided I'd call them. Miss Katie and Mr. Jack. It's like a totally southern thing, I guess."

"See?" Sailor pushed at Emily. "You didn't tell me that. You're always leaving things out."

"Whatever." Emily sat cross-legged and began tying stems together to make a fairy chain. Emily and Sailor believed that when they each made a perfect circle of white flowers with stems end to end, and then placed those garlands on their heads, wishes were heard. Of course so far none of their wishes had been granted, but there was always next time.

The lawn was circular, a tidy oasis behind Sailor's uncle's house. Since his wife had died, he'd made a garden for her. When Sailor's aunt was alive, he'd always been "too busy" to make this garden he'd promised. When she died, he devoted his weekends and evenings to the magical place where he gave Emily and Sailor special permission to hide on boring and searing summer afternoons. He was the one who told them about the fairies, and they believed him.

Silent under the July sun, tying flowers together while their fingertips turned green with brilliant stem-juice, they each thought of their wishes. As with every afternoon that summer, far-off thunder was the broken promise of much-needed rain that never came. A fat blue bird dipped into a nest above Emily's head and glared down at her as if she might try to take the speckled eggs that she would never touch or hurt.

Emily finished her flower circle first and placed it on the crown of her head. "I wish I could meet Mr. Jack." She closed her eyes and fell backward onto the grass under an oak tree thick with dense summer leaves, a shadow, and an umbrella over her face.

Sailor placed her own wreath on her head. "Me too. I wish you could meet Mr. Jack."

"A double wish," Emily said.

"The fairies will hear us this time. It'll for sure work this time. Totally for sure."

twenty-two

. . . .

BLUFFTON, SOUTH CAROLINA

2010

Families were formed of many combinations and with one Facebook "friend request" Kate's family had increased plus five. As weeks passed, Emily asked questions as they came to her; Kate answered and then asked her own. They learned about each other's habits and likes and dislikes, about what they had in common and what they didn't.

Kate fought the urge to act like a "mother," but what else was she? What was the plan for a birth mother who reentered a young girl's life? Did she just send notes of adoration? Did she try to see her? Become involved in everyday life? What she'd give for a blueprint or outline. She'd read so many books when she was pregnant—there was not an absence of advice then, but now?

None.

While the rest of the world returned to their normal routine, Kate oscillated between jubilation and melancholy, between joy and fear.

All these years and time, and her daughter was now part of her life, but what if she messed it up now? Every day seemed a new way to ruin the good, the newly found goodness. Finally two months after her visit, the Jackson family wrote to say that they were heading to the Florida panhandle for vacation and would love to stop in Birmingham and meet Jack.

Jack had taken three days to think about it before calling Kate.

"Why wouldn't you want to meet her?" Kate asked, cradling her cell phone between her shoulder and ear as she arranged shirts on a rack.

"This isn't something to be taken lightly."

"I didn't say it was. I just wondered."

"I've told you. This isn't something anyone in my life knows about. This isn't common knowledge. I tried to forget." Each sentence seemed a word of its own: simple and complete.

"But you didn't."

"Didn't what?"

"Forget. I mean, how could you?"

"At times I did. And now, when life has some kind of balance, I don't want to mess it all up again."

"Jack, she just wants to know her story. That's all anyone wants, I think. To know where they came from and why. You never have to see her again. Just give this to her. To me."

"Yes," he said. "Okay."

"Great, so I'll see you soon." Kate hung up, leaning her head against the wall.

"You okay?" Lida asked, coming from behind Kate.

"Yep." She shook her head. "I really don't get Jack at all. Here is the one person he has wondered about and worried about for his whole life and he almost doesn't want to see her?"

Lida smiled, but her lips were closed and the smile sad. "It must be hard for him."

Kate nodded. "I know."

And she did know. Jack's heart had long since healed, and opening doors and windows to this piece of the past might make him feel and remember things he'd obviously kept far from his life. She did know.

The edges of Kate's body felt frayed and loose as she waited on the outdoor patio of the pizza place in downtown Birmingham. This was where they'd agreed to meet. Jack hadn't invited them to his house; he hadn't even invited her to his house. This meeting was separate, a thing outside his life. A secret.

Kate again looked out to the streetscape, cars passing, heat mirages working their way across the sidewalk like water. Her cell phone rang and Emily's dad, Larry Jackson, informed her that they were running late, as they were lost.

"Jack isn't here yet either," she said. "Take your time." And just as the words came out of her mouth, she saw him: Jack walking toward her with sunglasses covering his eyes, a smile when hearing his name.

"I'm here." He sidled around the round iron table and hugged Kate. "I was hoping I'd get to see you alone for a second before they showed up. I'm nervous as hell," he said.

"Don't be. They are so easy to be around. So sweet. They aren't here to judge you."

"Okay." He shuffled from foot to foot, his hands loose and unsure where to go or what to do.

She loved so many things about Jack, from the way he smiled to the gentleness he had with other people. The way he moved with surety through his world and then quickly showed, through the smallest gesture, a vulnerability she believed only she noticed. She adored his need to do the *right thing* always, his hand always finding the small of her back when she needed steadying, the way he looked at anyone and everyone when he spoke to them, as if they were the only ones in the room or even in his life. These were the things, the things of him, that she hoped the Jackson family would notice, the beauty of him that made her heart so full that nothing else fit.

"They'll love you," she said with absolute conviction.

"You might be biased." He laughed that low, beautiful laugh just as they looked up and saw the Jackson family walking toward them.

"Sorry we're late," Larry said, holding out his hand to the father of his daughter.

"No problem," Jack said, shaking Larry's hand. "I'm Jack Adams."

"Nice to meet you. I'm Larry and this is my wife, Elena, and my daughter, Emily." He turned to face his wife and daughter, protective in his stance and words.

Jack shook Elena's hand and then stood before Emily. She ignored his hand and threw her arms around him. "Hi, Mr. Jack. I am so happy I finally get to meet you. So happy."

In this stunning moment, Jack forgot to hug her back. His arms dangled at his side, useless until Emily laughed and he lifted those arms and hugged her in return.

She stepped back and stared at him. "I look more like you, don't I?"

He nodded. "I think so, yes." He paused. "Where are your brothers?"

"Camp," Elena said. "They go to the same camp in Maine every summer, but Emily hates camp. Hates being away from home."

"Me too," Jack said. "I'm a homebody, too."

The air lightened and they sat at the table, shuffling positions in the awkwardness of the moment. When they'd settled down and the menus were handed out, it was Emily who spoke first. "Okay, I want to hear some stories. I want to know about you," she looked at Jack. "I mean, I've talked to Kate a ton on e-mail and stuff, but I don't know anything about you except the facts. And who cares about the facts?"

Elena touched her daughter's arm. "Emily, don't push."

Jack smiled at Elena across the table. "She's not pushing. I want to tell her everything. I just don't know where to start. Ask me something."

"Well, I mean if you guys didn't have a first date, I wouldn't be here, right? These are the things I've wondered for my whole life. How did you meet? Isn't that what you'd wonder?" Emily looked at her dad and he nodded.

"Yes, Em. But I was just thinking that might not be where I'd start the conversation," Larry said, his hand placed over hers, his large fingers covering his daughter's smaller ones, her hand disappearing all together beneath his.

"Yep, Dad because you're you and I'm me."

"Help us all," Elena motioned to the sky.

"We never really had a first date," Jack said. "Katie and I grew up in the same town. I don't remember not knowing her or loving her. We went to elementary through high school together until my family moved here to Birmingham at the end of my junior year."

"So," Emily broke into the conversation. "You always knew each other."

Jack laughed. "Always. She was unavoidable." He smiled at Kate. "Inevitable."

Kate's skin expanded to allow his warmth to settle inside. For so many years she'd felt tight and small as if she needed to keep things enclosed and locked, as if her insides might explode if she didn't keep control, and this unfolding was a relief.

"Inevitable?" Emily said the word as if she tasted an exotic flavor. "That's so cool. Like *I* was inevitable."

"You were," Jack said. "Of course you were."

"So you fell in love when you were my age?"

"I did, yes. I won't answer for Katie."

The conversation broke apart as the waitress came over and took orders. But it was Emily who picked up threads and continued as if they hadn't stopped. "So, you fell in love and then what?"

Jack looked to Kate. "You want to take it from here?"

She shook her head. "Nope. She asked you. Go on."

"Well, my family moved here and then Katie and I went to different colleges. When she graduated, Katie took this amazing job far away and we tried to see each other when we could. It was when she came to visit me here that you came to be."

"Wow." Emily sat back in her seat, sipping Coke through a straw. "That is awesome."

Unasked questions, unanswerable questions, grew from "I loved her" to "adoption," but those were left alone for the moment.

Emily slurped the last of her Coke and the lunch order was placed before them. Facts were shared about life and jobs and school. "You know," Jack said after Emily said her favorite class was creative writing, "your aunt is a writer."

"I know," Emily said while taking another bite of pizza. "I read this funny blog she wrote about finding the right preschool or something like that."

"Don't talk with your mouth full," Elena said, handing a napkin to Emily. Elena laid her fork on her uneaten salad and leaned forward. "Yes, that's actually how we found you guys. We went on the Internet looking for Kate, but her sister Tara kept coming up. Hopefully, she's handed down some of those writing skills to Emily."

"No way I can be that good and get published for real and all that," Emily said.

Jack took her hand. "You're already that good. I mean, I haven't read your writing, but you're already that good because I know . . ."

Elena stood and turned. "I hate when you say that. I hate when you say you're not good enough." She rushed toward the bathroom, her exit so sudden that the awkward silence was unsettling, a cold wind.

Kate turned to Larry, "Is she okay?"

"Yes, this is hard for her. She just needs more space with it than the rest of us," Larry said, glancing over his shoulder and then taking his daughter's hand again. "She gets upset when you say you aren't good enough at anything. She feels like it's her fault."

Kate's eyes filled with tears and shame. "Is it because we were talking about my family? I'm sorry. Should I go after her?"

"No."

"No."

Larry and Emily spoke simultaneously.

"She'll be fine," Emily said. "But never, ever go after her when she leaves. Right Dad?"

He nodded. "It's not because you talked about your family."

Jack stood. "I think I should go now. I don't want to cause problems. I just wanted to meet all of you." He looked down at Emily.

Emily stood and faced him. "Mom will be sad if you leave without saying good-bye and . . . just stay a little bit longer. I promise it will all be fine. I promise. Just stay."

"And who can refuse you?" he asked, that smile again on his face.

When Elena returned with her red eyes and stoic smile, good-byes were said, and shaky hugs offered. Jack and Kate stood together watching the Jackson family get in their car and wave.

"You think I made Elena upset?" Jack asked as he sat on a bench at the edge of the sidewalk and Kate sat down next to him.

"No, I don't. But I can't imagine how this must be for her. I mean, I don't think this was something she imagined. We dreamed of it, but I can bet she didn't."

Jack nodded, his arm slipping over Kate's shoulder, familiar.

"Can we just stay here in the warm sun for a few more minutes. Just stay here knowing that our daughter is good and fine and well?" Kate asked, quiet and leaning against him.

"We can stay here as long as you like."

Eyes closed, warmth rushing through her hollow body, Kate felt somehow reborn and new. "The waiting was worth it. My God, she is so beautiful. And all of us sitting there together."

"It's more than I'd ever hoped for," Jack said, and yet his voice was colder than the words were meant to be.

"The waiting was terrible though," Kate said. "There were days I would've combed the earth for her if I'd known how."

"Me too," he said, his voice warming slightly. "But I couldn't. It would've been terribly wrong. You can't give something up and then ask for it back."

Kate lifted his sunglasses so she could see the green, see the truth. "Are we talking about more than just our daughter now?"

He shrugged.

"Say something," she pleaded.

"What do you want me to say?"

"I don't know. Whatever you want. Whatever you want to say, say."

"I'm glad we saw her. I am. That's the truth. But it has to stop here." He looked away. "To bring in all that pain again makes no sense at all and surely you don't want to either."

"What if it's not pain?"

"Of course it is." He removed his arm from her shoulder and slid to the other end of the bench.

"I don't get it." She was thrown off-balance, as if he'd slid to the other end of the world, an adult teeter-totter.

"Don't you think I wanted to be with you? Days I wanted to go to Arizona and talk some sense into you?" A haze of summer heat and anger settled between them, palpable. "Shit, even after I was married I wanted to do that. It never seemed to end."

"How was I ever supposed to know that's how you felt? You only wrote that one letter. That one yearly letter." Kate's voice shook.

"I can't always do exactly what I want to do. None of us can. If I'd done every single thing I wanted over the past thirteen years, I can't imagine how many people, including myself, I would've destroyed. This is not about what I did or didn't *want* to do; it's about what I *had* to do. Don't you even get that? You act like I didn't want to write to you or see you."

Kate dropped her face into her hands. "Then why didn't you?"

"There was always something, Katie. Always. A real something. And then it did end. I did finally stop wanting it all."

"Why not now?"

He stood then and looked down at her. "You have a boyfriend who has an engagement ring in his bedside drawer."

She looked up at him. "I know that."

"Just because Luna found us—" he seemed to stumble. "Look, Katie—*Kate*—that was then and this is now. We can't dig into the past and fix it. It's already happened. Done."

"But our daughter isn't in the past anymore. Our *daughter*. Luna." Kate stood now, facing him with her voice strong. "This is not a small thing. She found us and this changes everything. She's here."

"She's always been here. We just now saw her again, but she's always been here."

"With us, I mean. She's here with us."

"No." He waved his hand toward the street. "She's still with her family. Her *mom* and *dad*."

Kate sat, and she looked up at him through the tears that made him appear murky and wavy, a dream almost.

"You can't always make things come out the way you want them to come out." He took a breath and then spoke on exhale. "This was a perfect day and I just don't want to ruin it with anything we'd do or say now. I think we should just go. Just leave this the wonderful way it is." He looked away. "I heard what you said when Rowan came to get you, about ending one chapter and starting another. And that's exactly what we both need to do."

The ground was slipping, moving away as if she could for the first time feel the roundness of the earth. "I understand," Kate said.

"I'm not sure you do. I've never told my son. My ex-wife. My family." Jack ticked each name off on his fingers. "If I focus on all of this—on you, on her—it takes away from living my life right now. She has a great life. Let's leave her be."

"It's not like that. You can't pretend her life doesn't exist so you don't have to upset yours."

"You never told Rowan," he said. "So let's not forget that. You might not ever have told him if he hadn't shown up at my house."

Regret rolled around inside Kate's belly, trapped under her ribs. "You're right. I hadn't told him, but I was trying to find a way. I wasn't taking that engagement ring until I found a way to tell him."

He avoided her gaze, staring off as if she weren't pleading with him. "I don't know how to fix this for us." His voice was as distant as the years between them.

"I'm not asking you to fix it."

"I think it's best if we give ourselves some time to think about this. Let it be . . ."

"Okay," Kate said. She touched the side of his face, a last gentle gesture, and then walked away. She wanted and needed him to call out to her, to call her back, but he didn't, and she continued to walk until she reached her car.

Once, a day, a time, and a place had existed when Kate had believed that nothing could separate them—not anger, not un-forgiveness, not other loves, nothing at all.

twenty-three

. . . .

BIRMINGHAM, SOUTH CAROLINA

2010

Emily sat in the back seat trying to read her parents' every move and glance. Were they mad? Sad? Glad?

"Say something," Emily finally asked.

Elena turned in her seat. "That was a nice lunch, didn't you think?"

"Of course I did. Why did you run off?"

"Can't you for one second imagine that was hard for me?"

"Of course, Mom. Mr. Jack thought he hurt your feelings with the 'aunt' comment. I could tell. He didn't mean it though."

"That wasn't it. I was upset because my heart breaks every time I hear you doubt yourself, every time I hear you talk about how you're not good enough or smart enough or pretty enough. I don't know what I've ever done to make you believe that. You're amazing and you can do anything you want."

"What are you talking about?" Emily scooted up in the seat, straining the seatbelt across her chest.

"When you said you'd never be as good at writing as Tara. Why do you say things like that? I didn't raise you that way, Emily. I've always told you how . . ."

"What you tell me and what I feel aren't the same thing, Mom. Not the same thing at all. And it makes me crazy when you tell me how great I am over and over and over. Of course you're supposed to believe I'm the most wonderful of all wonderfuls, but guess what?" Emily took in a long breath and hollered, "I'm not!" Her words echoed inside the tiny rental car.

"Yes, you are."

"Damn GPS," Larry said. "It keeps taking us in circles." He stopped at a red light and turned in his seat. "Okay, that's enough. You're both emotionally fraught and tired. Please."

"God, Dad, why do you have to be so freaking logical? Can't you just let us freak out?"

He laughed and shook his head. "Nope. No freaking out."

Elena attempted not to laugh, but the sound bubbled up and she turned in her seat to face the windshield, pulling down the visor to check her face. "I look a wreck."

"No, you don't." Larry reached across and took her hand. "All is well."

The GPS's robotic voice announced, "Stay left and keep in the right-hand lane."

The three of them burst into laughter. "How do I stay left and keep in the right-hand lane?" Larry said as they drove past the restaurant for the fourth time.

Only Emily saw them on the bench: Mr. Jack and Miss Katie. Her head was on his shoulder and his face was lifted to the sun.

"Just turn left anywhere and see where it leads us," Elena said.

Emily settled back into her seat and ran through the list of questions that still remained, but not one of them was as important as this answer: Yes, they'd loved each other when they'd made her. She'd been made of love instead of the other options she'd imagined in her worst moments.

It was important, she thought, to know where you started. It seemed to her that where you started just might have something to do with where you ended. And love was a good place for a start and a finish.

twenty-four

· · · · · · · · · · · · · ·

BLUFFTON, SOUTH CAROLINA

2010

Days passed until September leeched summer from the ground and Kate felt herself becoming as cold as the arriving autumn. The months moved forward toward the holidays, time marked by the falling of leaves, the marsh grasses turning from brightest green to sage. Even the slant of light resting on the leaves marked time, becoming weary and faded. Kate worked the boutique, watching the crowds increase. She and Rowan were still together and she waited, patiently, for her heart to join her mind.

Emily sent funny e-mails and photos as Kate measured every answer, word, and note as carefully as an exact recipe and made sure to copy Elena. Kate longed to see Emily again, but she waited. The old ache, like an old bruise that wouldn't heal, returned when Jack disappeared as he had during the years between his letters—silent and gone.

Then Thanksgiving arrived with its companion of a record-breaking cold spell, frosting the live oak leaves into silver-flocked exclamation points. The heat had gone out in the middle of the night and Mimsy Clothing was as cold as the refrigerator; Kate's loft felt encased in rime. Kate and Rowan stood at the window of the boutique, waiting on the technician from Bluffton Heating and Air. They were bundled up in coats and scarves.

"Damn how did it get to be Thanksgiving?" Rowan asked.

"Thanks for staying in town," Kate said and burrowed closer to him. "I'm so glad you'll be here for dinner. I'm not sure I could take it without you. Tara with her perfect husband and the kids, Molly getting drunk on champagne because she thinks champagne doesn't really count as alcohol, Dad asking again and again about Luna. This should be a great, great night."

Rowan laughed, "Everything works out in good time."

"And an apple a day keeps the doctor away," Kate said.

"Can't teach an old dog new tricks."

"Damned if you do and damned if you don't. It's all a lie," Kate said, laughing and leaning into Rowan's shoulder, staring out the window at the potted mums outside the front door. They drooped under the weight of winter, now dead. "We need to throw those away," Kate said, pointing outside the window. "Winter killed them."

He pulled her closer as if the cold would do the same to them. Finally, the technician banged on the front door announcing that this would be double-price for working on Thanksgiving.

"Of course it is," Kate said.

She walked to the back of the store and checked e-mails while Rowan took the technician to the heating units.

Dear Kate,

Happy Thanksgiving to you and your family. This is a hard note to write, but I need to ask that you please not e-mail Emily for a lit-

tle while. I know you love her, and I know you have no ill inten-
tions, but we are seeing a sadness and belligerence in her that we've
never seen before. Every time she is angry (as all teenagers can
be), she announces that she is running away to live with you or
Jack. She's even asked a few of her friends to call her Luna. So, I'm
asking that you give us some space to be what we've always been—
her parents.

  With Warm Wishes,
  Elena Jackson.

"Warm Wishes?" Kate spoke out loud, her voice echoing in the room.

"What?" Rowan called from the side room.

"Elena sends me this e-mail that could break any heart in any world and then ends it with 'warm wishes.' Seriously?"

Rowan came to Kate's side and read the e-mail. "I'm sorry."

"Nothing to be sorry about." Kate scooted away from the table and from her emotions, wanting to soothe Rowan as much as herself. "I'd do the same thing. I probably wouldn't even have let her meet me. I could've been a serial killer. A crazy, insane person living in a cult in New Mexico. But she did let me meet her, and that has to be enough for now."

"Let's go to your loft and skip your parents' dinner. We'll drink all the champagne you have."

Kate smiled at Rowan, sensing an eagerness to be alone, to mend, and then make their own holiday. "That is the most brilliant idea I've ever heard," she said.

Kate awoke with her leg wound around Rowan's, her head on his chest. She smiled before she opened her eyes. Maybe she'd come out on the other side of a long-gone fantasy. Maybe now her desire and her touch could be in the same place, the same bed.

Rowan wiggled his arm out from under her head, moving silently.

"I'm awake," she said, opening her eyes.

"Stay in bed. I'll go get us some coffee and donuts."

"Boston cream?" she asked, turning over to wiggle further into the pillows.

"Anything you want," he said.

"I want."

He kissed her before he left and she again closed her eyes, content to sleep, but across the room, her cell phone rang. She climbed out of bed and stumbled to her dresser to answer. It was Jack's voice that brought her to full awake, a jolt more potent than coffee.

She sat upright then, finding her way into day and time: the day after Thanksgiving. Six in the morning. "Hey," she said.

"Emily ran away. She's on a Greyhound bus on the way to Birmingham. Her parents are freaking out."

"Oh, no." The room wavered; she closed her eyes to focus. "Okay, I'm coming."

"Wait. Not here though. We looked up the bus she took and it's a twenty-five-hour drive with a stop in Richmond, Virginia, and then again in Atlanta. She should hit Atlanta in about five hours. Her parents are flying there, and Greyhound knows she's on the bus. The driver is watching out for her. So meet me in Atlanta—we can get there before her parents."

"Yes." Jack's words erased the night and intimacy with Rowan as if it had never happened, a blurred dream. "Elena must be freaking out."

"Pretty much, yeah."

"Why did she do this?" Kate cupped the phone between her shoulder and ear, fully awake and in the bathroom. She turned on the sink water to brush her teeth.

"They wouldn't let her go to a party or something parental, and she snuck out in the middle of the night and left a note saying she took the Greyhound to Birmingham. They didn't know until late morning because they thought she was sleeping in, and they hadn't checked her room."

"This is terrible." Kate spoke through the toothpaste froth filling her mouth.

"What?"

She pulled the phone away from her mouth and spit. "Sorry, I was brushing my teeth. I'm coming now."

"I'll meet you in Atlanta," Jack said, and he was gone.

Kate dressed without once thinking about what she wore or how she looked. The only image imprinted on her mind was the picture of Emily on a bus, scared, and alone. Kate wrote a note. It was cowardly, but all she knew to do to leave quickly.

> Rowan,
>   Emily ran away and I'm intercepting her bus in Atlanta. I'll call you.
>   xo
>   Katie

Quick decisions—her leaving without a phone call and signing the name Katie—were the only two things Rowan mentioned when he called her in the car, and the only two things he would remember about that day after Thanksgiving.

twenty-five

· · · · · · · · · · · · · ·

ATLANTA, GEORGIA

2010

Emily Jackson felt nauseous, sick, and mostly scared. The bus smelled like too many people who hadn't taken enough baths. This had all seemed like such a perfect idea when she was so mad that her stomach hurt. She'd asked to go to Chaz's party and her parents had done the most embarrassing of all embarrassing things: they'd called to see if his parents were going to be home for the party, which of course they weren't and which of course busted Chaz.

Now she wouldn't be able to show her face at school, and she'd never be invited anywhere for the rest of her life. And all of that had seemed the worst of all possible worlds until about eight hours into the bus trip when she was tired, hungry, and shaking.

It had been easy enough planning the trip; she'd done it in her head a hundred times since meeting Mr. Jack in Birmingham.

At Sailor's house, she'd gone on the Internet and found the

Greyhound schedule from New York to Birmingham. She took the MasterCard from her Mom's wallet and instantly she had a ticket. Done. That easy.

She wrote a note and left it on top of her pillow. She'd signed it in capital letters: LUNA and then drawn a tiny crescent moon under the name.

The thought of her mom reading the note made Emily's hot tears start again; her eyes ached. The note would hurt her mom's feelings, but Emily had been so mad, and signing "Luna" had seemed smart and funny. Changing her name was something she and Chaz had talked about doing for weeks. They'd even practiced with him calling her Luna to see if she liked it, and she did.

It was all a brilliant plan until she tried to sleep and the creepy man, who smelled like the bottom of the trashcan behind her garage, sat next to her and showed her his snake tattoo. Until she needed food and even the ten dollars she took from her Mom's purse wasn't enough. Until she called Mr. Jack's cell phone ten times and he didn't answer. All she'd imagined as wonderful turned into awful.

It had been such a great image: walking off the bus in Birmingham and having Mr. Jack standing there, taking her home. And then Miss Katie would come visit and tell stories about working in the desert. Then Mom and Dad would be sorry and let her do whatever she wanted whenever she wanted and not ruin her life.

Emily leaned against the oily window where someone else had left a smear of something white, sniffling into the pillow she'd been smart enough to bring. She curled her legs up underneath her bottom and wished, in the most desperate way she knew how, that the tattooed man sitting next to her would go away. She imagined the snake coming alive, writhing its way into her seat. Then she heard her name and she turned her face only slightly.

"Are you Emily?"

She nodded into her pillow, wiping at her eyes. The bus driver's eyes were blue and crinkled around the edges like a shirt before it was ironed. "Your mom and dad are pretty worried about you. I want you to come up to the front seat and sit behind me until we get to Atlanta."

Emily nodded again, her voice hiding somewhere behind her tears. She grabbed her pillow and Hello Kitty duffel bag and followed the driver to the front seat. He placed a reserved sign in the seat next to her and smiled down. "I'll watch out for you until we get to Atlanta. Your family will meet you there."

The bus driver's name was Eric, and he smelled like cologne and cigarettes all mixed up.

Atlanta. Her parents would meet her in Atlanta. She found her voice. "How much longer?"

"Five hours, darling."

"Okay," Emily said and closed her eyes, curling into the double seats, and under the eyes of a kind bus driver, she finally fell asleep.

Kate waited in front of a coffee shop in downtown Atlanta, a block from the Greyhound station. Cold seeped through her jacket. She grabbed mittens from her purse and pulled them on. A work crew was outside hanging Christmas lights and ten-foot wreaths on the street-lamps. Kate had never understood people who said, "Oh, this is my favorite time of the year." For her, the holidays only brought expecta-tions, sleeplessness, and money spent that she didn't have.

Christmas seemed to her a frenetic and twinkly-light-filled attempt to ignore the fact that it was winter and cold and bleak. The holidays were a desperate grasp at something beautiful. And if she'd ever felt desperate, it was right at that moment as she stared toward the street waiting for Jack to appear.

She held a cup of coffee, the warmth sending smoke up to her face. She took a long sip, and shuddered against the searing heat. "Damn," she said out loud.

"What's wrong?" Jack's voice asked.

Kate turned to face him and involuntarily, a muscle memory in response to his voice, she smiled. "So much is wrong."

"Like?" He smiled in return, an answer to her own.

"The coffee burned and I have a horrid hangover." She took a deep breath and then exhaled. "Our daughter ran off on a Greyhound bus and it's freezing cold and I hate how holidays make me feel so behind on everything."

"Anything else?" He laughed into the words.

"I think that about covers it. Okay, what time does the bus get in?"

"Thirty minutes." He pulled her coat closer around her. "You're shivering."

"I know, it's ridiculous cold out here and my South Carolina wardrobe isn't exactly Patagonia worthy."

"I love the way you say things," he said and shook his head. "Even in the middle of a crisis, you have something cute to say."

"Thanks, I think."

"Let's walk to the station," he said. "The parking lot is full because of the holiday."

She nodded. "It's only a block; I can handle it."

They walked together, huddled against the cold as they passed a Baptist church, a stone fortress, strong against the wind. "This," Kate pointed to the church, "reminds me of a church in Charleston." She stopped, staring at the front doors, remembering a plea she'd once made to a painting of the perfect mother, Mary. "Emily must be so scared. She's only thirteen. What was she thinking?"

"Guess she's got your spunk. I remember a thirteen-year-old girl who stood up to Principal Proctor and didn't care."

"Oh, I cared. I was a good faker. But this? Running off on a bus? I'd never have been that brave."

"I also remember a girl who ran off into the wilderness and wasn't scared one little bit. Spunk. Yep. She got that from you."

"Stupidity might be a better word." They stopped at the entrance to the bus station, huddled together at the sidewalk's edge.

"What did she get from me?" he asked. He spoke beneath his scarf and Kate pulled down on the wool to see his lips form into a smile.

"Hmmm . . ." Kate looked off to the sky where clouds floated like parodies, seemingly false imitations of what fluffy clouds *should* look like. "She got your kind eyes and sweet smile. She got your stubbornness."

"I'm not stubborn," he said and touched Kate's nose. "At all."

"Really?"

"No, but it seemed like something I should defend."

"Being stubborn can be really good."

"Like when?"

"When it's time to do the right thing."

He smiled and pulled his scarf up again as if he needed to hide his mouth. Kate shivered and glanced up the street. "Hurry, bus, hurry."

Jack pulled her close and she buried her face into his parka, finding warmth. After a minute, diesel miasma filled the air and Kate peaked out to see the bus pull up. She let go of Jack and stepped closer to the edge of the curb not wanting Emily to wonder if she was alone. There was, Kate knew, a terrible twisting moment when you hoped for something and realized that the something wasn't going to happen, and she didn't want this for Emily.

The bus doors opened with the swoosh of warm, stale air falling down the bus stairs and into Kate's breath. The driver, dressed in a blue suit and hat, stood in the opening, blocking the view inside. He stepped down and then turned to hold out his hand to a girl who jumped from the top step to the curb in one leap, landing in Kate's open arms. Sobs shook Emily's tiny body and Kate wrapped not only her arms, but also her scarf and coat around her daughter. Then Jack's warmth was around both of them, and they stood on the curb of the Greyhound station as one tight, round bun of comfort.

"I'm sorry." Emily's words were stuttered and damp. She looked up. Her face was pale and blotched with red circles; her copper curls scrunched behind her head and flattened against her left cheek. Her green eyes were circled with red, her eyelashes mashed into moist clumps.

"Shhh . . ." Kate said. "Let's get somewhere warm."

"Where's your bag, honey?" Jack asked.

Emily pointed to the strap of her backpack. "This is it."

Jack took each hand—Kate's and Emily's—and led them away from the bus stop. He then squatted down and looked directly into Emily's greenest eyes. "You scared us so badly. Are you okay?"

"I am now. Yes, now I am. I'm sorry I scared you. My parents must be so mad. I didn't know it would feel so bad. I didn't know it would be so scary. I just didn't know." Emily dropped her head onto Jack's shoulder, into the same soft spot where Kate had just rested.

"How could you know?" Jack asked.

"How about hot chocolate while we wait for your parents?" Kate asked, pointing toward the coffee shop a block away.

Emily nodded. "Are they going to kill me?"

"Unless kissing your whole face will kill you, I doubt it," Jack said.

Wound tight together and bent low as one tree with many branches against the icy wind, they were passing the Baptist church when Emily stopped.

A crew of four men emerged from the church, lugging various figures that would add up to a nativity scene. They carried scraggly animals and then the half-limp hay. Mary and Joseph were carved of wood and weathered to a fine sheen. The manger and baby Jesus lay in the grass facedown with Jesus' carved bottom faced toward the sky.

Emily stepped onto the grass and walked toward the crew until she stood in front of the wooden baby. The four men stopped, frozen as if they were carved wooden statues themselves. Emily bent down to pick up Jesus, her hands as gentle as if the baby were real. Then she turned the manger right side up and placed the figure inside.

Jack and Kate watched without saying a word, as if they were in church and their daughter had walked up to the altar for communion. Emily turned around and walked back. "Sorry," she said, "I have a thing about manger scenes. I just can't help it."

"That was sweet," Jack said.

A breath of ice blew across the yard. From the corner of her eye, Kate saw it—a feather winding across the nativity scene to land at their feet. It was large, red and brown, torn at one edge. Kate bent over, but when her fingers went to grab it, Emily's hand covered the feather. Together, mother and daughter stood and laughed at their coordinated motions to fetch nature floating past.

"I kind of have a thing about feathers," Emily said. "Nativity scenes and feathers."

"Me too," Kate said. "I collect them."

"Weird. How do you collect nativity scenes?" Emily asked. "Where do you keep them?"

Kate laughed. "Feathers. I collect feathers." She glanced at Emily. "That's a red-tailed hawk."

Emily smiled. "That's awesome that you know that."

"Why do you love feathers so much?" Kate asked.

"Because of that one you gave me when I was born. The white one."

"You have it?" Kate asked, her love lifting high, a wing.

"Why wouldn't I?"

"I just didn't know if your mom gave it to you."

Silence fell over them and in the warmth of mere words, no one noticed the cold. Then together they ran into the coffee shop and occupied a back booth. Jack had grown a beard, and Kate wanted to touch it, gather its warmth. He wound his gloved fingers through hers as they sat together.

Emily sat across from them and held her mitten-covered hands over her face. "That bus smelled really bad and now it's on my favorite mittens."

Kate smiled. "We can clean them."

"I'll never do anything like that again. Ever. I was mad and wasn't thinking. I would never leave my parents. This was stupid." She yanked off her mittens and pulled her hands through tangled hair.

"I have a present for you," Jack said.

"Really?" Emily looked up and smiled.

"Yep, but nothing fancy."

"I don't care about fancy," she said.

He reached into his coat pocket and yanked out a crumpled packet of Sour Patch Kids. "Here." He handed her a packet that looked as if it had been put through the washing machine, wrinkled and faded.

Emily reached across the table and took the package from him. "Oh, thanks. These are my favorite. How'd you know?"

Jack just smiled. "I just knew. And I've had those for a very long time."

Emily looked down at the candy and laughed. "Yeah, I can tell."

Kate squeezed Jack's hand.

He nodded and his eyes filled, and then just as quickly he turned away from Kate, looking at Emily. "We're here for you, Emily. We are, but you can't run away," Jack said.

"I know." She cast her gaze downward, avoiding their eyes. "I know. When the bus driver told me you'd be here, I was able to use my brain again. It's just that I had this made-up life with you. Sailor and I used to make up all kinds of stories about you and I thought . . ."

"We all do stupid things when we're mad," Kate said, reaching across the table and taking her hand. "We all do. But next time, just call."

Emily looked first to Jack. "Why didn't you answer me when I called all night?"

Jack pulled out his cell phone, glanced at the screen. "Em, I don't have a single call from you."

She lifted her own phone, flicked it open to the front screen and held it up to Jack, showing him the numerous calls.

He leaned forward and squinted. "That's my work number. Oh, I am so sorry. I had no idea . . . it was Thanksgiving. I wasn't there. . . ."

"I'm so stupid." Emily dropped the phone onto the table.

"No . . . I should have given you my cell number. I'm so sorry." He reached across the table for her hands, but she turned away.

Emily glanced between Jack and Kate and then the tears that had filled her eyes ran down her face. "I'm going to ask you something terrible. I know it's rude that I'm asking, but . . ."

"What is it?" Kate asked, softly, prodding.

"Do you want me now? Would you take me if I asked?" Emily asked, her voice muffled.

Jack jumped from the booth, moving to Emily and sidling up next to her to wrap his arms around her. "I wanted you more than I've ever wanted anything in my life. Ever. I love you more than I've ever loved anything in my life. But take you now, Emily? You're not ours to take. You know that, don't you?"

Emily looked up and nodded. Her face was mottled, dirty with a combination of Jack's coat, bus grime, and tears mixing into a muddy wetness that covered her cheeks and ran down her chin. "Did you always love me?"

"Yes," Jack answered. "Always yes."

"But I'm a terrible secret, aren't I?"

"No!" Kate measured her words as carefully as if the combination of letters were the keys to the secret of the universe, and to Emily they were. "We've been here. All along we've been here loving you."

Emily looked up at Jack as if to verify the truth. He nodded, unable to speak.

Yes, Kate thought, this was the pain he'd wanted to avoid. Yes, this was what he'd meant when he'd told Kate to let it all go. He couldn't bear to feel any of this again.

A real smile, the kind that reached all the way to her green eyes, came over Emily's face. "Yes, I guess a call would have been the better thing."

Jack stood up and for a breath-stopping moment, Kate thought he was leaving, that yes, this was all too, too much for him. Then he held out his hand. "I want to show you something."

"Okay," Emily wiped at her face.

"Stay here. I need to get my laptop out of the truck."

"You carry your laptop around?"

"I was headed into work when I got the call. So hold on."

"Do you know what he's doing?" Emily asked.

Kate looked over her shoulder, watching Jack walk away. "Nope. But whatever it is, I'm sure it's good. He's always full of good."

They grinned at one another—Emily and Kate—a conspiracy of almost identical smiles.

Jack returned and scooted next to Emily and patted the corner of the bench. "Here, Katie." Then he gently placed his laptop on the table and opened it to the slight whir of a booting computer. He clicked a few times until a photo emerged on the screen. Large and vivid there was her name: LUNA in zinc letters, the A covered in a shaft of light.

"Oohh," Emily said, an involuntary child's voice of awe. "What is that?"

"Your name," Jack said.

"Well, I know that. But where?"

Jack clicked on another photo and the same image emerged, but pulled backward to show the entire front of the studio on a brick-lined street in Birmingham. "It's an art studio in Birmingham. It's mine actually. A small studio for emerging artists."

Emily stared at Jack like a child who was being read a fairy tale, wanting to believe its truth. Then she looked at Kate, who nodded. "Yes, it's true."

"It's true? You named something after me?"

Jack smiled and pushed her hair back from her face. "Yes."

Emily smiled at the photo, ran her finger along the screen. "I want to go there someday."

"Of course, as long as your parents are okay with it." And with that his phone dinged. He looked down "Speaking of . . . your parents are almost here."

Emily nodded.

They consumed the remaining minutes as if they were a huge buffet containing all the food they'd ever wanted. Kate and Jack listened to Emily chatter about Sailor and Chaz; about hating reading, but loving stories; about her brothers being the most annoying creatures on earth; and about how she wanted to go home and sleep for days.

Elena and Larry burst through the door, worry covering their faces like a mask, Emily jumped up and buried herself into the folds of their coats, disappearing almost altogether.

"Parents." Kate looked toward the three of them.

Elena came to sit in the booth. "I am so sorry to put you two through this. She's never done anything like it. I was scared almost crazy."

"Don't say sorry," Kate said. "We love her. It's okay."

"I know you'll understand if we just leave now. Larry got us a hotel room and I think we all just need a good shower and some sleep."

"Absolutely." Jack stood.

The good-bye hugs were quick and efficient, and then the Jackson family was gone, daughter and parents together, leaving Jack and Kate alone.

"Is it terrible that I wish her parents hadn't shown up so quickly?" Kate asked.

"No, it's not terrible," Jack said. "I wish the same thing. But . . ."

Kate held her hand up. "I know there's a but. There's always a 'but.' You don't need to say it, Jack."

"You're mad."

"No," Kate said. "Just sad."

They paid the bill as the waitress took the empty coffee cups and hot chocolate mug. "I have to get back to Caleb. I threw him at Mimi Ann and she has to work."

"She lives with you now?"

"No, I took him to her apartment. But I need to go get him." He paused. "How was your Thanksgiving? I didn't even ask."

"It was good. I just drank a little bit too much champagne." She paused. "And yours?"

"Fine," he said and then stood and held out his hand for her to join him.

She shook her head. "No. I'm going to stay here for a little bit. It's a long drive for me, so maybe I need some more coffee."

"Are you going to be okay?" he asked.

"I'm sure I will be." Then in one last hope-drenched request, she asked him. "Can't you stay for a little while?"

"I can't." He closed his eyes and when he opened them, he seemed gone. "I just can't. Caleb and all."

She nodded without speaking. Words no longer changed anything at all.

twenty-six

· · · · · · · · · · · · · ·

BLUFFTON, SOUTH CAROLINA

2010

Rowan's dark house was ominous instead of comforting, and in bed Kate pulled the blanket up to her neck. December had settled into South Carolina and into Kate's bones. The opposite side of the bed was empty and it was two-thirty in the morning. Where the hell was Rowan? She'd called his cell phone ten times and it had gone to voice mail. He hadn't said anything about staying out after their argument that night. He'd left to "walk it off."

Kate had tried to focus on her life with the store and her friends and Rowan; with her family and her loft and the success of Mimsy. She'd avoided talk about Emily and Jack, but that night she'd spilled her hurt to Rowan, telling him that Emily was calling Jack and she hadn't even known they talked.

"Why should he tell you he talked to her?" Rowan had asked, and then for the third time filled his glass with straight whiskey.

Kate had thought the answer obvious and only stared.

"Tell me something, Kate who used to be Katie. What did I do yesterday?"

"You worked on the Cavanaugh landscape plan and obsessed about tree size for the side yard." Kate answered. "Why?"

He looked away and then back. "I didn't think you'd notice."

"What are you talking about?" she asked.

"It seems like all you talk about lately is Luna and Jack. Jack and Luna."

Her heart fell sideways. "No."

"Seriously. It does."

"That's so not fair," Kate said, squeezing her napkin under the table, winding it through her fingers. "I just saw her in Birmingham three days ago."

"Three days and how many hours, Kate?"

"What is that supposed to mean?"

"You are obsessed with all of it."

"Why are you being so mean? This is about Emily. She's not some cute kid I met on a trip, or my second cousin." She hollered and everything seemed to bounce off the house walls, a rubber ball of words.

"I know she's your daughter. Don't you think I know that part of the story by now?" He stood and looked down at Kate. "This is falling apart."

"What is?"

"This conversation is falling apart. I am going to take a long walk and I'll be back."

That had been hours before.

"Oh, Rowan, where are you?" She rolled over and spoke to his empty side of the bed. She thought about taking a sleeping pill to ignore the panic, but then what if there really was something wrong and the police came knocking at the door and she was out of it? What if Rowan was in the Emergency room, mangled from a car accident, and she blissfully slept?

Waiting for Rowan, she again had the same terrible feeling—the exact helpless, hopeless feeling she'd had during that trip to Charleston with Norah so many years before.

On a girl's getaway before Norah got married, they'd sat at a poolside hotel bar in Charleston, South Carolina, on the first day of spring. Norah had understood what that day was to Kate, and together they sipped mint-infused vodka drinks made by the hotel bartender with the Elvis hairdo. The pool was on top of a lavish hotel overlooking the spired city. The Holy City, the tour guide had told them, for all the churches.

When Norah fell asleep on the pool chair before the sun had set, Kate found herself at the bar drinking alone and discussing the intricate theory that Elvis was still alive and well, hiding somewhere to live a quiet life. Eventually she wandered out of the hotel to walk through the circuitous streets of Charleston. The Ashley River moved at the city's side, a faithful companion, snakelike and sultry. Kate stood at its banks, aware of the slow buzz of vodka sliding its way through her body just like that river.

She walked on, turning into blind alleys and backstreets until she stood in front of a lavish Gothic cathedral so highly wrought that Kate's eyes didn't know where to rest. She pushed open the double wood doors and walked into the dark, quiet sanctuary, an otherworldly hush made of ancient whispers. Wandering in the rear of the church, she found herself face to face with an oil painting of the Madonna and child. A scholar, she thought, a woman better than herself, would have wanted to know the history of this grand church, the painter of this masterpiece, the origin of this edifice. But Kate merely wanted to kneel before this painting of the perfect mother: the kind of mother Kate couldn't be to her own daughter, the kind of mother for whom statues were crafted and paintings were formed and religions were founded.

Kneeling on a worn velvet bench, Kate didn't close her eyes when she prayed. She spoke directly to the painting. "You're a real mother and I'm asking you to watch over my daughter. I have no right, but I'm asking anyway. Please watch over my daughter, Luna, born on this day four years ago. I won't ask anything else, just that." Kate then closed her eyes. "Just that."

She stayed there on her knees long enough for them to hurt, long enough for the sunlight to move from one side of the stained glass Ascension to the other, long enough to cry and then stop. When she did stand, it was to light a candle and repeat her only plea, "Just that."

The March air in Charleston was cluttered with the competing forces of air and water. Kate sat on the front steps of the church and realized she had no idea which turns she'd taken to get where she was—in her life, at the church. Water won the battle over air and rain began to fall, nestling in Kate's hair, working its way through her clothes to skin.

The man who found her, the Italian man with the broken English, the tailored suit, and the umbrella, was charming and witty. He sat next to her on the church steps and tilted his umbrella to shield her from the rain. "I saw you today at the hotel pool," he said.

Kate turned, her head dizzy. "Oh, yes. That was the beginning of the end," she said, attempting to smile.

"What end?" he asked, and the word end sounded like "eend," which made Kate laugh too loudly.

"This end, right here. Where I'm lost and half-drunk and . . . wet."

"Aha," he said and then held out his slim hand. "I'm Nico."

"I'm Kate," she said, leaning back against the step and scooting closer, under the dome of his umbrella.

"Kate." He seemed to taste her name. "Are you lost?"

"In more ways than you can possibly imagine."

"Well, I don't believe in coincidence, so we meet again. Maybe I can help you be not lost."

"Be not lost." Kate laughed again. "Well, can you get us back to that hotel?"

"These are things I can do."

"Show me?" she asked.

Nico walked her through the maze of streets and alleys, and Kate willingly followed, feeling safe and shaky. She needed, God how she needed, to outrun the fear that the way she felt would be the way she would always feel—Lost and Lonesome, a permanent penance.

Damp, they arrived at the hotel where they sat at the restaurant bar. Nico ordered her a sandwich and a beer, telling her that the "heaviness would save her lightness." She laughed at his mixed-up words. He told her stories of Italy and how he'd come to Charleston to open a restaurant. A stranger who spoke her language in broken ways, he made her feel oddly safe, like another girl completely.

Satiated with food, they left the bar, and in the elevator their mouths came together in warm kisses. Then they were falling into his room; his hands found skin, running along her spine with deep pressure until he reached the hollow of her lower back and she gave into the sensations so opposite of what she'd been feeling. She tasted his skin, moist with rain. In dull amusement, she wondered how he could so neatly fold his suit over the chair while she was so carelessly ripping off her own clothes. When they did come together, she couldn't blame him for pressuring or pushing, as she was the one who begged, "Now. Please."

Kate actually believed, for the moments it was true, that giving her body to this kind Italian stranger would end the agony of wonder and loss. And it did, until it was over and she found herself again full of aching shame and the knowledge that she'd—once again—tried to fix something with someone. While he slept, she crept out and returned to Norah, spilling her pain to her best friend and then reaching for Jack's yearly letter.

Then in a vow inside what remained of the first day of spring, Kate promised herself to never again believe a man to be an answer.

And until she met Rowan Irving in New York, she'd stayed far from that idea.

Now, curled up and alone in Rowan's bed, the images in her mind grew. She'd tried to cover the pain and unknowing in so many ways. But it never ended. Yes, she thought. It stayed. And stayed. The need and want for what she lost never went away.

Eventually she drifted off and when she finally felt the bed tip, she inhaled the stale beer aroma of Rowan crawling under the sheets. It was five AM. She sat up.

"Where have you been?" she asked.

"Out," he mumbled. "Go back to sleep."

He turned away and she stared at the back of his head, at his shoulders squared away from her like a wall she could never climb. "I've been up all night," she whispered, reaching to touch him.

He rolled toward her and squinted. "Looked like you were sleeping to me."

"I've been worried sick."

"Why?"

"Because I didn't know where you were and you didn't call or answer my calls."

"Are you now my mother?"

"What?"

"I mean, I'd think you were worried because you love me, not because you couldn't find me or keep tabs on me."

"What?"

"Stop saying "what?" You sound ridiculous." He sat up. "I didn't want you to worry. I just needed some space and time to think, and I fell asleep on Mark's couch after the poker game. I had my phone turned off. I'm exhausted. Can we please talk about this tomorrow?"

"It is tomorrow. What did you need some time and space to think about?"

"Are you even kidding? You've been happier the past few months than I've seen you since I met you and you don't think I know that you're happier because *they* are back in your life? So not only did you keep this from me, but they bring you more happiness than I ever could?"

"No." She took Rowan's face in her hands. "I don't know how to say sorry again. But it's not 'they' who bring me happiness. Don't say that. Yes, I am relieved and full of lots of emotions because my daughter found me, but it has nothing to do with Jack or having him back in my life."

He stared at her for too long; long enough that she thought he might not answer, and maybe it would have been best if he hadn't. "I don't believe you," he said and rolled over. The sentence was spoken into his pillow. "I just don't."

Kate pulled at his shoulder. "Please."

"Stop. Let's sleep. Nothing good can come of this discussion right now."

Kate flopped back onto her pillow. When the alarm buzzed, she turned it off as Rowan snored. She would fix this. She would not let old feelings ruin something wonderful that was right here, right now.

The dinner party with friends was every other month and it wasn't until four o'clock that afternoon when Kate remembered it. She was responsible for an appetizer. In a quick run to the grocery store, she grabbed a premade cracker and cheese tray wrapped in cellophane. They were late to the dinner party and Kate almost dropped the plate on the way to the front door. Rowan grabbed her elbow and steadied her. "You okay?"

"No, and you?"

"I'm just fine."

"How?" she asked and turned to face him, balancing the plate and fighting tears.

"What?"

"I mean, how are you fine when we had a big fight and we haven't talked about it all day and now you're just pretending everything is okay?"

"Let it go. It's over."

"Over? You came home at five in the morning and said you think I care more about Emily and . . ." She stopped, biting back *his* name.

"You can say his name. Jack. Jack. Jack. Isn't that what you wanted to say?"

"See? You're not okay. This is ridiculous."

The front door opened and Bessie Lovett stood there in the doorway in her pink shift dress and kitten heels. "What are you two doing just standing on my doorstep without ringing the bell? Silly you, especially when you have the appetizers, my dear." She reached over to hug Rowan first and then took the plate from Kate as she stepped aside to let them enter the house. "Come in."

Rowan placed his hand on Kate's lower back and they entered the house. He leaned down to whisper in her ear. "I'm sorry, baby. It's been a long day; I have a helluva hangover, and I don't mean to be an ass."

Kate stopped in the hallway and grabbed his hand. "Please don't be mad at me. I can't bear it."

He nodded and kissed her.

"Look at you two lovebirds," Larson's voice bellowed, which is what his voice always did, and he joined them, slapping Rowan's back. "How you feeling today, buddy?"

Larson's wife, Cindy, tall and wearing an orange tunic as bright as her personality, walked into the hallway. She handed a glass of white wine to Kate, nodding between Larson and Rowan. "These two should be in bed after the night they had."

"Huh?" Kate took the wine from Cindy and smiled through the stomach-dropping realization that Cindy knew something she didn't.

"Last night. These two out all night at some club in Hilton Head, pretending they're young, single, and cool. Ridiculous."

Larson grabbed his wife around the waist and dipped her backward. "I only have eyes for you, baby."

"Yeah, but unfortunately last night, you only had lips for your beer."

Kate looked to Rowan. "Mark's house?" she mouthed.

"So," Larson said and turned to Kate. "Last night, Rowan told me your story. Unbelievable. It's like a sappy movie, but better. Are you floating on air?"

"What?" Cindy pulled at Kate's arm. "What's he talking about?"

"I'll tell you later," Kate said as the four of them entered the kitchen.

"No, tell me now," Cindy said, "I can't stand it when Larson knows something I don't. It kills me. Tell me," she hollered, slapping her hands together. Everyone in the kitchen quieted, waiting.

Tasting Rowan's lie and feeling her gut fold inside out, Kate shook her head. "No." she took a long sip of wine. "Not now. Maybe later."

"Oh, you've got to tell the story," Larson said. "It's amazing. I mean, shit, I've known you since high school and I had no idea."

The hushed room stared at Kate and the floor below her feet shifted, altering her world in the same way an earthquake shifts a coastline, changing the view.

"It's kind of . . . private," she said. "I haven't really told anyone yet."

"Well, Rowan was telling the world last night," Larson hollered.

Bessie lifted the tin foil off the crackers and cheese, staring at the prepackaged appetizer.

Kate cringed. "Sorry, it's nothing fancy. I had an insane day and . . ."

Bessie laughed. "No problem, sweetie. But to make up for it, you must tell all of us the story Larson knows that we don't."

Rowan had moved to the other side of the kitchen, sitting on a barstool and drinking straight whiskey. The four other couples in the dinner club stood around the granite kitchen island waiting in various poses of expectancy. *A story.* Who doesn't love a good story? But this was her story.

"The story." Kate leaned against the counter.

"Yes," Rowan said from the other side of the kitchen.

"Fine, a story it is then," Kate said, using a singsong voice of sarcasm, the voice that as a child had sent her to her room one too many times. "Once upon a time, a long time ago before I knew Rowan, I slept with someone else."

The kitchen sank into unsure silence, the friends not knowing whether to laugh or play along.

"Shocking, isn't it? I mean, I'm sure Rowan never slept with another soul before he knew me. Right? Well, then . . . even more shocking, I got pregnant with Jack Adams and we had a baby and then we chose adoption. This baby, this little girl, found me and found us." Kate took in a long, deep breath. "So, there you go. That's the story."

Larson came to Kate's side. "Jack Adams? Are you shitting me?"

"No, I don't think I am."

"But you and Jack were . . . the perfect and inseparable couple. If he was the father . . . why?" Larson looked to Rowan and cringed. "Sorry, buddy, I didn't mean it that way. Damn, why am I still talking? I should shut up now."

"Good idea," his wife said and took his hand.

Larson looked to Kate. "I just think it's unbelievable that you got to meet your daughter after all these years. That's the part of the story I wanted you to tell. It's . . . surreal."

"Yep, surreal," Rowan said and stood from the barstool. He left the kitchen and then the house shivered with the slammed front door.

"Damn, I'm an ass," Larson said. "He told me all about it last night and I thought it was common knowledge. You know, something you'd want to talk about. A cool reunion story. Forgive me."

"It's not your fault, Larson. It's mine." She glanced around the kitchen at the faces of the couples she'd known for years. Oh, she thought, the things we don't know about friends. They were all staring at her as if they'd just met her, as if they hadn't laughed and cried, as if she'd never babysat their kids or cooked them dinner.

Bessie spoke first. "Girlfriend, it's not a big deal. We . . ." she motioned to the women in the room. "Are here for you. We can't wait to hear everything. But I know you gotta run off and catch that Rowan."

"Thanks. I'll call later . . ."

"I'll repeat myself," Larson said. "I'm an ass."

"No." Kate shook her head and hugged him. "You are not."

Rowan sat in the car waiting on Kate, which brought relief. She climbed into the passenger seat and placed a hand on his leg. "I am so, so sorry this is hard on you. I don't know how to make it any better. I just don't. What do you want me to do?"

"Stop talking about it."

"I wasn't. You're the one who told Larson."

Rowan stared out the windshield. "Stop talking about it. Stop obsessing about it. Stop seeing your old love. Just stop." Then he looked at her and his eyes were cold, marbles from a bowl, not real. "Tell me now, Kate. Look me in the eye and tell me that you don't love Jack Adams. If you say that, I'll believe you."

There it was—the small space in a world where everything changes with a single answer, an honest answer. "I can't," she said, closing her eyes. "I can't say that."

"I didn't think so."

"But I want to move on, Rowan. I do. I'm with you because I want to be."

"I wish that was enough. God, I wish that was enough. You should see the way you look when you talk about him. You should see the way you smile when you talk about both of them."

"No," she said so quietly she wasn't sure she even said it.

"Look how we're hurting each other. Look at the things I'm doing and saying. This is turning us into people we don't want to be. It's turning me into someone I don't recognize."

"You told your friends without asking me."

He held up his hand, stopping her. "No. These aren't just my friends. Supposedly they're *our* friends. They've tried for years to be your friends, but you don't let anyone in, Kate. Don't you even sort of see that? You keep your distance, always on the surface of things, always a little bit not-there. It's killing me."

"Don't do this," she said.

"Do what? Tell the truth? Well, here it is: We need to take a break. We need to breathe our own air for a while."

Kate wanted to find a way to talk him out of this, to continue trying to be happy inside their life, but she couldn't and didn't.

twenty-seven

. . . .

BIRMINGHAM, ALABAMA

2010

The baggage carousel turned endlessly, suitcases and golf bags a jumbled mass. People pushed forward as they grabbed their belongings. Kate spied her own luggage—a small black bag with a pink tag. The Birmingham airport was crowded on that Friday afternoon and yet when she walked outside, she didn't need to wait for a cab, because no one else was in line. It seemed as if the whole world had someone to pick them up and she alone was alone.

She could have called Jack to get her, but she wanted to surprise him. Or maybe she didn't want him to tell her not to come. She waved at the cab. *This is real.* She was in Birmingham and she was putting it all on the line: *I want you and you alone,* she would say. She hadn't said that yet. She'd told him she wanted him in her life, that she missed him, but not yet that confession.

The cab driver took Kate's bag, throwing it into the open trunk. "Where to?"

She recited Jack's address and slid into the backseat. The short drive into Forest Park took her past downtown. She looked up to Vulcan and she wanted to whisper a prayer to the iron god, but he wouldn't be any help at all. And she wasn't sure what would help. Telling the truth seemed the only thing that mattered.

His house was dark in the afternoon shadows, and she stood on the flagstone front porch for longer than she wanted. Her bravado had fled. Finally she lifted her hand and pressed the buzzer, hearing the sound echo through the house, the empty house.

Again, she hadn't thought through her plan. He wasn't home. For all she knew, he could be on a two-month trip to Europe. Or out with a date he wanted to bring home. She turned around and faced the street, her back to the front door. She slid down, leaning against the doorframe and then sitting on her suitcase. Far off, a train called a mournful sound as it passed through the city without stopping.

The December air changed its mind every few minutes, calm and then lifting a cold-draft reminder of winter's stay. Kate pulled her coat closer and waited. What was there left to do?

An hour later, but what seemed many hours later, Jack's truck rounded the corner and turned into the driveway. He spoke to someone in the passenger seat, laughing, and he didn't see her. She wanted the flagstone to crack open, create a crevice to hide inside. She dropped her head onto her knees and closed her eyes: maybe he'd go in the back door, never see her, and she'd call a cab.

"Katie?"

She looked up and tried to smile, feeling the shake at the outline of her mouth. "Yep. It's me." She stood to face him.

"What are you doing?"

She glanced around. He hadn't been alone in the truck. "I came to tell you something," she said.

"A phone won't do?"

"Not for this," she said, doubt turning to embarrassment and running along the cliff of humiliation.

"What is it?" he asked

"I love you, Jack."

He closed his eyes. "Katie . . ."

"I'm not done," she said, taking his hand. "Rowan and I—we're over."

He opened his eyes and shook his head. "I'm sorry. What happened?"

"He knows."

"Knows?"

"He knows I love you, Jack. And he knows that nothing can change that." She held her breath, waiting, again waiting.

"Let's go inside," he said.

A roller-coaster ride, a plummeting feeling inside, took Kate by surprise. "That's all you have to say?"

"No." He shook his head. "But let's go inside."

He unlocked the door. "Who was in the truck?" she asked.

"Caleb. He ran next door to play video games. Dad isn't nice enough to buy the new Tiger Woods PlayStation game, so off he goes." Jack smiled.

She stood at the windows, again looking at the downtown view, which was becoming familiar, a touchstone.

Jack took her hands and pulled her closer. "I just don't know what to say or do."

"Maybe you could say it back. That you love me. That we can try this . . ." She moved closer, kissing him, her hands sliding under his shirt.

He took her hands and pulled them from his waist. "Not here."

Hot humiliation worked its way through her belly, rushing to her face. She carefully, like she forgot how to use her legs, backed away.

"Where are you going?" he asked.

"I don't know," she answered, hesitating.

"Please stop," he said, immediately at her side. "Let me make sure Caleb is staying at the neighbors. We'll go somewhere."

"Okay."

The cabin had one bedroom. The walls were formed of logs stacked one on top of the other, nestled together. Kate could sit in the stone fireplace if she wanted, so large and empty. Jack walked through the room, turning on lights. They'd only driven twenty minutes, yet they seemed states away, Colorado maybe.

"What is this?" she asked, whispering.

"My Dad's," Jack said. "It's his hunting cabin. And it's not really even his. He leases it with a couple other guys."

"For everything I know about you, there's even more I don't know." She shivered. "It's freezing in here."

Jack walked toward her and took her face in his hands, his mouth finding hers, and he kissed her deeply. She was no longer freezing. She pulled away to look in his eyes, and his kiss became more insistent, a hungry need she met with her own. One hand fumbling and trying to unbutton her jeans, the other tangled in her hair sending shivers down her neck. When she was half-undressed, clothes hanging off limbs, he picked her up. She wound her legs around his waist as he walked forward. Maybe he'd changed his mind, a game where he was now carrying her back to his truck, sending her home. "Where are you taking me?" she whispered.

He didn't answer, but carried her to the bedroom where two sets of bunk beds were shoved against the wall. He set her feet on the ground and then he sat on a bottom bunk, looking up at her. She bent forward to kiss him, her hair falling over his face. "God, you are so beautiful," he said. "I've never stopped loving you."

She answered with her body.

The night was a culmination of need. Years dissolved. With every touch, they drew closer to who they'd been—to who they'd been before the wilderness, before marriage, before Luna, before loss.

Between touch they talked of the past, they murmured about the years of missing each other and the things they'd each done to try and forget. Huddled beneath the quilts of a hunting cabin, he called her Katie and that's who she was. They talked about seeing kids who were the same age as Emily at any time and having to stop, gain their bearings. They admitted they'd been with others and imagined each other.

Desire would seem sated, and then rise again, a wave, a tsunami, and Jack's hands again found their way to the places she'd imagined for years. Their lovemaking was the same and altogether different, wiser and slower, insistent and gentler. They used their bodies to erase the pain and the wondering, to say without words what they'd wanted to say all those years. They told each other the secrets of their need.

Kate didn't believe she'd fall asleep, but then Jack was gently shaking her. "We need to go. Caleb will be home soon."

Jack was quiet, efficient in his movements as they left the cabin, as he drove them back to his house before dawn. Efficient in the way he parked in front of his house and turned to her. "You have to leave before Caleb gets home."

"What?" she asked, still sleepy. "I want to see him again, I want . . ." She wanted too much, too many things to list.

He shook his head.

Her heart woke completely, jolting her to reality, away from the bed and the warmth and the dream. "You don't want me to be part of this, do you? You need me to be separate like Emily. A secret."

"He doesn't know who you are. He doesn't know . . ."

Kate stared through the windshield. "I don't understand. He doesn't have to know everything."

"This was a mistake. We should have seen where this was going. We should have known better. We can *not* do this. It will hurt too many people."

Kate stared at his profile. She was still warm with his touch, with him, and there he was telling her it was a mistake. She wanted to hate him, but it wasn't possible, even in that terrible moment, it wasn't possible. "Known better?"

"How can I bring this knowledge into his life?" Jack pointed to the house, as if it was a living thing.

Kate was upside down, inside out, confused. "Then what was last night?"

His face was covered in the flashing hurt of truth, a cringing around his eyes and mouth. "I thought . . . I thought we could do this. I did. But there's no way." He motioned toward the house. "What am I supposed to do? Go in there and tell my son that you're the mother of my other child, his half-sister? Am I supposed to tell my parents that they have another grandchild I never told them about? Am I supposed to tell my ex-wife that I kept this from her for our entire marriage?"

"Yes, Jack maybe that is what you're supposed to do."

He stared at her, the green of his eyes seeming to turn grey and distant, changing. "We have to find a way to end all this. To really end this, to stay away from it all. It's too much for both of us. For everyone. We can't destroy anyone else. I can't."

"Destroy?" Kate opened her passenger side door. "If you think our love and our daughter would destroy someone else, then you're right, this was wrong."

She didn't allow him to carry her bag or even take her to the airport. She didn't allow him to look at her or talk. She climbed into a cab and didn't look back to see him standing on his front porch watching her leave.

twenty-eight

. . . .

BLUFFTON, SOUTH CAROLINA

2010

The Sunday afternoon before Christmas, Kate stood at her loft window, staring out over the May River. She loved that river and every movement it made. Kate wanted to be that river—changing and stable simultaneously, but she felt as if she were coming undone, unable to keep opposites coexisting.

Jack had been right—wondering and not-knowing was better than revisiting the pain and separation. She was, once again, trying to heal. Every time she wanted to call Jack, or when she reached for the computer to e-mail, she reminded herself that she couldn't talk him into giving her something he couldn't give. Loving her had hurt him more than almost anything that had ever happened in his life. How could she expect him to do that again? He'd made it more than clear—having her near made his life worse, not better. This was an awful knowing, and she reminded herself of it whenever she went to pick up the phone or type an e-mail.

Beautiful days needed to be lived, and Kate tried to plunge into them, determined to move toward gratefulness and joy. She turned her gaze from the river and grabbed her coat. It was Christmas tree–buying day with her parents and then a party with Norah and Lida that night.

Kate drove her parents through the Christmas tree parking lot for the third time, passing full and double-parked spots. Her dad, still angry Kate hadn't shown up for Thanksgiving, said, "Forget it. We'll just skip it this year. Just like Kate skipped Thanksgiving dinner."

"Skip a tree? What are you talking about?" Kate's mother asked. "Stop it, Stuart, you're being ridiculous."

A pickup truck backed out of a parking spot and Kate slammed on her brakes, flicking on the turn signal. "Look, we got one," she said, using her lightest voice, hoping to dissipate her dad's anger with kindness. She'd already tried the apologies and a bottle of thirty-year-old whiskey.

"Lookie there," Kate's mom said in a voice better used on four-year-olds. "It's a sign that we should stay." She pointed at the open parking spot.

"A sign?" he asked.

"Dad, seriously. Can you just stop being mad at me long enough to make this fun for Mom? It's her favorite thing every year, and you're ruining it."

"I'm ruining it?" He turned in the passenger seat as Kate put the car in park. "Because I'm the one who made her cry on Thanksgiving because her oldest child didn't show up? Because I'm the one who ruined the day?"

"Ruined the day?" Kate asked. "Listen, I'm more than sorry. Sorrier than sorry for not coming. I was in a messy place. I honestly believe you would have been more miserable if I'd been there."

"Well, you could have let us decide for ourselves," he said.

Kate opened the driver's side door. "Let's pick a tree. Come on."

The air was permeated with the sappy-sweet smell of pine. The ground was soft with the spongy feel of evergreen needles piled in layers. Lines and crooked rows of bent trees waiting to be chosen, to be taken home and dressed with bright lights, tinsel, and family ornaments.

Her dad climbed out of the car and slammed shut the passenger door with more force than was needed.

Kate rolled her eyes. "So, Dad, if you could just pretend to want me around for fifteen minutes, that would be good for me. Seems lately everyone needs me to stay away. . . ."

He stared at his daughter. "I'm sorry," he said, his voice softening as they wound through the rows.

"Here, here," Nicole called from a few yards away. "I found the perfect one."

Stuart and Kate walked toward her, and he circled the tree. "It's missing branches in the back," he said.

"We can put it in the corner," Nicole ran her fingers down a branch, allowing needles to fall into her palm. "I love this one."

"Why do you always pick out the one with the bald spot?" he asked.

"Guess I love bald spots," she said, reaching up and touching the back of her husband's head.

Kate laughed out loud and Stuart made a noise that was meant to sound angry, but carried humor inside. He walked away. "I swear the two of you will be the end of me."

Kate's mother looked at her and smiled. "He can't stay mad forever."

"I know." Kate walked toward the back of the lot where the smaller trees leaned against a makeshift wall, and her mom followed. "Now I want to get a small one for my loft."

"This year let's put more on your tree than just tiny white lights."

"Why? I like all the white lights and nothing else. It's nice. Clean and nice."

"Well, I think you need messy and bright."

Katie smiled. "Maybe you're right. Okay, this year, let's get loud and obnoxious: green, red, blue, everything."

"Yes." Her mother smiled. "I know just where to find such things."

"I am sure you do."

When Stuart had written the check and the trees were tied to the top of the car, the annual dance of the Vaughn Christmas tree buying ended on a good step. Michael Bublé sang "I'll Be Home for Christmas" on the car radio and Kate sang along with her mother's voice as background and her dad's "humph" as an endnote.

Kate parked her car in front of Mimsy Clothing to allow her dad to undo the trees, taking one to tie to his own car and propping the smaller one against the brick wall. "I'll take it up," Kate said.

"Wait," Nicole said, opening the hatchback. "These are for you. Have fun at your party tonight." She handed Kate four boxes of bright, large, multicolored light strands.

Kate laughed. "Thanks, Mom." She hugged her parents good-bye.

The tree dropped needles in the elevator and across the apartment floor as Kate dragged it to the corner and set it up in her small tree stand. Her iPod was plugged into speakers and she clicked the playlist titled "Holiday Music," filling the room with the sounds of Diana Krall singing "Let It Snow," her voice convincing enough to coax white flakes from the Low Country clouds. Lida and Norah were coming over that night for their annual Mimsy Celebration, and Kate wanted the tree to at least have lights on it when they arrived.

She filled the tree stand bowl with water as her cell phone buzzed across the room. She reached for it without thought, fumbling at the side table and answering.

"Hey, it's Jack." His voice broke across her complacency.

"Hi, what's up?" she asked in a voice that wouldn't betray her mood. It had only been days since she'd left him. She'd told him she loved him and he'd said their relationship needed to end. It seemed impossible that he was on the phone talking as if the hurt hadn't happened, as if she hadn't made a fool of herself.

"I want to talk to you." he said.

"Oh?"

"I know you left mad. I am so sorry if I hurt you. This is all such a mess."

Kate didn't answer, her breath held, her eyes closed.

"Are you there?" he asked.

"Right here . . ."

"Remember when Luna called herself a *terrible secret*? And then you said the same thing? Well, now I keep hearing it in my head, over and over. Since you left, I've been sick with all the hiding and secrets, but I don't know what to do."

"You don't know what to do?" A voice can hide tears, and hers did.

"I just need more time to think about it all, talk through it."

"More time?"

"Yes . . ."

"Thirteen years wasn't long enough?"

"I don't know who else to talk to about this, Katie. I don't want you to hurt. I don't want anyone else to get hurt, but no matter which way I turn I'm messing this up. . . ."

"I'm sorry this is hard for you, but listen, I'm having a party here in a few minutes and truthfully, Jack, I don't know how to be with you right now." Kate paused, taking in a breath, exhaling the next words. "I just don't know how to be."

"You don't have to be any kind of way; I just wanted to talk to you about it." His voice was quiet, moving away.

"You asked me to stay away from you."

"That's not what I said."

"Yes. Yes, it's exactly what you said."

"I'm so sorry. That all came out wrong."

"I can't stay away from you and be here for you. I can't do both at the same time." Humiliation and hurt spoke for her. "What good can come of all this talking?" she asked. "The good already happened."

"Okay," he said. "I get it."

"Bye, Jack."

When Kate hung up, she was again that girl on the monkey bars, swinging off and landing, and if for only a moment, triumphant. But this time instead of trying to get Jack to love her, she was trying to love herself.

Crystal and colorful beads nestled inside small bowls set on Kate's coffee table. Wire and pliers were set on a tray to the side. Round glass balls and small jars of paint were lined up on the kitchen counter. The ornament-making party with Norah and Lida was a yearly ritual. Each year they made decorations that were more extravagant than the last and then placed them around the boutique. Customers often asked where the one-of-a-kind ornaments came from.

Kate whipped the last of the lights onto her tree and turned the music up just as the elevator buzzer rang. Norah arrived first with the salsa, guacamole, and chips. She wore a bright red dress and her hair hung loose around her face. "Merriest," she said to Kate and kissed her cheek, balancing and carrying her bowls and a wrapped present to the kitchen. "Did I beat Lida?"

"You did." Kate took a bag from Norah's hand. "Nothing says Christmas like salsa."

"Shut up, you. I was swamped today and this was the best I could do."

"Trust me, it's better than anything I did."

"The apartment looks great." Norah walked over to the tree, laughing. "Did your mom do this tree?"

Kate smiled. "Nope. All me." The tree was covered in bright red and green lights, every branch buried and bending under the weight of the heavy cords. Kate touched an unlit bulb and twisted it harder into the socket until it popped on. "Just thought I needed something completely different this year."

"Well, this is most definitely different." Norah slid her wrapped package under the tree, a green bow poking its head from the square box.

"*Everything* is most definitely different," Kate said.

The buzzer sounded again and Kate pressed the button to allow Lida to enter the room. When hugs were finished and compliments given, they sat down to craft ornaments. Lida entertained them with stories of her date the previous night, of the woman who came into the boutique the day before and asked for "anything that would make her husband want to touch her. Just anything."

"I swear," Kate said, picking up two small beads and slipping them onto the wire, "people will say anything to you. I mean, when people come in and ask my opinion, the most risqué they get is, 'does this make my butt look big?'"

"Damn," Lida leaned over the coffee table and squinted. "That ornament is so gorgeous it could be jewelry. What can't you do, Kate?"

Norah laughed and shoved Kate to the other end of the couch. "Nothing. There is nothing this girl can't do."

"You two are crazy." Kate stood. "Lots of stuff I can't do. For one, I can't dance." With Vince Gill singing a jaunty "Winter Wonderland," Kate jumped up and attempted to move with the music, her arms and legs in disjointed patterns. "I look like those Gumby arm-waving things at the car dealership."

Norah and Kate's laughter overcame the music, blocking it out. "Oh, Mary and Joseph," Lida said. "You're right. You can't dance." She jumped up to join Kate, moving her hips and upper body in synchronistic sway.

"Damn Lida, you dance like a sexy version of jeans-and-dreadlocks ballet," Norah said through her laughter. "I'm not even gonna try next to you."

"Well, if you think that's so funny," Kate said. "There's more I can't do. Like sing."

"Don't even go there," Norah said. "I know you can't do that. You proved that years ago on the high school stage."

Lida sank onto the couch. "Girls, if you two want a celebratory drink or something, don't not-drink cause of me. I promise I'm all good. It won't bother me."

Norah's hands stopped in mid-motion as she strung a wire with all clear beads. "I can't have one anyway." She looked to Kate as she spoke.

"Nah, not in the mood," Kate said. "Long day and I love just being here with you two. Plus I want to make better ornaments than you so I have bragging rights."

"What, are you preggers or something?" Lida asked, a mirror-upon-mirror image repeating itself in a changeless question from the wilderness past.

Kate's throat clenched with a flinching of her heart and she glanced at Norah. "Oh . . ."

Norah nodded.

Together, as if connected by the wire on the table, Lida and Kate jumped up and hugged Norah, but it was only Lida who found words. "Oh, my God and Christmas and Craziness, you are having a baby. We are having a baby." Lida stood and raised her hands to the sky. "This is the best news in the world. Oh, you must be so excited."

Norah nodded. "I am. Scared as hell, but yes, I am excited."

Kate held Norah in her hug. "This is so great. When did you find out? How far along? When are you due? What did Charlie say?"

"Two weeks ago. Eight weeks. July. And he said *I* and *love* and *you*." Norah answered each question in order. "Crazy, isn't it?"

"No, not crazy at all," Kate said. "Not at all. Amazing. I thought . . ."

"I know. You thought he didn't want kids. But, sometimes things change."

"Sometimes?" Lida laughed and sat on the couch. "I love living my life near both of you. Every day is an adventure of nothing staying the same."

The three women celebrated and made ornaments, eating chips and salsa as if it were a delicacy. When her best friends left, Kate cleaned up and piled the ornaments in a box to take down to the boutique in the morning. She unplugged the Christmas tree lights, already regretting the multicolored strings.

After slipping on her pjs, she found herself sitting on the closet floor, digging behind her boots and long dresses to a wooden box shoved against the wall.

Are you preggers or something?

Hidden behind the clothes, the box found its way into Kate's hands without being seen. She pulled it out and set it in the middle of the closet, staring at it as if the long-ago rattlesnake might pop out.

The box was made from juniper wood, carved and sanded by Kate's hands over months and months in the desert. It was the box she'd made when she couldn't sleep, or she was afraid one of the young girls might run. She'd not known—then—what would ever be held inside, but she knew, under the stars and phasing moon, that the box was important.

She picked it up and carried it to bed. She slipped under her white covers and sat cross-legged with the box balanced on her knees. She was crying, but hadn't remembered starting. Opening the lid, Kate rifled through the contents: Jack's yearly letters; a single white feather (the pair to Emily's own); her pregnancy journal; a photo of Emily the day she was born; and finally a faded black-and-white picture, cut from the Wesley Junior High yearbook, of Jack and Katie at fourteen years old, standing next to a rocket from the time they'd gone on a school field trip to the Space and Rocket Center in Huntsville.

"I'd get on that rocket right now," fourteen-year-old Katie had said. "If it would take me to the moon."

"Someday," Jack had said, sincere as if promising his life to righteous war. "I'll take you there."

This was the last time Kate would allow herself the misery and pleasure of going through the box. She'd once believed that the greatest pain came from saying good-bye to her daughter, that if she chose the agony of letting go at that moment, then she wouldn't feel it so sharply later. God, how wrong she'd been.

She needed to find a way to carry the wounds, the damage, without hurting anyone else, which of course she'd done. Just ask Rowan or anyone who had dared get close.

Kate read every letter, and then the journal. She stared at every photo and then closed the lid, placing the box on her bedside table. Like dreams of flying to the moon, of having her own child, or once more loving Jack Adams, nothing was to be gained by holding onto the idea or the box or the dream.

Norah, her best friend, was having a baby. Life endured that way: moving on, changing. Like Lida said, "the adventure of nothing staying the same."

Kate glanced out the window at the bruised sky and held up her palm, and by closing one eye she blocked the bright crescent from sight, knowing that Luna's name was as close to the moon as she would ever get.

twenty-nine

. . . .

BLUFFTON, SOUTH CAROLINA

2011

Through and after the holidays, Kate's days felt as fragile as glass. She stepped into them carefully, gently. Then it was that day—again the first day of spring—when she found herself laughing with Norah over the child who kicked inside Norah's belly.

Kate's mom walked through the front door of Mimsy while Kate's hand sat on Norah's stomach. "What's so funny? What did I miss?" Nicole asked.

"Chase is kicking." Kate waved her mom toward them. "Come here, feel."

"Oh, you've already named your baby?" Nicole walked toward them, shaking her head. "You really shouldn't name your child an action verb, dear, it's a bad omen. You'll be chasing him all over God's green earth with a name like Chase."

"I hope so," Norah said, standing to hug Nicole.

Kate laughed again and her mom looked at her. "I just love when you laugh so good like that."

"Kate's always laughing." Norah said, glancing sideways at Kate.

"Not like that though. I mean, it's been a rough few months for our Kate, right? And I love to hear her laugh."

"Mom, please. Rough?"

"Yes, rough. It just kills me that nothing has turned out for you, Baby. And we just wish we could fix it." Nicole touched Norah's arm. "I mean, don't we wish we could fix it?"

"Nothing has turned out for me? What do you mean?" Kate twisted the jewelry display on the counter.

"I mean that you've lost Rowan and Jack. You can't hardly talk to Emily, and everything just seemed to fall apart."

"Mom, nothing fell apart. It just didn't come out the exact way you or I would want. But I've got everything good in my life. Everybody misses something or somebody. It's the way . . . of the world."

"But it's sad."

"Of course it is," Kate said and hugged her mom. "Of course it is."

And Nicole was right—nothing had turned out *exactly* right: Kate hadn't talked to Emily since Christmas, when Elena had allowed Emily to call and say "Merry," but then Elena had decided that until Emily turned eighteen it was best that all communication go through Elena. A mother's love was protective that way, and what was there to do but agree?

Jack hadn't called since the night before the ornament-making party. For weeks and then days and then not at all, Kate had believed he'd return and try to begin again. Hope dissolved with winter's thaw.

When Kate had run into Rowan with his new girlfriend, Gail, at the grocery store, he'd been happy. Kate had heard about Gail and her extravagant themed parties, about Rowan and Gail shopping together at the Farmer's Market, about Rowan and Gail training together for a marathon. She wondered again and again why she couldn't have been "that" girl for him. What if she'd loved him enough to be the party girl or the doting girlfriend?

But on the first day of spring Kate was determined to revel in all that was good and right and true: her sisters, her found daughter's birthday, and spring's arrival.

Molly walked through the door carrying a white box wrapped with an oversized pink ribbon. "Kitty-Kat, I come with cupcakes," she hollered across the room as she walked in. "Seriously amazing cupcakes. We're going to eat until we're sick."

"You're crazy," Tara said, her voice arriving before she was seen coming behind Molly.

Norah grabbed the box and set it on the counter, opening it. "I'm going to be as big as South Carolina by the end of this pregnancy. I swear all I want to do is eat."

"What are we doing today?" Tara asked, dropping her purse behind the counter. "What's the big plan?"

Kate picked up the newspaper, pointing to an advertisement. "There's an art festival in Savannah. I thought it would be fun."

Molly groaned. "An art festival?"

"There are bands and cute guys and bars," Kate teased, poking at her sister.

"Then I'm in." Molly picked up a cupcake, licking off the icing without taking a bite.

Nicole stepped forward then, placing her hand on Kate's arm. "Did you get a letter?"

Kate shook her head. "No. I didn't think I would," she lied, not wanting to again taste the dry-mouthed regret she'd awoken with. "There's not much he could tell me about his year. I was there for most of it." She smiled, but turned away.

"Look what I've got," Molly said, digging into her bag.

Kate glanced at her sister, and for the briefest moment, that moment of hope that often came with the ding of incoming mail or a ringing phone, Kate thought her sister might have *the* letter. Instead Molly pulled out a tiara. "I found this and I want to mail it to Emily for her birthday. You think that would be okay?"

"Absolutely," Kate said. "I sent her a set of oil paints. Elena said she was really into painting these days."

"Let's go to Savannah," Tara said, changing the subject and then also grabbing a cupcake. "I have to be back before car pool."

"Car pool." Norah groaned. "God, my days are numbered, aren't they?" She touched her stomach, but smiled.

"Numbered in ways in which you have no idea," Tara said. "If I were you, I'd go to sleep now and not get up until you go into labor. Cause I'm telling you, you're not sleeping again for a long, long time."

"Let's go, Miss Encouragement," Kate said. "Get out of here."

"Hey, Katey-Latey," Tara said. "What's your First Thing today?"

Kate stopped and turned to her sister. "I haven't decided. Sometimes it just shows up and I know. You have any ideas?"

"I do," Molly said, holding her hand over her mouth to stifle laughter. "I think you should skydive."

"Not happening," Kate said. "Never. It would be a First Thing that might be my very last thing."

Laughing, the gathering of sisters, mom, and best friend walked to the front door and stopped as Kate, once again, opened the iron mailbox to peek inside. Hope was having its say.

Nothing.

Empty.

"You looking for a letter?" An impossible voice asked.

Kate looked up and into those green eyes. "Yes, I am." She tried not to smile, but some happiness can't be stopped. Morning sunlight settled between them, a puddle on whose edges they stood. A dogwood tree bloomed overhead, a green umbrella dotted white. Time waited. It seemed as if all of nature and future held its breath with Kate, wondering what Jack's arrival meant.

Behind her, Kate's mother let out a cry. "Jack."

Norah spoke softly. "Let's go back inside for a minute. I want another cupcake." The double front doors swished shut, leaving Jack and Kate on the sidewalk.

"Maybe I'm better than a letter?" he asked.

"Maybe. But those letters are pretty special." Her toes inched toward the middle of the sunlight puddle.

He laughed, holding out his hand. She took it and he pulled her toward him, sliding his hand around her waist to hold her lower back. "I am so sorry, Katie. I said and did so many stupid things in the mess of these past months. I wish I could take back every word. Please forgive me."

She nodded. "We were both a mess." She paused. "But what are you doing here?" she whispered, both wanting and scared of the answer.

"I just happened to be in town for the Sand Gnats baseball game and . . ."

"Yeah, right," she laughed, "Baseball was my excuse. You have to find a new one."

He pulled her closer, if there was a closer. "I've told everyone about everything. How could I have not wanted to tell the world?"

"Told them about Luna?"

He nodded. "Of course about Luna, but also how I love you. How I've always loved you."

"You told them before you told me?" She smiled.

Their bodies, so close together, allowed her to feel his laughter. "I love you," he said. "And I have a great idea for your First Thing today."

"You do?"

"I do."

"And what is it?"

"For the first time, you promise me forever. You. Me. For good and all."

"That's not a First Thing. I promised that a long time ago."

"Then for the first time, let's make it happen. We might have ended, but love didn't. Staying together will be *our* First Thing."

She leaned into him then, and said only one word, one she'd said alone at night in the dark. "Jack."

He took her face in his warm hands and kissed her. "Guess I should've asked first," he said into their kiss.

"Ask me now," she said.

They touched foreheads, basking in the repeated words of long ago when he'd kissed her for the first time on the day of First Things.

"You know," he said. "I'm so happy Luna found us."

"Yes." Kate slipped her hand under his shirt, as if to make sure he was real, solid and there. "Found."

Found.

The word held the loveliest sound—lighter than any feather; softer than a kiss; a song in a single word.

thirty

· · · · · · · · · · · · · ·

BIRMINGHAM, ALABAMA

March 20, 2012

When people ask how they met, Katie and Jack say they loved in retrograde, backward. They'd both wanted to do things the way others did—to tell a story about meeting and falling in love and having kids—but they didn't. They met; they gave birth to a daughter; they unraveled and then loved again.

Their wedding was a celebration of years falling away and looping back. They married in Bluffton in a small chapel overlooking Katie's beloved river. She wore a simple cream silk strapless dress. Her copper hair was piled on her head, loose pieces falling onto her bare shoulder. A ring of white peonies circled her head. It was Emily, waiting in her pink junior bridesmaid dress at the back of the chapel, who whispered in Katie's ear just before she walked down the aisle. "That's a fairy ring on your head. Anything you wish today will come true." And Katie had kissed her daughter and said, "Anything I'd wish has already come true."

After they'd moved to Birmingham, Katie had sold her part of the store back to Susan. Lida became the full manager, her creativity taking the boutique in new directions. Katie took over Luna Studio, filling the space with the varied works of local artisans, from jewelry to letterpress to leather creations and more. Now exhibits and shows with live music and food were monthly events. Luna Studio had become a gathering place to celebrate new art and creativity of all kinds.

On the first day of spring, Jack and Katie threw a party at their Tudor house on top of the hill overlooking downtown Birmingham. Twenty guests crowded the backyard, including Katie's family and nephews; Norah, Charlie, and their nine-month-old son, Chase; neighbors, and friends. Jack and Katie were celebrating their love and also Emily's birthday, and although Emily wasn't there, she'd sent a daffodil painting with a single feather glued to the top right corner. "Happy First Day of Spring," was scrawled in her handwriting across the bottom of the artwork. "I Love You."

Caleb was on the tire swing and Jack stood behind him, pushing him higher with each holler. Claire, the woman who now ran the art studio, sat next to Katie and clinked her champagne glass against Katie's own. "You know," Claire said, "there really are easier ways to fall in love and get together, my dear."

"Yep," Katie said. "That's what I hear."

Jack caught her gaze across the yard and walked toward her. She was often stunned into wonder when she looked at Jack—the pureness of the way she loved him without regret or restraint. He reached her side and then touched her rounded stomach where their child was just starting to flutter inside, a tickle at the bottom of her belly that could have been anything, but was only one thing.

Caleb bounded across the yard and then bent down, picking something off the grass. When he reached Katie, he held out his palm and looked up at her. "Isn't this yours?"

Katie looked down and spied a small white feather fluttering in the bowl of Caleb's hand. "No, sweetie, I just like to find them."

"Well, I think this one got lost."

Kate plucked the feather from his hand, immersed in the beauty and sacrament of all things lost and found.

Dear Reader,

Over two years ago, in the middle of an ordinary day, the extraordinary happened, and my family will never be the same.

Some twenty-one years ago my little sister placed her baby for adoption. It was the most heartrending, courageous, and difficult decision she had ever made, and we all wept with her when she handed her baby girl to an anonymous, yet hand-chosen family. Then . . . two years ago, I received a Facebook friend request from a young girl with the same birthday as my adopted niece. It was too much to hope for, almost too miraculous to believe. But it was true: My sister's daughter, my niece, found us on Facebook.

Our family had often talked about my niece, using the name my sister had given her. We remembered her whenever we saw a girl who would be her age at that time. Everytime my parents moved into a new house, they planted a tree for her and we all prayed for her happiness and safety. We knew nothing about her—all those years we didn't know where she lived or with whom. Although we knew that legally she could find us when she turned twenty-one, there was no way for us to find her. And then finally, all those years of unknowing and all those years of wondering culminated in a reunion that most dream about.

My sister's story was the inspiration for this novel, And Then I Found You. It is my way of exploring the way we live with unknowing. We want certainty, we want solid ground under our feet. We want to be sure of our place in the world, and yet we rarely, if ever, have that certainty. So then, how do we live? And what happens when the lost become found?

Although the personal facts are left for my sister to tell, the fictional story in And Then I Found You explores the emotions and extraordinary change that reunions bring to a life and to a family.

I hope this story touches your heart.

Warmly,
Patti Callahan Henry

1. This novel was inspired by a true story. Is there an event in your life that you think would make a good novel?

2. Kate is so devoted to her work with damaged girls that she postpones her life together with Jack. Do you think that Jack should have been more patient in waiting for her? Or was Kate taking their relationship for granted?

3. Kate hears a lot of "terrible stories" from the girls at Winsome Wilderness. How did these experiences contribute to her decision to place Luna for adoption?

4. Kate seems to take great comfort in rituals. Have these rituals served a positive purpose in her life—or have they held her back?

Discussion
Questions

5. Do you think Kate and Rowan's relationship would have had a different outcome if she had been able to confide in him about her past?

6. Lida is much more than an employee to Kate, who seems to turn a blind eye to the younger woman's shortcomings. What do you think they offer each other?

7. When he was married, Jack didn't tell his wife about Luna. Do you think that this compromised their marriage?

8. Kate mentions that she "wants to love" Rowan. Can Kate—or anyone make themselves love someone? Can you want to love enough to love?

9. Jack says in one of his letters, "of all of the awful parts of missing their daughter, the non-knowing was the absolute worst." Why did Jack feel this way? Do you agree?

10. In the opening of the novel we see that March 20 is a significant date for Katie Vaughn, and it remains so throughout the remainder of the novel. Is there a date that is deeply significant to you and if so, why?

11. Thirteen-year-old Emily wonders about her "birth parents." Do you know any adopted children and if so, do they often wonder about their birth parents?

St. Martin's
Griffin

12. Emily is deeply loved and has a close family, but still she struggled with feeling wanted. Why do you think this is?

13. Emily wants to know "her story"—don't we all? Did hearing her story directly from Jack and Kate help Emily? Do you think that hearing "your story" helps you understand your life? Do you believe that telling "your story" helps others?

14. At one point in the novel, Emily believes that it would be nicer to live with Kate and Jack. Can you see why she would believe this?

15. Kate has a very close family and they often talk about Luna, and yet her birth and adoption are also a tightly held secret. Do you believe families can hold these kinds of secrets? How do they affect the family and those who are close to them?